No Safe Ground

No Safe Ground

Julia Pomeroy

FIVE STAR

A part of Gale, Cengage Learning

GALE
CENGAGE Learning·

Detroit • New York • San Francisco • New Haven, Conn • Waterville, Maine • London

GALE
CENGAGE Learning®

LIBRARY OF CONGRESS CATALOGING-IN-PUBLICATION DATA

Pomeroy, Julia.
    No safe ground / Julia Pomeroy. — 1st ed.
       p. cm.
    ISBN 978-1-4328-2682-6 (hardcover) — ISBN 1-4328-2682-4 (hardcover)
    1. Life change events—Fiction. 2. Fathers and daughters—Fiction. 3. Women veterans—Fiction. 4. Upstate New York (N.Y.)—Fiction. 5. Suspense fiction. I. Title.
PS3616.O578N6 2013
813'.6—dc23   2012037321

First Edition. First Printing: February 2013
Find us on Facebook– https://www.facebook.com/FiveStarCengage
Visit our website– http://www.gale.cengage.com/fivestar/
Contact Five Star™ Publishing at FiveStar@cengage.com

Printed in Mexico
2 3 4 5 6 7 17 16 15 14 13

To Raif and Liv, peas in a pod. I miss you every day.

ACKNOWLEDGMENTS

The two people I want to thank, first and foremost, are my agent, Richard Parks, for hanging in there and working so hard; and his friend and mine, our beloved Dale Davis, who read this in its earliest form and, prejudiced as she was, loved it. Many thanks to Michele Slung, who teaches and entertains me; to all the kind and hard working people at Five Star—thanks for taking me on board. To my friends and family—Jarrett, Francesca, Rennie and Phyllis, who read the book and gave me the feedback I needed to keep working, thank you. My brother Eugene, king of soldierly tips: it was with him, driving to Rome, that I first kicked around this idea. Thanks to John Dax, who donated good money so I could sully his name; to Jarrett and Alicia, both strong women and inspirations for Vida; to a handgun instructor I had once, five years ago, who got me thinking about Millie; when I started this story, I needed to be inspired by courage and strength, and I have to believe she has both. Thanks to Anne, always, for her unending support; to Algy, for becoming the man he is. To my dear sister-in-law, Connie—not only do I miss her, I miss her tremendous love and enthusiasm for the genre and for those of us who work in it. And finally, thanks to John Gregory, for helping me whenever I need help and always making me feel like a star.

AUTHOR'S NOTE

As a writer, I am often asked if I put people I know into my books. Here's the deal: each character I write has a little of myself in him or her, because that's what I know. And many of my characters are inspired by one aspect of someone I meet or am familiar with, a phrase heard on the street, the way someone dresses, or how they read the paper on the subway. So no, no one person in this book is meant to be real or represent any person, living or dead. No offense was intended to anyone.

And for those military-minded readers out there, I apologize ahead of time for any mistakes I've made regarding weapons, Iraq, or the Army.

CHAPTER 1

A mud-splattered black Town Car pulled up in front of the Hudson, New York, train station, and a man in a well-cut black suit scrambled out from the rear, unassisted. As soon as he slammed the door, the limo pulled away into a U-turn, tires squealing. The passenger stood on the sidewalk, briefcase in one hand, brushing himself off angrily with the other.

Unconcerned about the dust that had transferred itself from the back of his car to his passenger's clothing, the driver took the limo up Columbia Street and out of town, northbound. Twenty minutes later, he drove slowly through the small village of Bantam, bypassing Main Street, and continued on. He slowed down again as he passed through the cluster of houses known as West Bantam and took a left on a narrow county road toward New Canaan. The trees formed a canopy over him at first, then dropped away as the road wound through fields and by farmhouses.

One last turn-off onto a dirt road. The farther he drove, the deeper into the woods he went and the lower the property values dropped. The only car he passed was a dirty white wagon parked by the side of the road, a quarter of a mile from his house. Hikers, maybe, or prospective buyers looking at land.

Eventually he arrived at his short, rutted driveway. Home was a rundown seventies ranch, once dark red, now a grayish pink, sitting in a weed-ridden clearing. The garage was below ground level, the surface of the ramp cracked and pocked with holes,

11

the overhead door frozen half-open with all the landlord's unwanted possessions visible—crib parts, a playpen, bicycle wheels, and cardboard boxes piled haphazardly on top of each other.

Reynolds Packard climbed stiffly out of his limo. He was a man in his fifties, tall, built like an aging bull, with old, thick muscles in his neck and shoulders. He had the start of a paunch that pushed his belt low on his frame, making his legs look shorter than they actually were.

Like the man he had just dropped off, he wore a black suit, but his was cheap, the elbows and knees shiny and bagging. His pale blue eyes were hidden behind dark prescription glasses, and his white hair stood out from his head in a grown-out brush cut. Attached to his lower lip was a dirty-yellow soul patch. In his ears were small white earphone pods that, along with the glasses, made him look like a bodyguard for the president of a war-ravaged third-world country. The wires met and hung down on his chest, disappearing into his pocket.

Inside the house, the kitchen and living room shared the main space. A narrow hallway disappeared to the left toward the bedrooms. Pack pulled out the ear pieces and dropped his keys and mp3 player on the worn dining room table, took off his dark glasses, and stood still as his eyes adjusted to the change.

He was oblivious to it, but the place was dirty. The corners of the room were no longer angular, but rounded with years of compressed spider webs and hair. The stove was enameled yellow with food and liquids that had spilled and been baked to a hard finish. Across from the front door was a pair of sliding glass doors, filmed over and greasy. The place had the sour smell of unwashed clothes, mice. Used-up air.

He took a package of ground beef out of the fridge. He was standing at the kitchen counter, making himself a couple of loose patties of meat, when his phone rang. He listened as he prepared his food.

"Reynolds! Megan here," a high, nasal voice began. "I've got an airport run for you tomorrow at 11:30 from the Hilton, please confirm. Also, we got a complaint from one of your rides this afternoon. Mel says to call as soon as you get this."

Pack ignored her and went over to a tape deck that sat on a side table, two beef patties in his right hand. With his left, he maneuvered a cassette out of a library boxed set, and slid it into the machine. After the initial click and silence, a voice engaged and began to speak gently and firmly about personal potential. Pack stood still for a second, listening, then turned up the volume and walked toward the patio and slid open one of the glass doors. He had a small Hibachi on the patio. Tonight, like most nights, he would barbeque.

The deck was about twenty-five by thirty, ringed by a moat of weeds and shrubs, the encroaching woods only a short distance beyond. The land sloped gently down from the house, so the far edge of the deck was at least four feet off the ground. Once, there had been a short flight of rough-cut steps from the level wooden planking down to a lawn, but the grass hadn't been cut in years, and the steps had long since rotted and broken through. The grill was on the patio, however, so he didn't need the steps.

He was trying to decide if he would call Mel back, or just blow him off. Mel wouldn't fire him; Pack was a good driver, had his own car, and showed up on time. The fare today was a jerk, shouting on his cell phone for the entire trip, only shutting up long enough to complain about the dusty seats. "Listen, bud," Pack had finally said to him, "we're in the goddamn country, okay?"

His mind on the passenger, he stepped onto the patio and slid the door closed, turning as he did so.

Straight into the barrel of a gun.

Pointed at him, close, not even six feet away. A big, ugly handgun.

He made a sound like a truncated bark. A chemical rush tore through him and all sounds around him ceased, as if he'd gone deaf. He threw his weight away from the gun, arms out to the side, and stumbled backwards.

No explosion came, and it took a few seconds for him to realize he was still alive. He saw the person behind the gun, hands together and arms extended forward, still aimed at him. Dressed in dark clothes, it was a small person or a child. A kid? "Jesus Christ!" Pack's voice came out hoarse.

"Don't move," the gunman said in a voice tight with tension.

"It's okay, it's okay!" Pack raised his hands in a gesture of compliance. He was still holding the raw meat, but it was now squeezed through his fingers.

He realized with shock that his intruder was a girl, or woman. She was holding the stainless steel pistol in a two-handed grip, legs apart, knees slightly bent. Businesslike. Her head was low behind the gun, as if she were taking aim at him. Her expression was hidden behind the gun barrel and her hands.

"Who are you?" she said, her voice harsh.

His heart was hammering heavily in his chest. He stammered, trying to get the words out. "I live here. Packard, Reynolds Packard."

Slowly, she lowered her gun, so that it was now pointing at his groin instead of his head. She looked at him, expressionless, and said: "You're Pack?"

"What the hell is this?" The raw meat fell on the deck. "Shit, look at that."

"Don't pick it up, don't touch it." She raised the gun again.

"Who the fuck are you, anyway?" he said, the wasted meat causing an unexpected surge of anger.

"You alone?" she asked.

14

"Yes, I'm alone! What's it look like?"

"Are you armed?"

"Jesus Christ! No, no, I'm not armed."

She slowly loosened the white-knuckle grip her left hand had around her right hand. He didn't breathe until he saw her finger come out of the trigger guard.

She bent her elbows and pointed the gun skyward, as if she might change her mind and take a shot at him at any moment. "I'm Vida." Her smile was stiff and arrogant.

"Who?"

"Who? You're kidding, right?"

He stared at her, trying to understand what she was saying. "I've got to sit," he said, more to himself than her. He grabbed the one and only deck chair, a frayed red and white folding number, and pulled it toward him. He sat down heavily, legs wide, head back, eyes closed.

Vida watched him. She cleared her throat. "I scared you, huh? I thought you were someone else."

"Oh yeah? Like who?" He spoke without moving, his eyes still closed. "I should have you arrested. What are you, a junkie? In case you can't tell, I'm broke. There's nothing here worth taking. So you can get the hell out."

The girl didn't say anything. In the silence, they could both hear the drone of the self-help guru, coming from inside the house.

Finally, he sat up slowly and turned to look at her. He sounded tired. "Shit. You're still here. So tell me, you come here to kill me?"

"No," she said, looking affronted.

He took a deep breath. "Okay, then. I need a drink. Ah, god, I think my heart stopped there." He stood up slowly, one eye on her gun hand. "I'm going inside to get a beer. Okay?"

She pointed her gun at him, more as emphasis than a threat.

15

"No, stay. Sit. Don't move. I'll get the beer."

He sat back down and she went inside, leaving the sliding door open, and watching him as she went. He leaned back and closed his eyes again, his breathing still erratic. "And turn off that fucking tape," he called out, without moving. He could hear her moving around inside, then silence from the machine.

She came out a moment later and put the frosted can on the ground a few feet away from him.

He groaned and lifted out of his chair just enough to reach down for it. Then he sat back, cracked it open, and took a long pull. He sighed. Neither of them said a word for a full minute.

He was the first one to speak. "You say you're Vida?" He asked the question as if the name itself was strange to him.

She gave a quick nod.

He looked at her carefully and took another swig of his beer. She was about five-foot-two, with dark brows that stood out against pale skin. Her eyes were a dark brown, sunken with something like fatigue. Her brown hair was pulled back at her neck, exposing a fresh scar on the left side of her face: starting at her hairline, it skirted her eye and disappeared at her jaw. Though the wound had been well repaired, it was recent, and still looked as though someone with a magic marker and poor motor skills had been let loose on her face.

"That was your white Subaru, right? Back a ways?" he said.

"Yup."

He shook his head, as if he were a fool not to have known. "Okay, let's hear it. What do you want?"

"I need your help."

He felt an urge to stand up and smack her, but he didn't have the energy and she was still holding the gun. He made a sound that was distantly related to laughter. "You sure know how to ask nicely."

"I didn't hear you coming in, you surprised me."

"That's funny, too."

"Hey, I said I was sorry."

"Yeah? I must've missed it. Okay. Truce. You put that gun down, right now, on the floor. And move away from it."

The girl hesitated. "What if you call the police?"

"Are you really Vida?"

"What, you want to see my ID?"

"If you are, I'm not going to turn in my own kid. Not yet, anyway."

The girl still hesitated.

The man sighed, long and heavy. He picked up the raw meat, moving slowly so as not to startle her. "I was about to eat. You hungry?"

She glanced down at the red mess and her nostrils flared in disgust. "That's gross."

He pulled back his arm and threw the meat hard into the wooded area behind the house. "I meant the diner. One condition, though. The gun stays here."

CHAPTER 2

They didn't talk on the way down the hill. Pack drove slowly, paying extra attention to the ruts in the road, his hands still shaky. The girl stared out the window into the woods, her body as far from his as it could get. Her cockiness seemed to have drained out of her, leaving her small and more fragile.

At the main road they turned right into New Canaan. The diner was in a rundown strip mall, a rectangle of low gray buildings around a sprawling, near-empty parking lot. They had to wait behind a family of five to be seated. Pack stood still, arms crossed, staring ahead, while Vida looked out the plate glass window, her eyes combing the cars, checking the people in them. When a police car pulled in, she lowered her eyes and turned away.

The waitress seated them and she slid along the banquette, positioning herself with her back to the wall. She took the menu and read it carefully.

Stubbornly sticking to his original supper plan, Pack ordered a cheeseburger. Vida chose the turkey and mashed potato dinner. They didn't talk while they waited for their food. He glanced occasionally at her. He looked at the long angry scar and the dark circles under her eyes. He watched her sneak looks at the cop as he came in to pick up his order. She seemed to relax only when he left.

It wasn't until Pack had worked his way through half his

meal that he said: "So, are you going to tell me what's going on?"

Her gaze swept the room. The closest table was occupied by the big family. The youngest child was standing up, alternating between eating and throwing French fries across the table. Overhead, Greek music was playing, a bouzouki twanging. She shook her head. "Not here."

He blew air out of his mouth, irritated. "Okay, but hurry it up. I've got work to do."

Vida went back to her meal. She slowly ate her way through the rest of the food, taking occasional sips of her soda.

As soon as she was done, Pack gestured for the waitress. "I'll take the check."

"Wait," Vida said seriously. "Ice cream. I'd really like some ice cream."

He started to protest, and then sighed: "What d'you want?"

"A hot fudge sundae. With one scoop of chocolate, one of vanilla, and one of strawberry. Please."

He looked at the waitress with a shrug. Kids, right?

"Thanks," Vida said when the waitress was gone.

It took her twenty minutes to eat the sundae. When she wasn't looking, Pack went back to studying her scar, with its small neat stitches. It was pretty new, but well done, given the extent of the damage. It was like the illustration for a train track on a tourist map: from her hairline it traveled down to the middle of her left eyebrow, then picked up again at her temple, thicker and more complicated, as if it had reached a major depot. And down, with a few jagged turns, to her jaw. A neat version of what he and his buddies in the military had called a "frankensteiner." He wondered if he was going to find out how she got it. Most likely a car crash.

Not that he really wanted to know.

CHAPTER 3

When they got back to the house, Pack followed Vida up to the front door. He saw she was limping, but he didn't say anything. Inside, he gestured to the couch. "Okay, let's hear it."

She sat down on the edge of the cushion.

"I'm in trouble." She looked, for the first time, desperate.

But Pack ignored any effect she might have on him. He stood in front of her. "Before you start, you should know I got nothing to offer. I don't have money and I don't know anyone with any influence. So what d'ya do, rob a bank?"

She looked at him, her eyes suddenly cold. "No. I'm no criminal." Then she looked away. "I ran away."

"You ran away?" he repeated stupidly. "Where, from home?"

"No. Not from home. I'm twenty, remember? Or maybe you don't. No, I'm a soldier," she snapped. "I was injured, in case you hadn't noticed. I went home on leave, and a few days before I was supposed to meet up with my unit, I ran."

"Holy shit." He looked around the room as if someone else might have heard her.

"You gonna turn me in now?" she asked, a sneer in her voice.

"Hey, maybe I will. I don't know you from a hole in the wall. You've broken the law, you *are* a criminal—" even to himself, he sounded sanctimonious "—so no, no, I won't turn you in, but I can't help you. I don't want to help you."

She stared at him. Her eyes grew shiny, but she didn't cry. She stuck her jaw out. "You *owe* me, shithead." She swallowed.

He was resenting her more and more. "Hey, hey, don't call me names."

"Like that's what matters."

Suddenly exhausted by the girl's intensity, Pack pulled up a hard-backed chair and sat down. "What do you want from me?"

"You're a vet. I need you to find someone for me at the VA hospital."

"Why should I?"

She looked out the window. "Something terrible is going to happen to me."

Pack stared at her. "That's dramatic. What do you mean?"

"Someone killed my roommate, and now they want to kill me."

"Your roommate?"

"In Iraq."

"You were in Iraq?"

"That's what I said, didn't I?"

"No. Explain."

"We were on patrol. We hit an IED."

He felt a stab of pity for her. "Right. Yeah, they *are* trying to kill you. But that's war. You signed up for it. Your first big mistake."

"No, this was something different. Something personal. Not the usual."

Now he was starting to see where the fantasy was most likely bleeding into reality. "What do you mean?"

She took a deep breath as if she were steeling herself. "I was at Tallil. I'd been there for about five months, give or take."

"What did you do?"

She looked irritated by the interruption. "Do? My job? Motor Transport Operator. Driver. We call it MOS 88M. I don't know what it was in your day. My roommate, Haley, was a Cargo Specialist. Six weeks ago, we were together in a convoy, taking supplies north on the MSR. A long, flat stretch of road. I don't remember much of the whole thing, but when the explosion happened, the bad guys were waiting."

"Okay. So what else do you remember?"

"Nothing much till I woke up in the hospital in Landstuhl, Germany. That's when they told me what had happened. Haley was shot twice, once in the chest and once in the head, and I got hit by shrapnel. Leg and face."

"Maybe I'm missing something. What happened to you is about as bad as it gets, but I still don't understand how you figure someone's after you. Other than the enemy."

"Because after I got back home to Alaska I started to remember little flashes of things. I think I saw the person who shot her, and it wasn't one of the insurgents. It was a U.S. soldier. One of *us*."

He didn't try to hide his skepticism. "That's one hell of an accusation."

"Listen to this. I was lying on my side. Well, twisted. I remember dirt, grit, rocks, stones digging into my face and head. When we hit the bomb, I must've lost control of the truck and gone off the road. But I don't remember that. I remember waking up, the dust was thick, choking, I couldn't see the truck, but I think it was behind me. Anyway, there was a sound, an engine or something. Thrumming. Or maybe it was the blood inside my head. My mouth was open, dry like a cave. I could hear my breath whistling in my throat but I couldn't swallow or speak. My eyelashes were caked with crap. I couldn't move anything, but I wasn't in pain. It was like I was suspended. I didn't want to try to move. It wasn't about taking in what I saw, or thinking logically, it was just about knowing I was me, just for a few moments."

She stared blindly, remembering. "And then, as I lay there, a soldier walked into my field of vision. I saw the uniform, I saw him outlined against the sky. And I thought, I should call him. But I couldn't make any sound. I remember thinking, he'll want to know about me. He's looking for me but I'm so dusty, I'm hidden in the rubble, he can't see me. He thinks I'm a pile of rocks. Next I saw him stop and nudge something on the ground with his boot. I followed his gaze. It was a soldier, one of ours. Then I saw the blonde hair in the dirt. I recognized the hair. As I watched, the soldier pointed his rifle at the hair, there was an explosion and his weapon bucked. Then, boom, it bucked again. That's what I remember."

Pack didn't move. "So you saw his face."

Vida shook her head. "No. I saw him from the side. He looked tall, but then I was on the ground, maybe anyone would look tall. He was turned enough that his face was hidden by his helmet. And he was wearing sunglasses."

"Did you see the skin on his hand? Was he white or black?"

"I don't know, he had gloves on. If I had to guess, I'd say white, but over there, you've got that fucking dust on you half the time. But if I had to choose, I'd say white."

"How do you know he wasn't a local in fatigues?"

"I just know."

"Why do you think he didn't shoot you?"

"He didn't see me."

"Do you honestly believe that?"

"Okay, no. Maybe he had no reason to, or he thought I was dead already. I probably looked it—I must've been covered in drying blood. And my eyes were open."

Pack didn't answer. He looked at her, those same dark eyes staring at him, her scar livid against her pale skin, a damaged version of a little girl he'd only seen in photographs since she was a child. She wanted him to save her. Too bad. She'd come to the wrong guy.

He went to the kitchen, opened one of the cabinets, and

pulled down a sugar bowl. He brought it over to the coffee table and put it down. Out of it he took out a baggie of greenish brown leaves and a small folder of rolling papers. He glanced at her once then started rolling a joint.

When Vida saw what he was doing, her eyes widened in hurt. She recovered quickly and shook her head in disgust. "Oh, of course. Mom told me. I guess it explains this," she gestured around the room, "and all the other lifestyle choices you've made. Or haven't."

"Hey, you should talk, Pip."

It was the first time he'd used her old nickname, and she said: "Don't call me that. Who the hell is Pip? The name's Vida."

"Fine." He took a small disposable lighter out of the sugar bowl and lit the joint, inhaling. It popped and burned, and while he was still holding his breath, he held it out to her.

"Yeah, right. That's all I need."

He gave a snort of laughter. "Whatever."

After a few tokes he put the joint out and sat back heavily in the recliner. Vida was still on the couch, looking out the window.

"Okay, so what d'you want from me?" he said.

She looked at him coldly. "I should never have come here."

"Why did you?"

"I thought maybe you and Uncle Mitch could help me stay alive."

He crossed his arms. "Uncle Mitch, huh? You afraid of being sent back to Iraq?"

"Hell no," she said, though he saw a flash of something like fear pass over her face. "But I need to find out what happened. If I rejoin my unit, I'll never figure it out. I want to go to the police, but I have to give them something real, or they'll laugh at me. And I need to figure it out before I go back, or one day the guy who shot Haley will shoot me."

"That's bull. Why would he shoot you? Even if this guy exists, he did what he set out to do, right? He killed the other girl."

She looked at him as if he were stupid. "He must know now that I survived, that I could remember him. *Might* remember him! He doesn't know I never saw his face. Anyway, maybe I did see him and I'll remember in a few weeks. Either way, I need to find out before I go back."

"Where'd you get the handgun?"

"Guess."

"Hmm. Your stepdad."

"No. He's not like that."

"Why not? You live in Alaska, don't you? Don't you all have guns there? He and your mother are still together, right?"

"Pops has shotguns and a rifle."

"Pops, huh? He a nice guy?"

"He's the best. But he doesn't like pistols. Keep guessing."

"You bought it."

"Nope."

"You stole it."

"Sort of."

"Great. Why sort of?"

"Because when you steal from relatives, it's not really like stealing."

"Oh yeah? Who'd you steal it from? Your fat old Uncle Thing-amajig in Chicago?"

"Uncle Bob? Nope. Guess again."

"I give up."

Her burst of laughter had an edge to it. "From you, *Dad*. I found it in your bedside table."

"Oh, shit. My Smith & Wesson."

She had a beautiful smile and, for the first time, she let it shine. "Mine, now, asshole."

CHAPTER 4

Within ten minutes the weed had kicked in, and any possibility of conversation between father and daughter vanished like old smoke. Vida sat on the couch a little longer and then, when Pack fell asleep, she stood up. She walked into the kitchen. She looked at the dirty floor and the baked-on filth on the stove. She opened the fridge and smelled the sour milk. The smudged windows reflected the two dim bulbs that now lit the dreary room.

Vida felt a wave of despair. She'd counted on him; she was sure that when she turned up, he'd be shocked, maybe even angry at first, but finally he'd realize he was glad to see her, and he would do what he could to help her. She glanced over at him, the shiny black jacket, the white thatch of hair. His mouth open. Snoring. The yellowing patch of hair under his lower lip moved as he exhaled. What good was he going to be? He couldn't help her. He'd probably end up getting her arrested.

She would take the gun and any spare ammunition, and get out. She hadn't told him anything important. She could leave now, and forget all about him. Plan A was a dead end; it was time for Plan B.

If only she knew what Plan B was.

CHAPTER 5

When Reynolds Packard started awake at three A.M., it was dark and he needed to piss. His mouth tasted as if he'd been chewing on burnt logs. He was disoriented, until his body recognized the feel of his recliner and transmitted the message to his brain. Slowly, with a groan, he pushed his legs down, righting the chair. He had forgotten about the girl, and when he remembered her he groaned again, this time with feeling. He wondered where she was. Probably asleep in his bedroom, he thought with some resentment. Which meant he'd have to spend the rest of the night on the couch.

After turning on the hall light, he went to the bathroom, not bothering to do it quietly. He wasn't going to change his habits to suit her. After flushing, he looked into his bedroom. He hadn't made the bed for a while, so, at first glance, it looked as if there was a body stretched out on the mattress. But when he looked more carefully, he realized it was just the bedding. He had a second room, but there was no bed in it. He looked in it anyway, but there was nothing but the desk and some cardboard boxes piled in the corner. No girl.

She was gone. Either temporarily, or for good. To his surprise, he felt a pang of something that wasn't relief. He filled the kettle at the sink and put it on the stove. He needed coffee. As he waited for the water to boil, he had the grace to be ashamed that he had smoked a joint in front of her. What was he trying to prove? That he had no intention of being a father to her?

27

That shouldn't have come as any surprise to her. But no, he'd gone out of his way to scare her off. That stuff in the sugar bowl was old and stale and tasted like crap. The last time he'd smoked had been more than two years ago. He'd lost interest in getting high long before Vida showed up.

Suddenly, he remembered his pistol. He dropped what he was doing and went into his bedroom. But the drawer of the small bedside table was empty, all the bullets gone. Christ! Didn't even recognize his own gun when it was pointed at him and then he slept while his daughter walked out the door with it. She was right, he was an asshole.

CHAPTER 6

Mitch Jedd lived on the main road in Goose Creek, in a small peach and brown Victorian he'd been painstakingly remodeling for the last twenty years. For most of that time, his mother, Dot, had lived with him, providing support, light labor, and hot meals. And then, five years earlier, she'd begun having speech problems. When the doctors took a look they found she had a growth in her brain the size of a peanut. She'd refused surgery, saying she was too old. The tumor grew, and five months later she was dead.

At the time, Mitch was a state trooper. Soon after his mother's death, he retired and started teaching a weapons safety course at the local Rod and Gun Club. For two years he was a model citizen: didn't miss a lesson; came early to all the meetings; volunteered for all the committees. And then, on the third anniversary of Dot's death, Mitch came to the weekly meeting at the gun club wearing his usual jeans and denim jacket, but this time he had added a cheap, shoulder-length red wig and pale-blue eye shadow.

To the stunned silence he announced that he now wanted to be known as Millie. His short speech met with hoots of laughter and good cheer. Good old Mitch, he sure knew how to make fun.

But Mitch crossed his well-muscled arms, waited till they settled down, and said that, hey, he wasn't kidding. His name was now Millie. At the age of fifty-eight, he was going to live the way he had always wanted to live, and if the rest of them didn't like it, they could shove it.

And then he said he'd see them at the next meeting, and walked out the door. In silence, they watched through the windows as he got into his truck.

It wasn't until he'd driven away that the shocked membership started going at it. Never, they said to each other! No goddamn way. It was disgusting, plain disgusting. It made a mockery of everything they stood for. Plus, it would make them the laughing stock of every gun club in the state. And what about their members in law enforcement? They'd never live it down. Jesus, what would Dot have said? Tell you what, they'd kick him out of the club, that was for sure. No two ways about that. Hell, they'd run him out of town.

Eventually someone got out the rule book. They looked up their mission statement; they went through the by-laws. But it wasn't a gender-specific club and there was nothing in the by-laws, no matter how close they read them, that forbade a member from cross-dressing. It had never come up before. For now, it seemed like there was nothing they could do.

During the months that followed, the members of the club and the local law enforcement community laughed at Mitch behind his back. And often to his face. A few of them discussed in detail what they'd like to do to him, in public or on a deserted back road. He got anonymous phone calls, voices in the night that threatened to remove his man parts and shove them down his throat.

But the threats were just talk: he was a tough old guy with a stack of carry permits and a serious gun collection, so no one really wanted to mess with him. And anyway, most of them had known and worked with Mitch for years. Some of them had even gone to school with him, and even now, if they could ignore the eye shadow, they still liked him. He didn't talk or walk funny. He hadn't really changed that much. But it was just so damn *weird*.

Eventually, without anyone noticing how it came about, it stopped mattering so much. At the club, when Mitch got up to go to the bathroom marked *Does* instead of the one marked *Stags*, no one bothered to snicker and catch anyone's eye. They kept on with the business at hand. Mitch was becoming a memory, and Millie had muscled her way into his place.

CHAPTER 7

Mitch Jedd was Pack's cousin; they'd practically grown up together. Mitch was like an older brother to him, and though Pack now called him Millie in public, when they were alone or he was under stress, he sometimes slipped up and called him Mitch. And Millie didn't fight it. She knew she had to be a little more tolerant with family.

Pack waited until seven-thirty before calling his cousin. A deep voice, undertones of gravel, answered. "Hell-ow."

"Mitch. Where are you?" he asked.

"Home, where'd you think? You?"

"Meet me now? I got a problem."

"Okay, but I have to be at the club in two hours."

"Won't take long."

Because Millie lived partway to Hudson, they usually got together somewhere in between, usually in Bantam. Their favorite breakfast place was on Main Street. They'd been going there on and off for thirty years, and though it had changed ownership a few times, it still offered all the important choices and strong American coffee to wash them down.

Millie was waiting at a table at the back when Pack walked into the narrow, darkened space. The latest owner, MaryLyn, had repainted and decorated the place with bunches of dried flowers and ceramic figurines, but wisely kept the heavy maple furniture that had been there for three decades. Pack pulled out one of the armchairs, and sat down.

Millie's eyesight wasn't great, and she did a lousy job with her makeup. The jarring blue eye shadow was patchily applied to her lids, and she had two angry spots of blush on her jowly cheeks. No stubble showed through, however, and Pack worried for a second that his cousin was having something done professionally to remove it. The thought gave him the willies. He had an unspoken hope that one day Mitch would wake up and shake Millie off, like a bad cold.

"How's it going, Pack? I ordered for you."

"Eggs and a short stack?"

"Yup."

"Except today I want oatmeal with raisins."

"You're messin' with me."

"Okay, I am messin' with you."

"So, what's up?"

Pack took a breath. It suddenly came to him that this was not going to be as easy as he thought. "My daughter, Vida, came to see me last night."

Millie smiled slowly. "You're kidding. The Pipsqueak? That's great. When do I get to see her?"

"You don't. She's gone."

"Why? Something wrong?"

"No. Yes. We had a disagreement."

Millie sat back with a frown, putting both meaty hands on the table. Her short fingernails were painted a bright red, the varnish chipped and wearing off. She drummed her middle fingers on the tabletop. "Did you know she was coming?"

Pack rubbed a hand through his hair. He avoided eye contact with his cousin. "No idea. She surprised me."

"And? Why'd she leave?"

"I don't know. She asked me for help, and maybe I wasn't too positive about the idea."

"She's in trouble?"

"Yup. She thinks someone killed her roommate."

"You're kidding. She's in college? She turned into a nut job or d'you believe someone's really after her?"

Uncomfortable, Pack shifted in his chair. "I don't know. The friend's dead, I guess. Though I still think Vida's imagining killers."

"I guess or is that the truth? That her roommate's dead?"

"Truth."

"Now you're pulling my leg, right?"

"No, I swear."

"No, I mean if this other girl's dead, how come you don't believe her? I think you should be giving her the benefit of the doubt."

"Hey, her roommate's dead because Vida's a soldier, they ran over one of those fucking IEDs, and the other girl got unlucky."

"Jesus. You're telling me your little girl's a soldier in I-raq? Christ almighty. She was hit by one of those roadside bombs? Is she okay?"

"She's got a pretty bad slice on her face. And a limp."

"Poor kid. So go on. She's on leave, comes to find her long lost dad, ask him for help. Then what?"

Pack paused. "Actually, leave's over."

"Leave's over?"

"She's on the run."

"On the run? You mean, she's AWOL? Come on, Pack, am I going to have to drag this whole damn thing out of you?"

Pack sighed. "She needs me to help her find someone at the VA hospital."

"Why?"

"I don't know. There's someone there she needs to talk to."

"That's it?"

"That's exactly what I said to her. I asked, is that it? If I get you into the VA hospital, are we even? She said, you left me when I was six, you never came to see me. We'll never be even."

"She's right."

"But that's not true, her mother left me, I didn't leave her."

"Keep telling yourself that, man."

By the time Pack left MaryLyn's, he'd been assigned one task. To find his daughter. Millie wasn't interested in his excuses and his personal interpretation of Vida's fears.

"Not the point, man," she said, rapping her knuckles against the table, rattling the dirty dishes. "The point is, your daughter came to you for help"—she raised her palms to the ceiling as if describing a miracle—"she came to you, no one else, not her stepfather, not her commanding officer, and you blew her off."

"Hey, she didn't have to—"

"Your kid's career, her future, and maybe even her life are on the line. Time to pull your finger out and grow up, Pack."

So, Pack's job was simple. Find Vida and do whatever she wanted. No more. No less.

CHAPTER 8

Pack didn't want to, but he knew the best place to start was at the beginning. So he used directory information for Talkeetna, Alaska, and asked for his ex-wife. Her married name was Gustafson. He was grateful when she, and not her husband, Bill, answered.

"It's me, Packard," he said.

"Packard? Reynolds Packard?"

"You know many others?"

There was a silence. He wondered if she was going to hang up. He also didn't know how far the Army would go in its hunt for absentee soldiers. Maybe they tapped phone lines. "I'm calling you about the money you say I owe you," he said, voicing the idea as it came to him.

The thing was, he didn't owe her money, and they both knew it. When she'd decided to leave, he'd given her everything he'd been left by his father, plus he'd told her to take everything that was in their savings. He didn't want to feel obligated or have to write a check every month. He'd intended to send her more whenever he could.

But somehow, that hadn't happened. When she remarried someone with a steady job and benefits, Pack figured both she and Vida were better off without him. So maybe their marriage hadn't turned out the way either of them had hoped, but she definitely wasn't expecting money from him.

He heard her intake of breath on the other end of the line.

She must've been holding the phone right up to her mouth. After a long pause, she said flatly, like someone who hadn't rehearsed enough: "Okay, good, finally. It's about time. How do we do this?"

"I don't want to discuss it with your loser of a husband nearby. I don't want him telling me what to do or interfering."

"Yes, I know. Okay," she said, calmly, throwing her gentle-spirited man to the timber wolves.

"Go to a pay phone that's not too close to home and call from there." He gave her the number of the public phone in Bantam near the gas station. "Twenty minutes from now, okay, Shelley?"

"I'm leaving." She hung up.

He stood holding the phone. It occurred to him that other than a few postcards in either direction and various legal documents, they hadn't communicated in at least ten years.

He was waiting there when the phone rang.

"Hello?"

"It's me. Is she okay?" Shelley asked, skipping any small talk.

"I don't know. She was here, but then she took off."

"Oh, god. Was she alright? How was her leg?"

"She didn't mention it."

There was a moment of silence till Shelley said: "What did you do to her?"

"Whoa, I didn't do anything to her. She broke into my house and was waiting for me with a gun."

"Oh, god," she said again, her voice cracking, "she must've been so scared. Where'd she get a gun? What did she want with you?"

He skipped her first question. "I don't know what the hell she wanted. She said someone was trying to kill her. She sounded paranoid and crazy."

"I knew it, I knew it! Oh, Pack, you idiot!" she burst out. "Your own daughter shows up and you think she sounds crazy? You didn't listen to her?"

"Shelley, come on. I didn't even know who she was."

Shelley ignored him. "She's a smart, good person. Hardworking, dedicated. We knew something was wrong, but we thought it was just the trauma, you know, from the attack. She wouldn't talk about it with me or Bill. And what do you mean, they're trying to kill her? You have to find her, okay? Goddamn it, you owe it to her."

Reynolds Packard shook his head, defeated. "Why does everyone keep saying that? Look, I don't know. Just give me her phone number, and I'll talk to her. I'll even go and see her, if she's nearby. She's still in New York State?"

"You're not listening! I don't know! She hasn't called us or any of her friends. She's alone out there. Her cell phone never picks up, and I don't know how to find her. Other than the MPs, this is the first I've gotten word of her since she disappeared two weeks ago."

"Jesus, Shelley. I need to hear what happened. From when she came home."

"Nothing special happened!"

"Okay, so tell me from the beginning."

He heard his ex-wife take a deep breath.

"After the hospital in Germany, they sent her home to recuperate. She was very thin, jittery, walked with a cane. For the first five days, she just ate and rested. At night, I could hear her cry out in her sleep. I'd go into her room and she'd be thrashing around with some kind of nightmare. I tried to talk about it with her, I suggested we go into the VA, but she refused.

"During the day, she did those exercises given her by the physical therapist and she watched television. Bill took time off from his job with the railroad to be with her. Pack, I had no idea what she was planning."

"You didn't notice anything else?"

"Well, a couple of times, we found her standing in the open front door, staring down the street past the other houses, as if she were waiting for someone. But when she saw us, she'd come back inside."

"Okay. What else?"

"Let's see, by the end of the first week, she began going for walks. Marci, her best friend from high school, went along if she wasn't at work, carrying Vida's cane in case she needed it. By the time they made it back, Vida would be sweating, her skin gray. 'If it hurts too much, don't do it, honey,' I told her. But the next day, she'd be out longer."

"Sounds like she was trying to push herself to get stronger," Pack suggested.

"It seemed desperate, is all. Then four days before she was due to report back to her unit, she told us she was going to take the train down to Anchorage early. She wanted to visit an old school friend. We were sorry to lose her, but it was her leave, and having a little fun in Anchorage seemed like a good idea. The only thing was, when she left she just had a backpack with her. I asked why she wasn't taking her duffel bags, but she said, no, no, this is plenty. Most of my stuff's at the base. Which wasn't true, because a week ago we found a lot of it in boxes in the attic. BDUs and the rest of her military gear."

"So how did you find out she was missing?"

"A week after she was due to check in at Fort Dix in New Jersey, we heard from the officer in charge. She'd never shown up. No phone call, no email. No word. He thought we were involved, we were hiding her, but eventually he realized we knew less than anyone."

"That's it?"

"No, that's not it. As of about ten days ago, they listed her as missing, whereabouts unknown. Absent Without Official Leave. Do you know that after thirty days, the Army could consider her a deserter? The police have been alerted, he said, in case she was involved in any criminal activity or met with foul play. Jesus god."

Pack tried to reassure her. "Hey, I just saw her, okay? She hadn't met with foul play, and as far as I could tell, she wasn't hanging around with felons. Look, are the MPs calling you a lot?"

"No, just this officer and another one out of Fort Benning. He seemed okay—polite, very businesslike."

"Don't talk to him again, or if you have to, be careful. Cry, say you miss her—just don't give him any information at all, nothing. Not about me, not about Mitch, nothing. And tell Bill the same, okay?"

After he hung up, Pack stood with his hand on the receiver, lost in thought. Shit. He walked to his car and slid behind the wheel, his rear settling heavily into the cracked leather seat. He leaned back on the headrest, staring unseeing at the street. The girl hadn't called him or wanted to see him since she was a kid, so why now, when he felt tired and old and just wanted to be left alone? When he was finally accepting his life for what it was?

Finally, like a bout of indigestion, the moment of self-pity passed. He let his thoughts start drifting back to the conversation. According to his ex-wife, their daughter was a model citizen. Enlisted out of high school, smart, hardworking, patriotic. Perfect little soldier, he thought wryly, not like the usual bunch of ADD boneheads that filled the ranks. So what happened? She ran into an IED and lost her nerve? Yeah, and why not? Who wouldn't, with half a brain? It goes under the heading: War is Hell.

But right in his living room she'd claimed that a fellow soldier had committed murder. And she might be the next victim. So either her memory wasn't playing tricks on her, and she was actually in danger, or else she was delusional. Okay, put aside the delusional for the moment. If what she remembered was true, what the fuck was going on?

He gave up on that question for now. What he had to figure out was how to find her. He tried to remember just why she'd asked for his help. Because he was a vet. She'd said he had access to the VA hospital and there was someone there she wanted to talk to.

What goes around, he thought. Once upon a time, Pack too had been in the pay of Uncle Sam. A Special Forces bonehead. Never was in-country, just spent his time with the 82nd Airborne at Fort Bragg, training new recruits in hand-to-hand combat. Teaching teenage boys to kill.

Sometimes the draftees he'd taught would show up after a tour. They weren't the same boys who left—many of them now had long hair and exotic tattoos, and some were so hard and crazy their COs seemed afraid of them. Plenty didn't come back at all.

At twenty-two, Pack had felt like an old man. As soon as he could, he left the service. One of the first jobs he found was driving for a long-distance trucking company. He liked it; just himself and the open road, accountable to no one so long as he brought the cargo in on time. He ate at off-ramp diners and slept in the cab of his truck, his rig parked in interchangeable, flat gray parking areas.

He might never have slowed down if he hadn't met Shelley. But it turned out to be only a temporary change of pace, one just long enough for marriage, a house, and a little girl. Six years later, he was on his own again.

And now that child was grown-up and on the move, just the way he had been. Only the reasons were different. And he was going to have to find her before the Army or anyone else did. Which brought him full circle.

So. Why had she come to this area? Not entirely for the pleasure of looking him up. No. Partially because, as a veteran, he had access to the VA hospital. Right. And not any VA hospital. This one. There was a particular person she needed to speak to there. Which meant said person was either a patient or an employee. Maybe someone she'd known overseas. He searched his memory for the name of the base where she'd been stationed. Fallujah? No, Tallil. And she said she'd run into the IED about six weeks earlier.

He could call Shelley back and ask her for all the details, but first he thought he'd give a look at the Internet. He didn't own a computer, but he knew his way around one well enough to get started.

At the small village library, there was one free machine. It was a few feet away from a girl of about twelve, a laptop and pile of textbooks on the scarred wooden table in front of her. Though she was probably supposed to be doing her homework, he could see she was in a cyber conversation, giggling to herself, her fingers hammering the keyboard at warp speed.

His fingers felt fat and slow by comparison. He typed the words: "American casualties in Iraq" into the search engine. One of his first finds was a list at a website called icasualties .org. It seemed to be a site that was collating and tracking data from the Department of Defense. It showed headings of information: names on the left, followed by nationality—U.S., U.K., Other—date of death, town and province, and cause of death. He saw a long column of IEDs under cause of death, interrupted by the occasional Vehicle Accident. Cause and effect. Death, straightforward and scrollable.

He plugged in the month when Vida would have been

wounded. The long list refreshed, this time with new names and places, but looking very much the same as the last—mostly IED after IED, hostile fire after hostile fire.

Finally, he found the only two female casualties listed during the week of the accident to Vida. One was a Sgt. Mary DiStefano, and the other a Specialist Haley Ann Flynn. DiStefano died in an accident to her vehicle. Haley Flynn died by Improvised Explosive Device, followed by small arms fire. He double clicked on her name, and up popped a Department of Defense memo, headed IMMEDIATE RELEASE.

Pack glanced through the announcement of her death. No surprises. "She died August 12 of wounds sustained when vehicle was attacked by enemy forces using an improvised explosive device and small arms fire." From what he'd heard, the IED was probably detonated under their vehicle, either through impact, or by remote control. Then, when the soldiers inside tried to save themselves, they were ambushed by the enemy, now using handheld weapons.

He sat looking at the chart, envisioning the sand and dust, the noise and chaos. The twisted metal and flames. The blood. He pictured Haley Flynn. He thought of the girl he'd met the other night, his daughter, asking for help. He shook his head and hissed, unaware he was making noise. The young girl next to him looked over; his gaze, raw with the brutality of the pictures in his head, must have scared her. As soon as he looked away, she started pulling her books together and shoving them into her backpack.

Oblivious, Pack glanced over the DOD announcement. Specialist First Class Haley Ann Flynn, of Delmar, New York. Hey. Delmar was a suburb of Albany. That was it—it couldn't be a coincidence. Had to be one of the reasons that Vida had come to his neck of the woods; the dead friend had family here.

All he had to do was find out who and where.

There were twelve Flynns in the Albany phone book. He ran the page through the copier and paid fifteen cents to the librarian on his way out. Once he got to his car, he started at the top of the list, looking for the family of Haley Flynn. Halfway down he found a listing for Flynn, Joseph, in Delmar.

"Who's this? Who's calling?" The voice at the other end was female, and agitated.

"Sorry to disturb you, ma'am," he said, flattening his tones out, letting his eyes rest on the street sign ahead of him, "this is Sergeant Woodbridge, calling from Fort Benning. How're you doing today?"

"How d'you think I'm doing? What did you say your name was?"

"Sergeant Woodbridge, ma'am. I'm sorry for your loss. Specialist Flynn was a valuable member of her unit," he continued. "Am I speaking to a family member?"

"She didn't have anyone but me, you must have that in your precious files, Sergeant. Don't you have that in your files?"

"Yes, ma'am," Pack continued. "I was just making sure. In case you were a family friend. Can someone from Grief Counseling come by and speak to you?"

"What about? What else is there to talk about? What do you want?"

"Nothing, ma'am. This is a courtesy call. We thought you might appreciate having someone in the military to talk to about your daughter. Her sacrifice means everything to her country."

The woman dissolved into slow, wet sobs. Pack felt like a rat, a mean, sharp-toothed rat digging into her heart.

"Fine, fine, come over. But not today. Tomorrow. Around three. I'll be back by then." Pack heard the clatter of the receiver, then a dull dial tone.

He underlined the number he'd just called, and went back into the library.

Inside, his computer was still free. He sat back down and reverse searched the number. Within seconds, up came a name and street address. Joseph Flynn, 3275 Birchwood Lane, Delmar, NY.

He was a little closer. Now to find out when Vida had last seen her dead pal's mother, because he was sure she had gone to see her. And was probably expected back.

Chapter 9

The night before, in Delmar, Vida had climbed into Haley's childhood bed, worn out. As she lay there, waiting for sleep, her mind drifted to a photograph she'd found back home in Talkeetna, the night before she left for Anchorage. It had snowed lightly, and she had stayed up late, packing, looking through old letters and pictures. She came across one of herself in dress uniform, grinning, her arms around the necks of a couple of friends. She thought of that moment now, trying to remember how it felt—the excitement, the confidence. But she couldn't. It was so long ago. Her eyes filled as she lay there and when she finally rolled onto her side, the damp on her pillow was strangely comforting, though she didn't know why.

Eventually, exhausted, she fell asleep.

In the morning, she could tell by the tangle of bedclothes and residual memory that her sleep had been filled with dreams. She lay still, trying to recall them. She could picture a face, close to her; something she was trying to grasp, but couldn't reach. She gave up.

Downstairs, she could hear Haley's mother moving around. Vida decided to shower, hoping that by the time she was done the woman would have left the house—gone shopping or something. Vida couldn't face her.

After she had dried off and dressed, she listened. The house was quiet and Vida went softly down the carpeted stairs.

But Lorna Flynn was sitting at the kitchen table, hands

folded. She looked weighted down, as if she would never move again.

Vida stopped short guiltily. "Good morning, Mrs. Flynn. You okay?"

Haley's mother was in her fifties, pale and doughy. Her gray hair was tied back into a greasy ponytail no thicker around than a child's pinky. A small mouth was lost between two soft, white jowls. It occurred to Vida it was like a down-turned lima bean between two dinner rolls, and she immediately felt guilty. Mrs. Flynn's large brown eyes might once have been beautiful, but now their whites were a dirty yellow and the skin under them puffy and dark. She was, truly, the saddest person Vida had ever met.

"Yes, dear, thank you," she said, her eyes wet, and they both knew she was lying. "Can I make you some breakfast?"

"Ah, no, I'll just grab some cereal, thanks."

But Mrs. F. stood anyway. She took a bowl out of the cupboard and placed it on the table. Then she found a spoon. She put a box of Froot Loops in front of the bowl. A carton of milk to the right of the bowl. She studied her handiwork. "I think that's it."

"Perfect, thank you." Vida sat down, and began pouring out the brightly colored shapes, wishing she didn't have to eat in front of this so-sad woman. "I was out late."

"I heard you." Mrs. Flynn sat back down.

"I hope I didn't wake you coming in."

"No, no, I like hearing someone in the house. Did you find the person you were looking for?"

"Yes, but nothing came of it. I shouldn't have bothered." She took a spoonful of cereal. She hadn't told Mrs. Flynn that she was AWOL, or about her memory of a U.S. soldier shooting Haley. The woman vacillated between believing her daughter's death was a terrible twist of fate, or a patriotic sacrifice. She didn't need to think that her child had been murdered by a fellow soldier in cold blood.

The only sound in the room was Vida's crunching. "Did Haley ever mention a John Dax?"

"It doesn't ring a bell. Is he the person you went to see?"

"No, I went to see my—someone my mother used to know."

"Oh."

Crunch, crunch.

"Who's John Dax?" Mrs. Flynn asked. Vida doubted she really wanted to know. The question was simply a reflex.

"A friend of Haley's. I'm hoping he can tell me more about what happened in those days before—before the explosion. You know, help me remember. I hate not remembering. Mrs. Flynn, did Haley write a lot of letters?"

Mrs. Flynn shook her head. "Some but not a lot, she was way too busy. She never said so, but I got the feeling her CO didn't trust anyone else to do the job right, you know? So she didn't get much personal time. I used to be proud of that, but now I wish I could give him a piece of my mind, 'cause maybe that's why she was shot—she was most likely tired and wasn't paying proper attention. I don't know. But she did tell me about going to chapel; she told me about the food, and how she wished she could wash more often. You can read them. I keep them in the drawer in the front room."

Chapel? Vida didn't think Haley ever went to chapel. On impulse, Vida reached across the table and touched the woman's wrist. "I'll be leaving in a couple of days. I really appreciate what you've done—putting me up, lending me the car. Haley was lucky to have you."

The woman responded to Vida's touch hungrily. She took hold of her hand and clutched it, her grip damp and warm. Her eyes filled up, as if human contact had opened little tiny faucets in them. "Don't go. You're all I've got left of her. Please."

Vida left her hand where it was. "Mrs. F., I've got to catch up with my unit."

The grip tightened. "Don't go back. It's too dangerous. You'll get killed too."

Vida flinched at the words. "No, no, I won't. Anyway, they're starting to pull troops out. They may not even send me back."

"Please. Don't go. There are people over there who want you dead."

Vida resisted pulling her hand away. "I have to go. I'll be leaving day after tomorrow. That gives me today to find John Dax, hopefully."

Mrs. Flynn sighed and changed direction. "Then I'll cook a big dinner for you tomorrow night, a goodbye dinner. And you'll leave the morning after. What's your favorite food? Tomorrow I can shop and cook. Haley loved lasagna. Do you like lasagna?"

Reluctantly, Vida smiled. "Sure. I love lasagna."

Mrs. F. gave her hand a last squeeze before letting it go. "You're a very kind young woman. Now tell me, this person you're looking for, John, was he Haley's boyfriend?"

"No, just a good friend, I think. They went to meals together, things like that."

"How did you find him?"

"A guy at the hospital with me in Germany, he'd spent a couple of months in Tallil when I was there. He'd heard that Dax was out and got a job here."

"So you want him to help you remember the accident?"

Vida looked up and to the side. "Not the accident, but some of the things that led up to it. What we were doing, what was going on. I feel like I've lost a piece of my life, you know?"

Vida was exaggerating. She hadn't really blanked out everything before the accident, but she couldn't bring herself to tell Mrs. Flynn what was really on her mind. She was hoping that Dax, one of the few people who had been friends with

Haley, knew what had been going on with her on base. Her mother was sure to have no clue because, by the sound of it, Haley had fed her a bundle of lies. Vida needed someone to shed some light. Explain away this feeling of some terrible secret.

As if she could read her mind, Mrs. Flynn said: "I think you're going to be disappointed, honey. That's the terrible thing about tragedies, they just come out of nowhere. No warning. I think you're looking for something to explain it all. But I've finally realized that it's all random. God doesn't involve himself in the small things."

"Maybe, but the more I know, the sooner I'll start to clear the fog out of my brain."

Haley's mother leaned forward and dropped her voice. "I was hoping you'd say this man was her boyfriend. I'd have liked her to have had a real boyfriend, once in her life. Haley didn't have one when she was home, she wasn't allowed to. Her father was very strict, he didn't approve of any of that." Her chin quivered and her eyes filled again with tears. Vida watched helplessly as they spilled over her lids and ran down her cheeks.

Then, Mrs. Flynn surprised her. Her chin, still wet with tears, came up defiantly and she wiped it with the back of hand. "I hope she had some sexy soldier she was in love with over there, and I hope she behaved badly with him. There, I've said it."

Vida smiled at her. "Amen to that!"

Mrs. F. gave a burst of laughter and quickly covered her mouth with her hand, as if someone in the next room might hear and punish her.

Vida said, "If I suddenly remember Haley behaving badly, you'll be the first to know."

"I'll be counting on that." Mrs. F. sighed, as if the little bit of laughter had cleansed her. And then, done with pleasure, face giving back into the pull of gravity and unhappiness, she said: "I'll need my car tomorrow."

"Can I use it once more today?"

"Sure. I just need it to get groceries."

"If you tell me what you want, I'll do your shopping for you."

"You're a kind person. I don't love shopping. All those people, pushing and grabbing." Her hostess stared at the fingers of her left hand and twisted her wedding ring.

Vida waited a moment, then she stood and started clearing the few things off the table.

CHAPTER 10

From the Delmar suburb, Vida reached downtown Albany within ten minutes. Pack's Smith & Wesson was tucked under the driver's seat and she drove carefully, making sure to stay within the speed limit. Bypassing the sprawling Albany Med complex, she turned onto the access road of the Stratton VA Medical Center.

The hospital was a drab collection of high-rises angled into each other, surrounded by a sea of parking lots. The only color contrast was provided by the Stars and Stripes and the black POW/MIA flag snapping in the breeze, planted on a patch of lawn in front of the main entrance. Vida drove around looking for a space and finally found one near the exit. Being in a military facility made her nervous, as if there was a camera focused on the area solely for the purpose of finding soldiers like herself, ones who'd broken the basic tenets of obedience and loyalty. She'd been sure she wouldn't have to do this, that Pack would come here and find this guy for her. Now she had no choice.

She backed into the space so she could see the front entrance to the hospital from the driver's seat. She looked at the car clock. Twelve-thirty.

She turned on the radio and waited, watching the people entering and leaving the building. The man she was looking for was somewhere in his early thirties, over six feet, regular features. She tried to remember something specific, but came up with little. Decent looking, in good physical shape, at least he had been the last time she'd seen him. And she remembered he had a big laugh. She could always pick him out in a crowd by the sound, a sort of inhaled bray.

Thinking of Dax's laugh caused her mind to drift back to those early days, as it often did. The immediate association for her was always the heat. It was like a subliminal flash, unavoidable. Her tour had begun in the spring, but it was already well over 100 degrees by midday. When she first stepped out of the plane in Kuwait, she'd recoiled as if slapped.

"Bad, idn't it, Alaska? Eskimo like you, you ain't gonna make it here," she heard Pascoe's voice behind her, heard the grin in the words. They'd traveled together from the U.S. Pascoe was from South Carolina, and this was his second tour. He was short and stocky and kept his head shaved, even though his scalp was peppered with zits. He usually made a point of adjusting his balls whenever he was around a woman, even if she outranked him. As if, as Haley would later say, they were so fucking *gi-normous*, there was just no comfortable way for them both to fit in his pants. Vida eventually decided he was obnoxious but harmless and did her best to ignore him.

But this particular time he got to her, maybe because she was afraid he was right, she wouldn't be able to hack the heat. She turned her head to the side and snapped: "Shut the fuck up, okay?"

By a quarter to two in the VA hospital parking lot, Vida was starting to second-guess herself. Maybe she was going about this all wrong: Dax might not even be at the hospital. He might be on vacation, or home with the flu. She should go inside and find out.

Before stepping into the lobby, she touched her hair to make sure it was covering the left side of her face; she didn't want anyone to notice her. Inside, she looked around. Most of the seats were occupied by older men, some middle-aged, some frail and shrunken, one or two possibly some of the last surviving World War II vets. None of the old men were amputees, just the middle-aged and younger. Her leg suddenly throbbed, as if in sympathy.

There was an information kiosk in the middle of the hall and Vida approached it, then changed her mind at the last minute and veered away. She didn't want to talk to anyone who might remember her, unless there was no other way. And for all she knew, they could have a closed circuit TV trained on it. The directory on the wall listed various departments. She looked over the categories, wondering where to start. Psychiatric. As good as any. Less likely to see bandages or blood.

The bank of elevators was at the back of the large main hall, and she waited with patients holding forms, doctors in their scrubs, nurses pushing wheelchairs. A few people chatted but most of them watched the slowly descending numbers.

On the fifth floor she followed the signs. She tried to walk as if she had purpose, all the time looking at the faces around her. She hoped she would recognize him when she saw him.

She walked through two small waiting areas on her way, every seat taken, televisions on. The canned laughter was occasionally overpowered by a page over the loudspeaker system, calling a patient or a doctor.

When she reached the main reception, she got in line behind an aging black man in a wheelchair. His legs were so atrophied they were mere ridges on the seat. His head was tilted to the side and he was moaning softly to himself, the sound crescendoing into yips and cries of pain when it was his turn to roll up to the window. The receptionist spoke firmly over his wails, as if he were simply hard of hearing.

When it was Vida's turn to step up, the woman shook her

head. "Any trick in the book," she said, apparently to herself, then looked patiently at Vida over the tops of her glasses. "Yes, hon? Can I help you?"

Vida smiled tentatively, as if confused or had lost her way. "I'm trying to organize my dad's visits and I wondered if you could give me an idea of John Dax's schedule."

The nurse shook her head. "I need the referral from his internist. What team is your father with? Silver?" Vida hesitated, and the nurse continued: "Just give me the last four digits of his social, hon, and I'll see if it came through yet." She looked expectantly at Vida, fingers poised over the keyboard.

"No, no, that's not what I want. My father really likes this John Dax. He's a nurse or an intern, so I thought I'd bring my dad back when Mr. Dax was working. A familiar face."

The woman shook her head. "Don't know any John Dax. You sure he works here?"

"I thought so."

"Give me your name and I'll try to find him for you."

"Oh, no, that's okay. Maybe I got mixed up with another floor. Thank you." Vida backed away.

The nurse smiled automatically, her attention already on the next person in line.

Back downstairs, Vida stood in front of the directory and picked another department. Oncology. Bad, but better than Surgery. Or Prosthetics.

She was about to get in the elevator when she saw the sign for the cafeteria. Not a bad idea. Everyone has to eat, right?

The cafeteria was in the basement, a small, windowless food court on the right side, tables on the left. It was past the lunch hour so if there had been a crowd, it had thinned out, leaving only half a dozen tables occupied. There was a young guy of Vida's age in a wheelchair, talking to an older man. Vida looked him over, but he was obviously a patient, not an employee of the hospital. Vida scanned the rest of the area, looking for men wearing scrubs or clip-on ID tags.

She had just turned away, when she heard him. He was laughing. Braying. She turned to the sound and saw him, sitting at a table at the far left. He was talking animatedly to two women, all three of them in hospital gear, the women with geometric patterned tops to their scrubs. One was a pretty blonde and the other was an older, heavyset woman with glasses on a chain around her neck.

Vida worked her way eagerly between the tables toward him. She had a surge of feeling so strong she felt tears prickle her eyes. Strange, because she barely knew him. But there was such a wave of relief in knowing she was about to see and talk to someone who knew what she knew, who had been where she had been, lived on the same base and breathed the same dry, infernal air in the place where she had nearly died. Not one more civilian she had to act normal with, or talk to about irrelevant crap.

"Dax?" she called out, as she neared the table.

He looked up, mid-laughter. "Hello?" And just when Vida was sure he didn't recognize her, he said: "Oh, wow, hey, I know you—Vida Packard, Specialist, right? Tallil?"

"Yeah." She grinned at him, happy.

He pushed his chair back and stood up. He was tall, maybe six foot three, well-built, with short wavy hair that was a pale orange, something like strawberry blonde. His complexion was mottled, the kind given to easy blushing. And in Iraq, she suddenly remembered, he sunburned quickly and his nose was always peeling. The memory made her smile again. "I've been looking for you," she said.

He said, "For me? Really? I guess that's good, right? Hey, let me give you a hug." He put his arms around her and squeezed her. She laughed. "You want to join us? Pull up a chair."

The older woman stood, shaking her head. "We're late already." She looked at Vida. "He's all yours. We've been having way too much fun, and Carla and I are both going to be in big trouble with the docs."

The younger nurse sulked sexily. "I'll see you later, Dax?"

He didn't answer, just raised his eyebrows suggestively at her. She seemed to find that satisfactory and, ignoring Vida, followed the older woman out of the cafeteria.

"She's crazy about me," he said, with a grin. "What's a man to do?" He gestured to the food court, as if it were his personal kitchen. "You want coffee? Some chow?"

"Coffee would be great. Thanks." With a sigh, Vida sat down. The chair was still warm.

"Milk? Sugar?"

"A little milk. Two sugars."

"Consider it done."

She watched him across the room as he dispensed coffee into a Styrofoam cup, his legs locking and unlocking as if it were impossible for him to stand still, or he had music running endlessly in his brain. She didn't remember that about him. There seemed to be no sugar, and he went over to an elderly woman in an apron wiping down counters. She could see from where she was that he was flirting with the lady, cajoling her. The woman laughed and flapped her hand at him. She disappeared and came back with a container of packets. Dax grabbed a fistful and held it in the air, playful, victorious. At the cash register, he threw money down without waiting for change.

"There's another lady that loves you," Vida said, smiling, as he walked up.

"Ah, yes. Old Janet. I won't deny it." He placed the coffee in front of her. "So, how are you, girl?" he asked, settling in across from her, his long legs spread, his forearms on the table. He was good-looking in an athletic, all-American sort of way, with a short nose, pale eyebrows.

She reached for the cup. "Fine. Not bad."

"You caught a break there, didn't you?" he said.

"What do you mean?" she asked, confused.

"I mean the IED. You were lucky, you walked away."

"Was carried, more like."

"Yeah, but what d'you get, a little shrapnel in the leg and a cut face?"

Blindsided, Vida felt a hot burn start up in her neck. She knew she was overreacting, but she couldn't help it. She wanted to get into his face and shout, "this ain't nothing, fuckhead—"

She took a deep breath, swallowing the feelings. "Just about," she said.

He watched her, then said: "Hey, I don't mean to make light, but Haley, she got the short end, right?"

"No question."

"So, what can I do for you?" He nodded, encouraging her, apparently oblivious to her suppressed anger.

"I heard you were here, and I wanted to see a familiar face."

"That's cool."

"Also, I'm looking for some information."

"Information? Anything you want. 'Bout what?" His foot beat time under the table, rocking it, spilling a little of her coffee. He didn't seem to notice.

"Haley. I'm looking for some insight into Haley."

He laughed. "Insight into Haley? Hey, you lived with her. Aren't females supposed to know all about each other?"

"Yeah, well, we weren't like that."

"What do you mean?" He frowned slightly, as if she was denying they were lovers, and by denying was making it truth.

Vida felt that their signals were getting all mixed up. She tried to clarify. "We didn't live together for that long and she was pretty private. So now I'd like to learn a little more."

"Why?"

"Why?" She was surprised at the new surge of anger she felt. What was with this guy? He wasn't what she expected. He was beginning to be a disappointment. "Because she was killed out in a field in the middle of fucking nowhere, right next to me. That's why."

"Hey, I was just kidding around. Take it easy." He sat back, as if satisfied that he'd gotten a rise out of her.

"No, you take it easy."

"Look, I apologize. I didn't mean to wind you up."

Vida was still trying to reabsorb the adrenaline that had rushed to the surface. She didn't answer, just nodded.

His expression turned suddenly sad, but he kept his eyes on her. He lowered his voice. "The thing is, I loved Haley."

"You're kidding, right?"

"Hell, no. In fact, we were going to get married. Once we got home for good. I'd told my Dad and everything."

"I'm sorry. I didn't know."

He ran both hands through his short wavy hair and looked away, desolation in his eyes. "No, no one did. It seemed like bad luck to talk about it."

"I wish I'd known."

Dax shook off the sadness and gave a snort of laughter. "Hey, maybe you did and you forgot. Those head injuries come with a lot of amnesia. Forgotten a lot from that time?"

Vida searched for the answer. "Not really. I remember quite a bit about the base, but I can't remember anything just before the ambush."

He shrugged. "That's pretty normal. Some of that may never come back."

"That's what they say. I'm getting some weird dreams, though, flashes. They feel like memories. Enough to make me wonder if something wasn't right."

"How do you mean?"

"Oh, nothing I can put my finger on. Just little slivers."

"Yeah, well, those recovered memories or whatever they call them, they can be total bullshit."

She glanced up at the huge digital sign above the cafeteria entrance. It was a continuous scroll, in blue letters, of surnames of pharmacy patients whose prescriptions were filled and ready for pick-up. Name after name, like a story slowly unfolding. "You think so?"

He laughed deprecatingly. "Hey, I'm no shrink."

"What department do you work in here?"

"Oncology."

"I was just about to look there for you. How long've you been here?"

"What is this, twenty questions?"

"Just wondering when you left Iraq."

He took a deep breath, as if resigning himself to sharing information with her. "My deployment ended a few days after Haley was killed. The date had been in the works for a long time. Weird timing, right?"

Vida leaned forward. "Tell me, was Haley having a hard time with anyone? Did she have any enemies?"

"Hey, I thought you were a truck driver, not a detective." He smiled, but there was a hardness to his eyes. "Did she have any enemies? No. She was a good, sweet gal. Never hurt anyone, never had a bad word for anyone." Each hand beat in separate, discordant rhythms on the table top. "It was my fault. I should have found a way to protect her, to be there for her. But instead I was just far enough away that some fucking towel-head blew her face off. Nothing I could do to stop him."

"Did you guys ever fight?"

He looked at her, confused. "Fight? You mean argue? Sure. We were a couple. All couples argue. So?"

"Just asking."

"Hey, we bickered, but we didn't fight."

"What happened to her diary?"

"Her diary?"

"You know, dear diary, today I fixed a tank. A journal."

He shrugged, watching her. "No idea. You think she kept a journal?"

"I don't think anything, I'm just trying to put together the pieces. I remember her writing. Lying in bed, writing."

"You're making me feel weird, like there was something about her I should've known."

"How could you?" Vida said. "I mean, you hadn't known her that long, right?"

He covered his eyes with his hand, just for a moment, as if to hide his emotions. "Not long. And there wasn't that much time together. You know what it was like, different schedules. She pulled a lot of night duty."

"Yeah."

He put his hand on Vida's forearm. The gesture seemed protective and reminded her of Haley's mother. "You know, you shouldn't go back."

Not from him, too. She pulled her arm away, casually, and scratched her cheek, as if that were the reason for breaking off contact. "Why's that?"

"You should get an Honorable Discharge, you were wounded."

"I'm fine."

"That's bullshit."

"I'm the one who walked away, remember? I'm fine. I just need to find a few answers."

"So what do you really want from me? Other than to remind me of a truly painful time in my life?"

"Oh, gee, I'm so sorry."

He stood up abruptly, rocking the chair. "Nice. Okay. Well, I gotta get back to work. I'll walk you out?"

"No need."

"I want the air."

He followed her out the entrance, toward the elevators, under the list of names. Still scrolling, still waiting.

Outside, the wind had picked up. The flagpoles clanked, a gust pulling at their moorings.

"So, where are you staying?"

Vida shrugged, unwilling to tell him anything about herself. "With friends. But I'm leaving soon."

"How can I reach you if I hear something?"

"What do you mean?"

"I don't know. Something comes to light."

"Comes to light? Forget it."

"Your call," he said, indifferently. And then he added, with a shake of his head: "Why *did* you come see me? You seem pretty hostile."

Vida didn't know what to say. "Hey, you're the one who jumped all over me. I was hoping maybe you could tell me something, something that would make me say, oh, right! That makes sense."

"I get it. Hey, I'm sorry. Maybe I can still shake something loose. Meet me for a drink after I get off work."

"I don't think so." At the corner she stopped and turned to him. "Well, bye," she said, raising her hand, palm toward him. She didn't want to shake his hand.

"Not so fast," he said, and he reached for her shoulders and pulled her toward him, taking her in an embrace, tight, hard.

She couldn't stop herself from struggling against him.

He opened his arms wide, exaggerated. "Wow, sorry. I didn't mean to freak you out." But he was smiling, very slightly. His face was flushed red, she assumed from the chilly breeze.

She nodded at him, turned around, and walked quickly to her car.

John Dax watched her walk away, her back stiff, as if she could feel his eyes on her. He saw her reach a small white car, open the driver's side, and before getting in, he saw her glance his way. He waved. She didn't wave back.

He stayed where he was, on the sidewalk. Vida had to pass right by him when she drove out. When she did, she kept her eyes forward, pretending she didn't know he was still there. She had to stop at the crosswalk to let a pedestrian by.

Boy, did she seem anxious to be gone.

He looked at the car while it idled at the crossing. A New York State plate. So this was not Vida's car, because Vida was from the West Coast. Washington State or someplace. He remembered that, because he was from out West, too. California.

And the car had a bumper sticker that read, "First Baptist Ministry, Albany." That was a dead giveaway. Hadn't Haley told him her mother was a bible-thumping Baptist? And they were from someplace near Albany. So, there was a good chance Vida was staying with Mom. Made sense; the girls were roommates.

What was going on with Vida? She seemed to have something to hide. Did she know something about Haley's death that she wasn't saying? And what was all this about journals?

Maybe it was time to pay his respects to Haley's mother. Probably should have done it sooner.

CHAPTER 11

On the drive back to Delmar, Vida found herself glancing every few minutes in the rear-view mirror, half expecting to see Dax following her.

Talking to him hadn't gone the way she imagined. She wished she'd never looked for him, never found him. So why had she? Because she was looking for a friend? That hadn't worked out. He'd just attacked her. Or had he? Hadn't she just jumped all over *him*, without provocation? And if she'd hoped he'd give her some answers, that hadn't worked out either, because she didn't have the right questions. All she'd done was draw attention to herself.

And what if he tried to reach her and found out somehow that she'd skipped out on her orders? That would be easy to do, she was sure, and he could report her before she had a chance to turn herself in.

Why had he made her so uncomfortable? He seemed to have cared about Haley; he certainly looked moved when he talked about her. Though here he was, already messing around with Carla-the-nurse. Not that it meant much. He was probably the type who always had more than one girl going, like the guy who juggles plates at the circus. It didn't necessarily mean anything. Still, there was something about him. She wondered if she'd ever liked him. She wished she could remember specifics about those last weeks in Tallil. She hadn't forgotten anything, so much as it had all been displaced, scattered, by what had happened on that patrol. She had plenty of memories, but they were non-descript events in her routine, one day indistinguishable from the other, like a photo album of shots out of sequence without names or dates. Nothing specific to those weeks, and very little about Haley.

Except for one night. She had alluded to it when she asked Dax if he and Haley fought. But she hadn't wanted to tell him about it.

She didn't know what date it was, how long before the explosion, but on that night, at about two A.M., Vida remembered being awakened by the slam of the door and Haley coming over and sitting heavily on the edge of her bed. She was whimpering and snuffling.

Vida sat up on one elbow, moving to make room for her. "What's the matter?" she asked, trying to clear her brain.

"I hate this place," Haley sobbed, her voice catching on the words, so it sounded something like: "I-ha-hate-thi-this pl-play-ss."

Vida turned on her bedside lamp, squinting in the sudden brightness. Haley's face was wet with tears, mucus bubbling from her nose. Her hair looked as if she'd been wrestling with a grizzly, and her army-issue t-shirt was streaked with dirt. Her shoulders were heaving.

"What happened to you?" Vida asked, shocked, sitting up in bed.

"I—I—I can't—" Haley said, unable to control her voice.

"Okay, okay." Vida hesitated, and then put her arms around her roommate. Haley leaned into Vida, but the embrace seemed to loosen something and the sobbing became even more uncontrolled. It was hard to make out the words through the wet hiccups.

When the worst of the storm had passed and Haley's sobs turned to dry shudders, Vida gently moved her away so she could look at her face, and asked again: "What happened?"

Haley wiped her face on her arm and looked at Vida. The edges of her cheekbones were sharply angled in the lamplight. "Christ, I must look like shit."

She stood up shakily, and went to her side of the room. She yanked a tissue out of a packet, blew her nose, and took a few deep breaths. "I'm in a bad situation."

"Why? What do you mean?"

Haley groaned, as if she were bone weary. "Oh, I'm so fucking stupid."

"What're you talking about?" Vida threw off the covers and sat up, swinging her feet to the floor.

Haley shook her head. "Trust me, you don't want to know."

Vida made a dismissive face. "Bring it on."

"It's just a bad situation. I didn't know how bad 'til tonight."

Vida felt a feather of fear run up her spine to the back of her neck. "Hey, nothing's written in stone. There's gotta be a way out of everything."

"You believe that?"

"Absolutely. It's *your* life, *your* show."

Haley looked at her, a cynical twist to her mouth. "Wow. I don't know if I buy it, but it sounds good." She looked away. "Let me sort it all out first in my own head, okay? I appreciate the concern, don't get me wrong."

She rifled through the stuff on her desk and found her earphones, put them on, and lay down on her bed. She closed her eyes. Vida realized she was being dismissed.

Frustrated, she lay back down on her bed and turned off her light. Though, if she were honest with herself, she was also relieved. Maybe it wasn't as bad as it looked, just drama with a boyfriend. She'd seen up close how Haley responded to rejection and had no desire to get tangled up in her roommate's messed-up relationships—they were theatrical, painful, and she,

66

Vida, was better off clear of them.

Eventually, she began to relax and drift off to sleep. And then she was pulled back, just a little, by a soft knock on the door. She heard the door open, and whispers. She considered waking up enough to see who it was, but couldn't quite bring herself to do it. She let go and sank into sleep.

CHAPTER 12

Vida woke up to the sound of Mrs. F.'s voice from downstairs. She looked at her watch: seven-thirty. What was someone doing here at seven-thirty in the morning? She rolled quickly out of bed and pulled on jeans and yesterday's t-shirt. There was no visitor that could be good news for her. If it was someone from the Army, she was up a creek if Haley's mother mentioned she was there. If it was anyone else, why so early?

She knew how sounds carried in the small house, so she walked softly to the door of her room and opened it, taking care not to snap the handle or let the door swing against the wall. She listened.

But there was no more talking. It must've been the phone. Haley's mom had a few friends from her church group, and she'd told Vida that sometimes they went to events together, or carpooled to the mall. Vida relaxed and closed her door.

In the small green-tiled bathroom down the hall she showered and washed her hair. Wrapped in a towel, she rubbed Vitamin E oil on her scars and examined them carefully. Some days it looked as if they were fading, but others, like today, they looked as angry as ever. Staring into the mirror, she looked behind her own reflection, at the bathroom Haley had used as a child and teenager. As that jerk Dax said, Vida'd gotten off easy. Haley would have been happy to come out alive, scars and all. Maybe that's why Vida hadn't liked her talk with Dax, because he'd spoken the truth and she hadn't wanted to hear it. She turned away from the mirror.

In Haley's room, she got dressed. She wished she hadn't promised to stay on another day; it was time to leave. She wasn't sure what the next step was, but she had a couple more people she could see in Plattsburg, and after that it was either Canada or turn herself in. Those were her only options. Because she'd be found eventually, and if she couldn't provide a really good reason for running, she'd likely go to prison.

Ten minutes later, she was downstairs. She heard Mrs. F. vacuuming in the front of the house, so she helped herself to a bowl of cereal and ate it quickly, leaning over the sink. When she was done she washed out the bowl and spoon, dried them, and put them away.

When she was ready to go out, she knocked on the wall, trying to get Lorna Flynn's attention over the roar of the vacuum. When she succeeded, the woman started, letting out a small scream before turning off the machine with her foot.

"Sorry about that," Vida said, when the sound died. "I'm going to the bus station. On my way back, I can stop at the store."

"Wonderful, wonderful. Here," Mrs. F. dug in her pocket and pulled out a piece of paper and a small bundle of bills. "I made out a list. Make sure you can read it—my husband always said my handwriting looked like the footprints of a headless chicken. Oh, and get some ice cream. Any flavor you want. You'll see, this is going to be fun. I'm so sorry you're going, I'm going to miss you so much. But at least tonight we'll have fun."

CHAPTER 13

Once she had finished cleaning and dusting, Lorna Flynn sat down at the kitchen table. She was beginning to feel some shortness of breath—must be old age creeping up on her. She thought of the call she'd had that morning from Federal Express. They had a package to deliver and wanted to know if she'd be home during the morning. She wondered who it was from. She never got packages—the last one was the flag, folded into a triangular plastic box, Haley's name on it.

She rubbed her hand over the worn surface of the swirling Formica, wiping away an imaginary crumb, thinking of those years when she and her husband and daughter had sat around it. She always took the long side nearest the stove and the sink, so she could deliver food and clear plates. Haley and Joe always sat across from her.

Today, for no particular reason, or maybe because it was Vida's last day, she had put on a Sunday dress. It was an old one, but it reminded her of Haley, as did so many things these days.

Sunday dresses.

She had been a bad mother to Haley. She knew that now, now that Haley was gone. She hadn't been there for her. She'd let Joe make all the decisions about their daughter's life, decisions that she, Lorna, should have had a part in. The truth is, mother and daughter should stick together against the father. They should give each other strength. Instead, she'd let Joe decide what their girl was going to eat, where she was going to school, even what she was going to wear.

See, right off, that was wrong. Mothers should decide what daughters wear. But Joe always said she had no sense of what looked right on a pretty little girl, because she was so fat. That's what he'd said. But she wasn't fat in those days, was she? Anyway, she was a lot thinner than she was now.

Why did she go along with it? Because she was afraid of him. Not that he hit her, but she was afraid of his contempt, his anger. She shouldn't have been afraid, but when he was angry he said terrible things to her. There were still dents in the wall where he'd thrown furniture. And then when the rage passed he ignored her completely or talked in circles, about how greedy she was, how she embarrassed him and their little girl when they were out in public.

She dreaded it. She felt so burdened, so worn down by it all. The truth was, she hated him. And sometimes she wondered if that was why, when Haley was a little thing, he started insisting he pick the precious little dresses she wore and what sweaters she'd put over them. And the shoes she wore on her tiny feet. Because he knew there was no better way to hurt Lorna. He didn't have to beat her up. He just had to steal Haley from her.

For the rest of Joe's life, that's the way it was. *He* took Haley camping and to the movies. *He* told her about her menstrual cycle, and *he* warned her about sex and boys.

Lorna sighed heavily, her finger drawing an endless loop on the table. She should have fought for her child, her little girl. But by the time Haley was ten years old, she treated Lorna as if she didn't exist. When she was fourteen and it was too late to matter, Joe fell off a ladder and died. Why hadn't he died when Haley was four? It would have been so much better. At sixteen, Haley left home. It was more than two years before Lorna saw her again, and by then Haley had enlisted.

If Joe came back to life right now, would she be able to resist him? If he reappeared in the kitchen, and six-year-old Haley walked in through that doorway, would Lorna be able to stand up to him and protect her little girl? She didn't know. She hoped so, but she didn't know if she could. She was still weak, maybe even weaker than before, softer, sadder. And fatter. She was like a sea cucumber she'd once seen on the TV, shapeless and full of liquid.

Just then, the doorbell buzzed, a sharp, drilling sound. Lorna started, wondering who it could be. Then she remembered the package.

She hoisted herself up from her chair, both hands on the table. She moved on her small feet out of the room, down the short hall to the front door. For a second she hesitated. Her front door had a half-moon window in the highest part of it, which did her no good because at five foot three, she couldn't see out of it. But from where she stood, she could see the sandy top of a head. Tall and male. And very close to the door. She didn't want to open it. But it would be quick; he was just delivering a package.

She unlocked the dead bolt and opened the door a few inches. The man standing on the porch wasn't wearing a uniform, nor was he carrying a package. "Yes?" she said.

The tall, fair-haired stranger was good looking, and had a warm, open smile. "Mrs. Flynn? Hi. It's so great to finally meet you. My name is John Dax. But you can call me Dax, everybody does. I knew Haley in Iraq." He held out his hand, waiting to shake hers.

For a moment Lorna Flynn wanted to shut the door. No more men in my house! But this nice-looking man was someone who'd known Haley. Hadn't she just been kicking herself for being weak and fearful? She shook her head at her foolishness. But she wouldn't just let him in, no questions asked; she wasn't the idiot Joe had always said she was. She'd ask to see ID first.

Ten minutes later, Lorna Flynn was happy. The young man she'd let in the door was a wonderful surprise. Heartbreaking, but wonderful. He was Haley's fiancé, just back from Iraq. Vida had found him at his new job the day before and he'd taken a day off to come and see her. Didn't Vida tell her he was coming? He'd held her hand while his eyes looked into hers. She could see they were filled with a deep sadness.

She led him into the front parlor and they both sat down, he on the overstuffed armchair, she on the loveseat that faced the window.

"If I'd known you were coming, I'd have worn something nicer," she said, and then felt foolish, as if she were trying to flirt with him.

"You're kidding, Lorna, right? I'm just so happy to finally meet you. You were such an important part of Haley's life. She loved you so much."

"She did?" Her vision blurred as her eyes filled with tears. Maybe she'd been wrong, maybe she hadn't been such a bad mother.

Of course, it was then she realized she hadn't offered him anything. She should see if he wanted tea or coffee. Joe, who was much better with people than she was, would have been irritated by her forgetfulness. "How about a cup of tea? Or some coffee?"

"I'd love some coffee, and then we can sit and you can tell me about Haley. No one knew her better than you."

Lorna pushed aside the memory of Haley sobbing at her father's funeral; and after the wake, when everyone had left, walking red-eyed into the kitchen and saying: "It's your fault Dad was so unhappy. You were never there for him. He told me once that you were frigid. You know what we called you? We called you Slushy—cold and sloppy. I hate you."

Lorna tried to smile, but it came out all wrong, as if she were pulling her mouth to the sides for the dentist. "No family is perfect, you know."

"I know that," said Haley's young man, his eyes still damp with tears. "Come on, let's make the coffee together."

Lorna took a deep breath. She didn't want to be a crybaby in front of this lovely man. Let him believe they were a happy family. "Come into the kitchen with me. I only have instant, but I can make it in a flash. In an *instant.*"

He laughed. A loud laugh, full of life. It was contagious, and Lorna joined in, pleased.

"That sounds just like Haley," he said. "She was always offering me instant coffee, in her room, because that's all she could swing. I told her, as soon as we got back Stateside, I'd get her a real percolator. She couldn't wait."

Lorna led the way out of the room but out of his sight her expression was puzzled. What percolator? Haley didn't want a percolator. This fiancé didn't understand that it wasn't for the convenience that Haley made instant coffee; it was because she preferred it. Just like her mother. It was something they'd shared. One of the few things.

Lorna glanced over her shoulder. Suddenly, her visitor reminded her of Joe. He was better looking and taller, but he was the same kind of person. A take-charge kind of man. The kind who liked to make you feel fat and worthless. The kind you had to be very careful around.

In the kitchen, she waited in silence while the water boiled. John Dax walked around the room, touching things. Occasionally he'd glance at her and she would look quickly away. She dumped spoonfuls of coffee crystals into two cups, quietly, angrily. She found a package of stale cookies she'd hidden from herself at the back of the cupboard and put them on a plate in

the center of the kitchen table. Milk, sugar. After she'd poured
the steaming water into the cups and put them on the table, she
sat down.

Dax sat opposite her, arms and legs crossed, one foot going
up and down fast, as if keeping time to an erratic inner
drumbeat. That was something else Joe used to do, Lorna
thought in amazement. She'd forgotten how his foot twitched
and waved from side to side, nervously, like the tail of an angry
cat. She hoped this man would drink his coffee quickly and
leave.

"It must be something to have Vida here, Haley's roommate,"
he said, breaking the silence. "They were pretty close. I was real
happy to see her myself, though it brought a lot of pain with it,
too. Is it hard for you?"

"No, not at all," Lorna answered. She avoided looking at
him. "She's a good girl."

Dax leaned forward, arms on the table. "Are you angry at
me? Have I said something to upset you?"

Lorna was horrified at the directness of his questions. She
needed the social cover, because her instinct told her it was the
only protection she had. She also felt a familiar response wash
over her: a desire to sink away and let the man take charge. Tell
him anything he wanted to know, agree with him, give in. "No,
not at all. I'm just thinking about an appointment I have to go
to soon."

"Well, I won't keep you. But how will you get there? Doesn't
Vida have your car?"

Lorna didn't know what to say. She'd been caught out in a
lie. "Vida won't be long."

"Good. Then I'll wait for her. There are some things we didn't
finish talking about yesterday." He sat back.

So he'd come to find Vida, not to see Lorna at all. And Vida
was her guest, a good girl who'd been hurt in the war, who'd
nearly died alongside her daughter. Lorna should protect her.

Something was unpleasant and Joe-like here, and though she didn't know what it was, she, Lorna, would handle it.

She stood up with an effort, leaning heavily on the table, instinctively exaggerating her weakness. "Vida's been through a lot. She needs to be left alone."

Dax stood up too. He towered over her. He put his hands in his pockets and locked and unlocked his knees, his eyes on her. His jaw moved from side to side. He seemed to be trying to decide what to do next. Then he shrugged. "Lorna, please. Sit down again. God, you're nervous. Why are you so damn nervous? I'm not here to hurt you. I just need your help."

Lorna was surprised. "My help? I can't help you."

"Yes, you can." He sat sideways on the edge of the table, one leg swinging, still taller than her. Lorna felt old and frail. By contrast, Dax seemed a mountain of muscle and moving, twitching energy. "I need to take a look at Haley's diary. You know, her journal?"

CHAPTER 14

Vida found a seat in the bus terminal waiting room and studied the bus schedules, looking at the names of towns and cities, many of them places she didn't know, all populated by strangers. She was afraid, but she shook off the feeling, disregarded it. Sitting there, she decided that, regardless of her promise to Mrs. F., she was going to leave that same night. She could get a late bus, after their goodbye dinner; go to sleep in Albany and wake up someplace new. It was the best way.

Eventually she found something that suited her: an eleven P.M. bus to Watertown, NY. Once she was there, she'd decide. Either find a way to cross the border into Canada, or get to Fort Drum and turn herself in. By ten P.M. dinner would be well over and Mrs. F. would have gone to bed. She felt comfortable with her decision. Lorna would understand. She shoved the booklet into her pocket and went up to the ticket window.

It was well past noon by the time Vida hefted the two bags of groceries out of the car and walked up the path to the front door. She'd taken her time coming back, enjoying the illusion that it was an ordinary day in an ordinary life. She'd stopped at a coffee shop, eaten a bagel, and people-watched. Like a regular girl.

As usual, the curtains in the front room were drawn. However, her eye was caught by something off-kilter. The bottom of the nearest drape was bunched, as if someone had pulled it aside momentarily and then let it fall, not noticing the way it gathered on the sill. Mrs. F. must've done that when she was cleaning. Had to be a first—the woman was so meticulous that if she weren't so soft-spoken, she'd have made a decent drill sergeant. Vida would have to make sure to tidy her room thoroughly before she left.

Once inside, she pushed the front door shut with an elbow and carried the groceries into the kitchen. There was no sound in the house. She put the bags on the table and noticed two coffee cups in the sink. Looked like Mrs. F. had had a visitor. That was good, she seemed to be alone too much. Maybe they'd gone out together.

After she'd unpacked the bags, Vida went upstairs. On the second floor, the house was divided into four rooms that opened onto the narrow landing: on the left side were Haley's room at the back of the house, and her mother's at the front; on the right, the bathroom, and next to it, a room Mrs. F. used for sewing. The master bedroom had one window onto the street and one facing the house next door, while Haley's room, smaller, had two side windows looking out onto the same neighbor's house.

Vida had to admit, she was grateful Mrs. F. wasn't around. She could pack her things peacefully, get organized, with some time to think. Later on, she could help with the cooking.

She tossed her backpack on the bed, unzipped it, and started collecting her few belongings. As she walked from the dresser to the bed, a movement caught her eye in the next door neighbor's window. The two houses were only about fifteen feet apart, and because of an uninspired architect's design, they were both the same height and size, with windows that lined up. The people next door usually kept their blinds down, probably for privacy. Today, the sun was shining, and the light reflecting off the window panes was creating a mirror effect. Vida was seeing herself in one of the windows across from Haley's bedroom. She raised her hand. The girl in the window waved back. Magic.

She started folding her t-shirts and wedging them into the pack. When another movement caught her eye, she couldn't help glancing once more at the other house. She was thinking about Haley, and how often her old roommate must have stood in this room looking out.

This time, however, she realized the movement wasn't coming from her reflection in Haley's room, but from the third window, the one opposite Mrs. F.'s bedroom. Looked like the neighbors had finally decided to open up and let some light in.

Yes. Someone was in that room across the way. Vida remained still, as if not moving would make her invisible. Embarrassing, if he saw her watching him. She could tell it was a man—a tall one—standing with his back flat against the wall, his head turned away from her. He seemed to be next to the door of the room, which looked like a bedroom. He was motionless, in a slight crouch. What was he doing? Weird.

Vida was just about to turn away when a detail at the edge of the window caught her eye.

She looked again, and her heart seemed to stop beating, before her thinking brain could process the information in front of her.

She could see the blind. It was down. Just like it usually was. She wasn't looking into the house next door, she was looking at a reflection, back into the house she was in. She had thought she was alone in the house, but she was wrong.

There was a man in Mrs. F.'s bedroom.

And just as suddenly, sickeningly, she understood what he was doing.

He was standing motionless against the wall, listening to her, Vida, moving around in the next room. The second he turned his head to the window, he'd see her reflection, just as she was looking at his.

Stealthily, she shoved the rest of her gear into her bag, picked it up off the bed, and moved as silently as she could out the door. When she got to the top of the stairs, she took them down two at a time, making no effort to be quiet. She ignored the shooting arrows of pain in her leg. She heard a crash behind her but she didn't turn to look.

She threw open the front door and ran, limping, toward the car. She still had the keys in her pocket and she fumbled for them, yanked open the door, and dived into the driver's seat.

"God, god, god," she said, her fingers suddenly thick and awkward, unable to get the right key, hold it the right way. At last she got it in, turning it hard. The engine roared to life. Quickly, into reverse. "Just run him down," she muttered, expecting to see the man blocking her way.

But there was no one there.

She stepped on the gas too hard and the car bucked backwards before fishtailing out the driveway. She jammed it into drive and leaped forward down the road.

At the corner of the street she slowed down and looked in the mirror. She was trembling with adrenaline, her hands unsteady on the wheel. She turned in her seat, looking over her shoulder.

Nothing. No one. She'd made it.

Her breathing started to slow.

There was nothing she wanted to do more than run. But she couldn't: in all likelihood, Haley's mother was back at the house. Vida couldn't just call the police from a public phone, even if she could find one—they'd take too long. No, she had to go back. Reluctantly, she turned at the corner. She'd circle the block while she figured out what to do.

A black sports car was pulling fast out of the Flynns' street just as Vida came back around the last corner. She guessed, from the squeal of his tires, that it was the intruder, but all she could see was the back of his head. And he was moving too fast for her to read the plate number.

She slowed down and opened her window, listening, waiting until she heard the sound of his engine as it made the rumbling stops and corners and finally grew distant. Then she turned down the street and pulled in front of Haley's house.

Engine off, she reached under her seat and found the black bag that held Pack's handgun, the magazines, and the ammunition. She pulled it out, making sure to keep it low so it was out of sight. She slid the loaded magazine into the gun, chambered it, and put it into her pocket. It was awkward and too big, but she could do it if she moved carefully.

She paused outside the front door, took a deep breath, and slowly opened it. She couldn't be completely sure the man she'd seen was the guy who'd broken in, nor could she know he didn't have a friend. As carefully and quietly as she could, she started up the stairs, gun held out in front of her. She tried to keep her body angled, the gun pointed where she was looking. But she kept her finger out of the trigger guard. Mrs. F. might be somewhere in the house.

On the landing, she glanced into the bathroom. She could see some of the area behind the door through the mirror over the sink. The room seemed empty, but she went in and checked behind the shower curtain.

Back on the landing, she went into the sewing room. The closet door was open and she could see the room was empty. She turned toward Mrs. F.'s room. She was gripping the gun so tight her knuckles hurt; she willed herself to loosen her hold on the handle, but she slid her index finger onto the trigger.

The door was pulled to, and she pushed it gently with the barrel of the gun. It swung open, slowly.

The first thing that hit her was the smell—the core of it was excrement, with a metallic overtone and hits of acid sweat. Vida moaned softly, put the back of her left hand over her mouth, and moved further in. As soon as she was actually in the room, she saw the chair. It was tipped over and its legs were pointed toward the door. She started to move around it, and as she did, the person in the chair was revealed to her.

She was wearing a flowered print dress or shirt, which had flipped up when the chair fell over, pathetically exposing pale, plump thighs. The face was hard to recognize—hidden under tangled gray hair, matted with black blood. But Vida knew it was Lorna Flynn.

For a moment she felt dizzy, and wondered if she was about to pass out. The way she sometimes felt in church, when she was a kid. Then a strange calm settled over her, as if she were floating a few inches off the ground. She put the gun carefully back into her pocket and slowly went to her knees in front of the chair. The woman was taped into it, though her shoulders sagged to the side and her head hung down awkwardly, making her neck look painfully stretched out. Her mouth and eyes were partially open, like a snapshot taken in mid-expression. Her face covered with discolorations and what looked like burn marks.

Vida could hear a faint buzzing in her ears, like a malfunctioning fluorescent light, but she ignored it.

Careful not to kneel in the blood, she felt for a pulse in Mrs. F.'s neck.

No rhythmic beat, but then she hadn't expected to feel one. Lorna Flynn's skin was cool to the touch. Vida stood and circled the chair. She saw that Lorna's arms were bound behind her back with duct tape, the same silver used to strap her to the chair. Vida knelt again and held a wrist. Nothing—no pulse, no flicker of a pulse. She moved her fingers and tried again, in case she missed it. But there was nothing.

She couldn't tell how the woman had died—she didn't know about things like that; but it looked as if she'd been struck hard on the head, because of the blood and matter.

Vida took one last look around the room. There was one dirty white canvas shoe near the body. The dresser drawers were pulled out and overturned. The small, walk-in closet was open, the pull chain light on, and a pathetic array of worn shoes thrown around. Nothing to give Vida an idea what the killer was looking for or who he was.

She walked out of the room.

She didn't realize till she was in Haley's room that she was crying, steadily, noiselessly. She stood in the middle of the room, the buzzing in her head still there.

She sat on the edge of the bed and covered her eyes with the heels of her hands. The total blackness was a relief.

After a few minutes, she dropped her hands and looked around. She forced herself back to the present. She had to leave, she had to make sure all her things were gone. She looked for anything she might have left behind when she ran out before. The few things she found she collected in her arms. In the bathroom, she took her toothbrush and pushed it into her pocket, next to the Smith & Wesson.

Downstairs, she looked in the front room, where Lorna had said she kept Haley's letters. There was nothing there, just empty drawers.

Before leaving, Vida dialed 911 and left the receiver off the hook next to the phone. She could hear the operator's voice, *Hello? This is 911. What is your emergency? Hello! Anybody there?* as she walked out the door. She hoped it would work.

Outside, she searched the car for any of her possessions, stuffed everything she had into her backpack, and swung it onto one shoulder. It was only two short blocks to the main road and the bus stop. With luck, by the time the police came she'd be out of the neighborhood. She looked at her watch. Five minutes to one. She set off down the street, her pace brisk.

The sky was overcast and a breeze was blowing. The fresh air helped to clear her head. What had the killer wanted? Was it something to do with her, or was it about Haley and her mother? The letters were gone, but were they connected to Haley's death, or had Lorna moved them for some other reason? Maybe the intruder was just a random predator who saw a woman alone and figured she'd have money or jewelry stashed somewhere. Somehow, Vida didn't think so.

As she walked, the tears cooled and dried on her face.

CHAPTER 15

Dax liked to tell people that the reason he joined the Army was for the $10,000 bonus. And that was true; it was one of the reasons. He had taken the money and put a down payment on a gleaming black Corvette. He loved the dense creaminess of it, the way the back end was raised, the way it took no prisoners. It looked the way he felt—sexy, hard, invincible.

The day before he was due to leave, he polished the car one last time, drove it into a rented storage unit near his father's small suburban house in Encino, California, covered it in a cotton blanket, and carefully locked the garage with the heaviest padlock he could buy. He arranged for the payments on the car and the monthly storage fees to be automatically deducted from his checking account. Satisfied, he went off to war.

The other reason he joined up was the one he didn't talk about. It was to do with the last job he'd had, working for a company that sold batteries over the Internet. He was employed by BatteriesForLess for three months, the longest he'd ever held a job. It was a small business, owned and operated by a married couple—the husband, Richie, dealt with the customers, while Carol kept the books. Dax was hired to fill the orders.

Three weeks into the job, he started having sex with Carol. She had fifteen years on him and was running to fat, but she was crazy about him. She was also angry enough at her husband that she made sure she and Dax did it in the husband's office, each and every time he went to the bank or the post office or

Costco. Which suited Dax just fine because doing it there, during the day, meant he didn't have to rent a room or give up his evenings. And it added something extra to the workday; made him feel that working for a lousy little battery company wasn't a complete waste of time. The best part was that every time the owner corrected something he'd done or chewed him out for something he hadn't done right, he'd think, yeah, and guess what? I'm screwing your wife, ass-wipe.

One day, about four weeks into the affair, the husband went out, and Dax went into the wife's office; he shut the door, went over to Carol, stood behind her, and started rubbing her shoulders. It was how they usually started. But this time she pushed his hands away and said: "Cut it out. Get back to work."

Dax was mortified. He stood behind her, blushing, thankful that she couldn't see the blood race to the surface of his cheeks in blotchy, uneven patches. But she glanced back at him and said: "Aw, you've gone all red. Sorry, hon. I'm just not in the mood, okay?"

Back in the front room, he was furious. The bitch. He'd gone out of his way to give the ugly old cow what she wanted and then she blows him off like that? Hey, *he* wasn't always in the mood, that was for damn sure, but he came through for her, didn't he? And it was a lot harder for him, he was the man.

But by the time the heat in his face had cooled, he had talked himself into giving her another chance.

However, the wife's change of attitude turned out to go deeper than Dax had anticipated. The heat she felt for her young employee had cooled and rational thinking had returned. She was beginning to realize she was playing a dangerous game. The whole thing was a dead end and she'd be a fool to risk her marriage over him; if she kept it up, sooner or later Richie would find out.

Two mornings later, when her husband had gone to pick up

a case of Jiffy bags, she called Dax into her office and told him their relationship was over—she loved her husband after all and it would be best for everyone if he quit. Less awkward. But not to worry, she'd give him a good recommendation.

On a slow burn, Dax thought about it until lunchtime. When Richie went out for sandwiches, Dax went into the wife's small paneled office. She looked up at him, irritated.

He opened his cell phone and showed her a picture he'd taken with it. It was an aerial view, the top of a bottle blonde head between a man's hairy thighs, his penis visibly disappearing into her mouth.

"What the hell is that—?"

"Look familiar?" Dax tapped on the screen, enlarging it, pointing out the familiar office carpeting and chair legs and the cute ladybug tattoo on her shoulder blade.

"That's disgusting, get rid of it—"

"I love you, Carol, and I'm not ready to give you up, so I'm going to have to send the photograph to Richie. Unless—" And he went on to tell her what he wanted.

Seeing no way out, the wife agreed. Making sure she understood that his finger was on the Send button and should he feel her teeth he'd push it, he wrapped his fingers in her hair and made her go down on him. It seemed like the right way to establish who was boss. Next, he told her to give him all the extra cash she had in the office, assuring her that he'd expect twice as much the week after.

He left work that afternoon with an improved outlook and a deeper understanding of himself. He saw now what he'd always sensed—that there was an area beyond everyday boundaries that belonged to him, a place that was his to make use of. The woman was nothing, just a two-timing slut who got what she deserved. Stupid, too. She assumed because he was young that she could push him around. But she didn't know who she was dealing with, that was for sure. He was a hell of a lot smarter than her, smarter and faster. And now he was calling the shots.

He liked the feeling. Hell, he might decide, one afternoon when the boss was out, that he wanted a quick poke. And somehow he knew he'd enjoy it more than he had any of the others. Yes, their relationship had definitely moved into whole new territory. She was wrong when she said it was a dead end. As far as Dax was concerned, it had a bright future.

However, Dax's problem was he didn't really understand Carol, no matter what he thought, nor did he understand the small battery business and the financial strain he began putting on it. Most importantly, he didn't understand what someone might do, when cornered, to defend themselves and their security.

He came into work one day, three weeks into his new off-the-books salary bump, to find the husband, wife, and two police officers waiting for him. Carol was sitting in a chair, crying. Richie had his hand on her shoulder. She cringed when Dax walked in. The police officers told him the woman had filed rape and extortion charges against him. She had told them he took pictures while he forced her to service him. And then he'd blackmailed her and she'd been so confused and torn up that she'd gone along with it. She sobbed some more. They took his cell phone with the photograph as evidence.

A few hours later, the woman agreed to drop the charges if all the photographs were deleted from his cell phone and she never saw him again. And he had to agree to repay the money he'd extorted from her. For good measure, she took out a restraining order on him.

He left the police station with a burning rage in his gut, his face dark red. He stopped at a strip mall for a pack of cigarettes. He sat in his car in the parking lot, smoking and fantasizing about killing her with a stone, a gun, a knife, a brick.

And then he saw it, a few doors down from the convenience store. A recruiting office. The poster outside showed a young guy, tough and proud. Carrying a rifle.

He didn't sign up right away, but he did go in and talk to the recruiter. Then he went home to his father's house and sat in front of the TV, thinking. He knew Richie and Carol's address, so that night and the next he parked down the block from their bungalow, dirty white with green drapes in the windows, and watched till the lights winked out one by one.

On the third day he went back to the recruiter and signed up.

On the night before he was due to leave for basic training, he covered his license plates with mud. He waited up until one A.M., then drove to the couple's neighborhood. He parked a few blocks away and walked to the house. The windows were open and he cut a hole in one of the screens on the side of the house and reached in with a wooden match and held it against one of the green drapes. It took three matches to catch. Then, being careful not to burn his fingers, he lit another one. Once lit, they started to go up nicely. He walked quickly away.

The next day, he got the bus out of town.

It wasn't until he finished basic training and came home on leave that he had a chance to drive by and see his handiwork. To his shock, he discovered that Carol and Richie's bungalow was untouched and the house next door was gone, in its place an empty lot.

He'd torched the wrong house.

However, when he got over his disappointment, he had to admit that his mistake could very well have saved him. With that restraining order, he would probably have been the first person the cops looked at. He'd been given a second chance. Next time he wouldn't be so quick to act.

But you know what they say about resolutions. Easier to make than keep.

CHAPTER 16

Two days after his telephone conversation with Mrs. Flynn, Pack drove slowly down Birchwood Lane, a curving suburban street dotted with boxy two-story homes. Once upon a time, they had probably all looked the same, but with time they'd mutated along with the tastes of their owners. Trees and shrubs had matured, garages were converted, porches added. Now they were like adult siblings, their DNA very similar, but clothes, hair, weight, and life experience giving each an appearance all its own.

The street was empty until Pack made the last bend in the road. Then suddenly there were a messy collection of vehicles ahead of him, pulled up to the sidewalk. One of them was an ambulance, lights off, and he counted three police cars. A smattering of people had gathered on the street and the pavement.

He slowed down and about two hundred feet from the crowd, he pulled up and parked. He turned off the engine.

He looked at the house numbers. The action on the sidewalk was definitely focused on the house he was looking for, number 3275.

His chest tightened. To confirm his suspicions, he saw what looked like a small white Subaru in the driveway, blocked by a squad car. The house was Spartan-looking, just two evergreen bushes, trimmed into lopsided globes, on either side of the front door. They looked like oversized, green beach balls that had come to rest against the white siding.

Pack saw one of the three uniformed officers outside the house begin to unwind a roll of yellow crime scene tape, attaching it to the fencing. The cop made his way down to the mailbox, looping it around the post.

Anxiety built and washed up through Pack like a wave of sound.

He threw open the door and climbed out of the car. Hands in his pockets, he strolled over to the growing crowd. He slowed as he drew near, circling the gawkers.

A woman, maybe in her early seventies, stood with her eyes on the house across the street, her hands up to her mouth. She had tears in her eyes.

"What's goin' on here?" Pack asked.

She glanced at him, but he made sure to be looking at the activity in front of the house, not at her. He didn't have to fake a look of concern.

"Terrible, it's terrible. They won't come out and say it, but I hear she was murdered."

"Who? Who was murdered?" He held his breath, waiting for the answer, waiting for the stone to drop.

The old lady wiped her eyes. "Lorna. She's been my neighbor for years."

"Mrs. Flynn? I'm so sorry."

"Poor thing, she just lost her little girl in Iraq, can you believe it? And now this."

"I'm so sorry," he said again, the emotion in his voice genuine, though it was a joyful relief he was feeling. Near the front of the crowd, he stopped next to a man in his thirties who was holding a can of soda on the top of his belly, the way a pregnant woman might.

"I can't believe it! Poor Lorna," Pack said, his eyes on the police activity. "Do you know if she was alone? Was anyone else hurt?"

The man shrugged. "Don't know."

Pack breathed out. "Was it suicide?"

"Someone said she was tied to a chair."

"Christ."

Now the man looked at him. "Who're you?"

"I drive a limo. Just dropped someone around the corner." Pack hoped the guy wouldn't ask how he knew the victim's name.

"A limo? You're kidding." The man looked around, maybe searching for a stretch pulled up by the curb, a few famous people in the back.

"More like a car service. I just brought a guy here from the airport."

"Oh," the man nodded, losing interest, eyes back on the house. He pointed with his chin at the house. "She was a nice lady. I didn't know her, but that's what I hear."

"Yeah?"

"At least they know who did it."

"You're kidding. That was fast."

"Yeah." He took a long swig of his soda. "Turns out some girl's been staying with Lorna. One of the neighbors saw her running out of the house an hour or so ago. Probably robbed her."

"Maybe she didn't do it."

"Not likely. They'll get her, don't you worry."

Pack waited around a little longer, but there was nothing more to learn. It had begun to drizzle and the crowd was starting to disperse. Not wanting to stand out, he drifted away with the rest.

It was pouring by the time he reached the highway. Sheets of rain that made the cars look as if they were moving fast on a dark gray river, their tires throwing up walls of water. He drove in the slow lane, his mind too busy to trust his own reactions.

He crossed the Hudson and headed south. At the last minute, he veered off the highway at Rensselaer, toward the train station.

CHAPTER 17

Vida found a molded plastic seat in a corner of the waiting room, as far away from the other passengers as she could get. She'd been there for more than two hours, but there were still six more to go for the Watertown bus. It had been raining steadily for the last forty minutes. She pretended to be reading a flier she'd picked up, her body hunched, eyes down. Though the waiting room was warm, she was shivering. The injured side of her face hurt and her leg ached.

All she could see in her mind's eye was Lorna Flynn, lying sideways on the floor, body duct-taped at the torso and legs to the scratched wooden chair, the weight of her pulling her away and down, like a sack of wet dog food. Though Vida had washed her face and hands in the restroom, she couldn't get the smell out of her nose, the iron taste out of the back of her mouth. Maybe whoever had done this to Mrs. F. was after her too. Or was she being paranoid? She couldn't think straight.

As the minutes crawled by, Vida slowly forced herself to focus. Eventually she had to accept that she couldn't sit there all afternoon and night, waiting for the bus. She had to turn in her ticket and go somewhere else, or leave the station and find another way of getting out of town. She looked at her watch. It had been only two hours since she'd called 911, but she had no idea, in Albany cop hours, if that was a lot of time or none at all. How long would they take to get there, call whoever was in charge, and start putting together the pieces? There were plenty of traces of her in the house, so it wouldn't take them long to figure out she'd been there. And neighbors, neighbors must have seen her around.

Yes, the police would want to talk to her. And once they did, she'd be put in prison or shipped back to the U.S. Army. She shut her eyes, wishing she could go back in time and erase everything that had happened in the past two months. For a second she allowed herself to pretend she could, and for that one moment, she felt soothed.

But the second passed and the panic flooded back in, stronger than ever. She felt she was sinking, and she let herself drift down, under the weight of it. Maybe her heart would just stop beating and it would all be over. Maybe she could will it to quit.

And then, with some regret, she lifted her head stiffly and straightened her spine. Stupid, weak talk. Time to get serious and come up with a solution. She had to get her shit together and make some decisions.

Through glass doors, she could see the buses, parked in the diagonal slips, noses up to the building. Each had its own gate into the waiting room, and above the doors were the destinations: New York City and Rutland, VT were scheduled to leave next. Just then, with a drawn-out screech of brakes and a tired hissing of air, a third bus pulled in. She watched the bifold door open, and passengers begin to step down. Two old ladies, slow and careful, followed by a woman carrying a small child. The kid seemed to be crying, but Vida couldn't hear through the glass. She wondered where they were coming from. A young guy carrying a backpack bounced carelessly down the steps.

The passengers began trickling into the waiting room. Sure enough, the child was emitting a steady, tired, could-keep-it-up-forever sound. The guy with the backpack—dark blond curly hair, nice-looking, wearing khaki cargo pants and a dark blue SUNYAlbany sweatshirt—looked at Vida and rolled his eyes.

He seemed to be referring to the child and, without thinking, Vida acknowledged it with a shadow of a smile. He grinned and she looked quickly away, immediately regretting the contact, however slight.

But she needn't have worried. He was pulling out his cell phone and within seconds was talking into it, laughing, as he walked to the exit. Vida felt a wave of loneliness wash over her.

She looked at the ticket window. There was no one in line, so she stood up and walked over. The young girl behind the glass was reading a textbook. She looked up at Vida, eyebrows raised. "Yup?"

Vida slid her ticket under the glass. "I have a ticket for a bus leaving tonight. Can I get a refund, or exchange it for a different destination?"

The girl glanced at it. "As long as there're no restrictions on your ticket, you get a year for a refund. Do you know where you want to go?"

"Yes. New York City," she said. Why not? It was leaving soon, and they'd be expecting her to head to Canada. She hoped.

The girl took her ticket and began punching in numbers on her computer. Vida looked out the front door. She could see the guy from the bus standing outside on the sidewalk. Probably waiting for his ride. Vida looked back at the window.

The young woman slid the new ticket under the glass. "Here you are . . . forty-five cents is your change. Gate #1 in fifteen minutes."

"Thanks." Vida pushed the ticket into her pocket. She looked at her watch. By now the police probably knew she existed. Soon, they'd be looking for her.

She stood where she was for a minute and then walked out through the glass doors. If she was going to be stuck on a bus for three hours, she wanted some fresh air.

Outside, the rain was finally ending. She hunched her

shoulders, happy to be out of the stale waiting room with its lingering smells of carbon monoxide and in-transit, unwashed bodies.

"You waiting for a ride?"

It was the guy from the bus. He was standing to her right, his hands in his pockets. He smiled tentatively.

She nodded, not wanting to give him any specific information.

"You go to SUNY?" he continued.

She knew she had to shut him out, or he'd never get lost, but she couldn't quite bring herself to do it. He had a good face—his cheeks still rounded, long nose, wide mouth. Scraggly bit of chin hair. A couple of freckles, as if to prove he was entirely trustworthy. But he was still a stranger, and she shouldn't forget it. "Why d'you want to know?"

Taken aback, he shrugged defensively, as if it was her loss. "Hey, I thought you might need a ride."

A police car turned the corner and came toward them, the interior invisible behind the wipers. Vida's heart hammered. The vehicle cruised along slowly, sharklike, and when it was just past them, it stopped. The engine turned off. Vida's pulse rate increased.

"Hey, I'm sorry. Suspicious by nature," Vida said. She moved a step closer to him, hoping they'd look like they were together.

Two officers climbed out of the squad car, their doors slamming in quick succession. They pulled up their heavy, gear-laden gun belts and walked together to the entrance. Vida had to control the urge to dart across the street and run.

She tried to look as if she were making up her mind about something. Aw, shucks, why not. "I don't actually go to SUNY, but I'm visiting a friend who does. It's frustrating. I was in there trying to find out if there was a bus or shuttle that would take me to campus, but the girl at the window didn't know anything about one."

Just then, an old blue VW Jetta pulled up in front of them. The driver leaned across the empty passenger seat and yelled: "Frostie! Yo, yo, my man!"

Vida's new friend burst into laughter and shook his head. "Cohen, you idiot." He turned to Vida. "Come on. We'll drop you wherever."

Vida glanced once into the waiting room. The cops were at the ticket window. One of them was leaning on the counter, talking. The other had his arms crossed. He was nodding.

She made up her mind. "Great. Thanks."

Frostie offered her the front seat, but she declined. She didn't want a stranger sitting behind her, and she'd feel less visible in the back.

After he'd sat down he said: "Cohen, this is—Sorry, what's your name?"

She hesitated. "Haley."

"Haley. Cool. Cohen, we're giving Haley a ride to school, so keep it under eighty. Haley, I'm Tom Frost, and this fool is Rich Cohen."

"This is nice of you guys." Vida kept her face turned away from the building until Cohen pulled out of the parking lot.

"No biggie. Where d'you want to go?"

"I don't care," Vida said. "I'm a little early to meet my friend, so if you just point me someplace central, like the cafeteria, I'll get something to eat and wait for her."

"Sure."

During the ride, the two boys chatted and laughed about friends, classes, friends, parties, friends, friends. How many people did these kids know? They were about Vida's age, maybe even older, but their lives seemed so light-hearted, so trivial. She thought of the other boys she knew about their age, also

98

gossiping and trash talking, but their subjects were different, and instead of backpacks filled with books and computers they carried supplies, weapons, ammunition. Death and survival vs. classes and professors. Common ground seemed to be women, boredom, and schedules.

Vida stopped listening, and her mind turned quickly back to the two cops. She had no choice but to assume the worst: that they'd come to the bus station looking for her.

The drive to the campus was only about fifteen minutes, just a few turns off the highway. It sat on a flat green expanse, the main buildings rising like white marble blocks among the trees, with four tall towers off to one side. "Dorms," Tom said, pointing to them.

They all got out of the car. Vida hitched her pack onto her shoulder. "Thanks for the ride."

"We'll walk you toward the Student Center," Cohen said. He was short and muscle-bound, like a wrestler. His eyes wandered over her, curious and intrusive.

She shrugged, content to be shown the way. She wasn't worried about Cohen and his muscles—hey, if he got fresh she had the Smith & Wesson. She could always blow his head off. For the first time all day she smiled to herself. "Thanks."

There seemed to be hundreds of students milling around, and Vida suddenly felt overwhelmed. They were aliens and this was their world. Dressed in jeans, t-shirts, flip-flops, and sweatshirts, they clustered together, talking, laughing, all with their backpacks or books.

She told herself she didn't look all *that* much different, at least on the surface. She was the right age, had the backpack, wore the uniform. But it was all she had in common with them. Under the thin camouflage, she was a different species. As if to confirm this, she felt the heavy handgun shift against her back.

"Haley," Tom said, but she ignored him, unused to responding to that name. "Haley, you there?"

"Oh, yeah, sorry. My mind was wandering."

"Straight ahead, across the quad, that's the Center. There's food, and all sorts of stuff."

"Okay. Great."

"I guess we'll take off."

"Tom, thanks a lot."

"No problem. Oh, if you and your friend are looking for something to do later on, Cohen and me and a few other guys are havin' a party in the common room on the seventh floor, Indian. DJ and everything. It's gonna be good."

"I'll remember," Vida said.

Rich had already started walking away.

Tom said: "I'm serious. Seventh: Indian."

"Seventh: Indian. Got it."

And with a nod, her one friend was gone. The friend who didn't even know her real name. But he'd helped her. Yeah, and his motives were as pure as the driven snow, no doubt. She shook her head, skepticism taking over. Seventh: Indian, my ass. She looked at her watch. It was a little past four. She turned away from him and headed for the cafeteria.

CHAPTER 18

The Amtrak Station was across the river from Albany itself, in a separate township, Rensselaer. It was on his way, so he stopped there first, turning down the narrow, shabby street that led there. He parked and ran in, trying to duck the rain. There was one train pulled up on the track, and he walked through it, looking at the passengers. Nothing.

Inside the building, he was about to go to the ticket counter when he noticed two police officers at one of the windows. He circled away and headed for the bathroom. At the Ladies, he pushed the door open a few inches and said: "Vida? You in here? It's Pack."

No one answered, but a white-haired woman, pulling a small wheeled suitcase, came out and looked at him suspiciously.

He went to the newsstand and was about to ask the sales clerk if he'd seen a young girl with a scar, when the two police officers came over.

"Hey, sir!" one of them said loudly, as if the clerk, a black-haired, dark-skinned man with pockmarked cheeks, were hard of hearing. "Do you recall seeing a girl today, could be as young as sixteen, dark hair, petite stature, might have seemed nervous or in a hurry?" He checked a small notepad. "She was possibly carrying a small backpack, either blue or brown, was wearing jeans and a sweatshirt, either dark blue or black?"

Pack was glad to hear they made no mention of her scar.

The man behind the counter thought for a moment. He

shook his head. "There are plenty of students who travel through here. Most look like that. I'm sorry, I can't help you." His sing-song accent placed him as Pakistani or Indian.

Pack spent the next five minutes pretending to be checking out magazines while he kept an eye out for Vida. But there was no sign of her.

After getting back on the highway, Pack turned west again and re-crossed the river toward Albany. He turned south, away from Troy, and followed the river. Two turns and he was on a side street, driving into the parking lot of the bus station. The rain was just beginning to let up.

A dirty blue Jetta, Wisconsin plates, and a SUNYAlbany bumper sticker, was pulling away from the curb just as he rounded the corner. In front of it, an unoccupied black and white cruiser was parked in the No Standing zone.

Pack circled into the parking lot and found an empty spot. He had a good view of the terminal and, turning off the engine, he stayed in his seat, watching the entrance. When he saw the cops coming out through the glass doors, he got out, took an old gym bag from the trunk, and locked the car.

He walked slowly to the entrance, passing the cops as he did. One of them was telling the other something. The second officer laughed.

He kept track of them until they climbed into their vehicle and pulled out of the parking lot.

Once inside the terminal, he did the same thing he'd done at the train station. He looked carefully at everyone, not just the solitary females. He had to assume that Vida might very well befriend someone so she wouldn't be seen alone. But she was nowhere in sight. He boarded the two buses that were ready to leave, over the protests of the drivers. Once again, he checked the Ladies Room.

He watched the young black woman who was selling tickets.

She was reading a heavy textbook, and when a customer came to the window, she barely glanced up. Just long enough to hand over the change, then back to the textbook.

He figured he would ask anyway.

"Miss, I'm looking for my daughter," he said, betting the truth was safer than a lie. "She bought a ticket today, and I need to give her something before she leaves."

"Where's she going?"

"I don't know. Look," he said, still sticking to partial truths, "we had a fight so I don't know where's she going and she won't answer her cell phone, but she forgot her bag." He held up the small blue duffel. "If I can just give it to her, I think it'd make all the difference. Her mother's at home, and if I come back with this, she'll never speak to me again."

An unwelcome picture of Mitch in his red wig flashed through his mind. He shook it away. "She's a pretty little dark-haired girl, with a fresh scar on her face."

He thought he saw a glimmer of recognition in the girl's eyes, but she said, her voice bored and flat: "Everybody's lookin' for someone today. How'd she get the scar, mister?"

"She's a soldier. Iraq."

The girl looked at him for a heartbeat, then said: "Look, it won't do you much good, but she exchanged her ticket just about half an hour ago. She was originally goin' to Watertown. Tonight."

Pack felt a surge of elation. Finally. Something.

"Where'd she change it for?"

"You missed her. Her bus left"—she looked at a schedule—"about four and a half minutes ago."

"Damn. Where was it headed?"

"New York City."

"Okay. Any stops along the way?"

"Yeah, this one makes a bunch of stops. First one, Kingston."

She worked the machine a little more, and there was a soft whirr of the printer and she flapped a sheet down in front of him. "Here's the schedule."

"You're a lifesaver." He stuffed the schedule in his pocket.

He was starting to walk away when she said: "You better not be telling me a tale, mister."

"I swear," Pack said, and walked quickly out the door.

The girl turned back to the line that was building up. Her voice flattened out again. "May I help who's next?"

CHAPTER 19

It was five P.M. when Pack pulled into the driveway of the little dark brown and peach house in Goose Creek where his cousin lived. It was a delicate house, the two colors used to highlight the curlicues of Victorian trim, lace curtains, and flower boxes in the tall, slim windows. An unlikely home for Mitch, but he'd fixed it up for his mother, Pack's Aunt Dot, who had been a tiny woman with a core of steel—steel that had been heated and hammered, then heated again. Then made into a samurai sword.

He found Millie in the dining room, sitting on a delicate dining chair. Next to her, on the veneered oval table, lay a dismantled Sig Sauer. It was on a hand towel; she was cleaning it. Spread out at the other end of the table was a jigsaw puzzle, still under construction. All the unfinished pieces were arranged to one side, turned over and divided by color.

The red wig was nowhere in sight and her gray hair stuck up from the sides of her head around a bald dome, glasses resting on the tip of her nose. She glanced up when Pack came in. She would have looked like an average old retired guy, except for the eye shadow. "Hey, buddy. What's up?"

Pack pulled a chair away from the table and sat down. "We've got a mess up there in Albany. Vida's in a shit load of trouble. I came close to finding her, but she slipped through my fucking fingers. I need Mitch to make some calls."

Millie sighed and kept polishing. "Tell me what's happened."

"First, it looks like the woman she was staying with got herself killed."

Millie stopped what she was doing and paid attention.

"And our girl was seen fleeing the scene, or whatever."

"Jesus. She's gonna hit the front page when they figure out who she is."

"You think I don't know that? I know that. I looked for her at the train station. Nothing. Then I tried the *bus* station." He leaned forward, elbows on the table. "She was there. Changed her ticket from Watertown to New York City."

Millie nodded. "Watertown, huh? That's near Fort Drum. And Canada. Okay. How'd you lose her?"

"The bus left five minutes before I got there, and the first stop was Kingston. So I jumped on the highway and chased it down to Kingston, figured I'd get her easy. Twenty minutes away, hell, I can make up the five minutes."

"And? You broke down?"

"No. I caught up with the bus just before the exit—followed it to the stop and everything. The driver let me on, no problem. But guess what? She wasn't on it."

Millie sat back. "Ahh. What happened to her?"

Pack shook his head. "I don't know. She must've changed her mind at the last minute. That was the first stop. She was *never* on it."

They sat still, both thinking, both staring at nothing.

Pack spoke first. "I wonder if I missed her, if she was right there at the bus station while I was looking for her."

"It's a small place. Could the person you spoke to have mistaken her for someone else on the same bus?"

Pack shook his head. "Nah. No girls or young women, not even any children. Just men, a few middle-aged women. A couple of teenage boys."

"So what do we do now?"

"Now I need Mitch."

Millie's eyes turned into gray pebbles. "Would you quit saying that, like I'm some kind of damn split personality? Just tell
me what you want me to do."

Pack ignored the outburst. "I need you to call the cops up
there and find out what's what. You gotta know somebody. And
then I need to find her. Right away. Shit, I was so damn close.

"I was going over it on the ride home. Someone killed the
mother of the dead girl. Why? No way it was coincidence, right?
I mean, what're the chances of that? What if Vida was right
about her roommate's death being an in-house job? Maybe the
dead woman knew something about it, who her daughter was
hanging out with, what her problems were. I bet Haley told her
everything."

Millie hesitated before speaking. Her tone was gentle. "Have
you considered the other option?"

"What's that?"

"That our girl did it."

"Are you nuts?"

"Hey, she was seen leaving the scene. She was under a lot of
pressure, PTSD, wounded. She had to have a short fuse. Maybe
the woman kept after her about something and she blew. It happens."

Pack had to hold back from grabbing his cousin. Instead, he
forced himself to think about Vida, waving the .38 at him, her
eyes hard, desperate. Was it possible? He gave it three seconds
of consideration. It was possible. He shook his head. "I know it
happens. But I can't even entertain that. Did it already and look
where it got me. Not this time. As far as I'm concerned, she's
innocent and running and needs help."

Millie smiled slowly. "Good. So what's next? Let's make a
list. I love a good list. What's first, the cops in Albany?"

Pack sighed in relief. "If you call them I'll call her mother.

See if she's heard from Vida. Also, I need to let her know what's going on and find out if Vida has any East Coast friends. New York in particular."

"Yeah, good idea. Also, family. Do Shelley or her husband have family nearby?"

"There's that fat slob Bob in Chicago. But Vida never liked him, she wouldn't go to him."

"She came to you, didn't she? She had to be desperate to do that."

Pack ignored him. "Christ, I nearly forgot the VA. I need to find out who she was trying to find at the VA hospital. Shit, if only I'd just listened to her."

"Don't waste your time thinking that now. You're listening now. And keep track of it all."

"Yeah, yeah. Do you have an email address?"

"Why?"

"I'll need it for Shelley. I want her to send me a picture of Vida."

CHAPTER 20

Pack called his ex-wife from Millie's land line.

"Shelley, remember what we did before? Do it again, okay?"

He got in the car and drove into Bantam and parked outside the police station. He went to the phone kiosk and picked up the receiver, keeping his other hand on the holder so the line was open. He turned his back to anyone who might be watching and he waited for Shelley to call.

"Did you find her?" were her first words, which disappointed him right from the get-go.

"You don't know where she is?" he said, hoping it was just a case of crossed wires.

"No, no. I haven't heard anything. I'm going crazy. I'm so scared, Pack."

"Don't, don't be, she's just trying to protect you."

"What d'you mean?"

"You know, she doesn't want you stuck in her mess. I'm sure that's it."

"That's what Bill says."

"See?"

"I think you're both just trying to—to sugarcoat things."

"Never mind that. Listen, something's happened here. You're not going to like it but you have to hang in there."

"What?"

"The woman Vida was staying with was murdered."

"Oh, my god."

"Yeah. And Vida was seen leaving the house a little while before the body was discovered."

"Oh, no . . . no!"

"Which doesn't mean anything, except the cops are looking for her. They don't know who she is yet, but they will soon. The house must be full of her fingerprints and such. Plenty to point to her. And when it does, she's going to be in a sea of trouble. And the fact that she's skipped out on her unit is going to make it worse."

"Oh, my god, what do we do?" Shelley's voice was tight with panic.

"We have to find her first."

"We can't find her faster than the cops. Oh, god, Pack. Jesus god . . ."

"Calm down."

"That's no—"

"Yes, it is. First thing we have to do is stay calm. We have to make lists, and follow through."

"But you stink at that—"

Some things never change. He took a deep breath. "Mitch is helping me."

"Mitch? You can't get him involved, he's a cop, he'll have to turn her in—"

"Not any more, he's retired. He's helping me, and we're going to find her. That's why there're some things I need you to do."

"Okay, okay. What?"

"For one thing, I need you to write down the names of all her friends. All the people you can think of that she liked and trusted. School friends, kids she went to camp with—"

"She didn't go to camp."

A real father would've known that, right? But Vida's mother wasn't accusing him of anything, just stating a fact. "Okay then," he said patiently, "people she worked with during the summers, or anyone from the military she talked about and whose name you know."

"I can do that." Her voice sounded eager, hopeful.

"When you've got a list, I want you to get in touch with them, get the word out she might come to them in need, and they should help her, but they should also let you know where she is, or be sure to tell her it's very important that she contact you. Get a disposable cell phone and give that number to her friends. Keep the phone with you all the time. And when you hear from her, call me immediately. Got it?"

"Yes."

"We need a point person, and you're it. Someone to field information."

"Yes, good. I can do that."

"Okay. Let's talk later today, when you get your phone. I picked one up already; I figure we should all have them." He read out the number. "Oh, and one last thing."

"What's that?"

"I need you to email me a picture of her."

"Why?"

"Because if I'm going to be asking people about her, I want to be able to show them a recent photo."

"Okay. Funny to think you don't have a picture of her." She sounded sad.

He paused. "We all set?"

"Yes. Okay."

"Good." He had no comfort to give her.

"Bye. I'll call you later, Pack."

"Okay. Hang in there, Shell."

CHAPTER 21

The VA Medical Center looked about as good as it was ever going to. The sun was shining onto its drab, pale brown outer walls as the Stars and Stripes snapped in the endless breeze whistling through the flat sea of parked cars.

There was something comforting to Pack about walking through those revolving doors. For starters, he didn't look any shabbier than the other old farts that littered the front entrance and had parked their asses in the rows of seats. And at least he wasn't dying of some fucking lung disease from smoking too many PX cigarettes. But mostly, he had to admit to a sense of belonging. Something tied him to these people—men and women, black, white, or anything in between. A shared what? He couldn't say it was a shared experience; he had to guess that everyone's experience in the military was different, but a shared set of laws, a common boss, a common direction and loyalty. Life was simple in the military. You did what you were told and kept going. For a moment he stood still, looking around, taking it in.

And then he caught the eye of a young soldier in a wheelchair and made his gaze go hard, not wanting the boy to see any pity there. It's what he signed up for, Pack said to himself. Nobody made him do it.

But he didn't really believe it. That kid didn't really know what he'd signed up for. The crapshoot. Some of them found themselves during their time. But others got lost, drifting away on a current, unable to swim to shore.

He went to the information desk. He found his VA card in his wallet and slapped in on the counter. The African American woman who was sitting behind it looked up, eyebrows raised, ready to be annoyed. "Can I help you, sir?"

"I hope so. Were you working here yesterday?"

"Yes, I was."

"Good. I'm looking for a young lady who came in yesterday. She's about yay-high big," he gestured with his hand held flat, about the height of his shoulder. "Dark hair, fresh scarring on her face. Walks with a limp. She was looking for a friend, and I'm trying to track her down."

The woman looked at him with raised eyebrows as if to say, "and I should tell you this *why?*" "I'm sorry, sir, doesn't ring a bell with me." She looked away.

Pack wasn't ready to give up. "Come on, please. She's my daughter, a wounded soldier just back from active duty. Suffering from severe amnesia," he lied. "She wanders, I'm afraid she'll get hurt. Are you sure you didn't see her?"

The woman weakened, irritated that he'd managed to pull one of the few heartstrings she had left. She said: "I mean it, no, I never saw her. But if she didn't stop here, it would've been easy to miss her."

"Do you have any suggestions, where she might have gone here?"

The woman shook her head. "No. She could've gone anywhere in the hospital. I mean, look around, everything's accessible. If she knew where to find her friend, she could've gone straight to the right department."

Pack held up both index fingers. "Okay, I get it. How about this: say she didn't know where to go, and didn't want to ask anyone, where d'you think she'd start?"

Exasperated, the woman laughed. "Look, I don't know! Go

from floor to floor and ask every damn person you see. Maybe someone'll remember your girl!"

Pack sighed, as if she'd let him down. "I guess that's what it's gonna take. Thanks."

He decided to work methodically from the top floor, down.

But no one remembered a young girl with a scar. The receptionist in Psychiatry said it was her first day, and if he came back, he could speak to the woman who covered it regularly. "She's having a small procedure," she whispered, "if all goes well, she'll be back in two days."

Back on the ground floor, he went again to the woman at the information desk. She was helping an old man decipher a thick form, so he waited.

When she finally looked over at him, she said: "No luck?"

"Nope. Maybe she didn't come in. Can I leave my number here, so if you see her you can give it to her, tell her to call? Tell her it's urgent?"

"I can't promise you anything."

"I know, I know." He wrote out his information on one of the information sheets sitting on the counter. She read it, folded it, and put it out of sight.

"Thanks." He patted the counter and turned to go.

"Why don't you ask in the cafeteria downstairs," she called after him. "Maybe they remember something."

Pack wheeled around. "The cafeteria. Of course. Smart lady."

Instead of waiting for the elevator, he walked the flight down, his footsteps echoing in the empty stairwell. Outside the cafeteria, vendors had set up tables and were selling gifts and handmade items—crocheted potholders and jewelry. He glanced at it, wondering who bought it.

Inside the cafeteria, he took in the people sitting at the tables, probably a mix of patients, staff, and visitors. He had no way of knowing who he was looking for. He walked into the food service area, where they sold coffee, sandwiches, salads, Burger King. A woman in a blue uniform jacket, wearing a pair of rubber gloves and a shower cap, was scrubbing down a shelf in the dessert cooler. She looked like someone who was there most of the day. She might remember.

"Ma'am, excuse me," he said. She didn't seem to hear him, so he rapped on the side of the cooler.

She stopped cleaning and looked up at him. "Yes?"

"Sorry to interrupt, but I'm looking for someone, thought you might be the person to ask."

She shrugged and stood straight. She was in her sixties, her face heavily lined and worn. "Try me."

She seemed willing to help. He took heart. "I'm looking for a young woman, early twenties, dark hair, limp, scar. She might have come in here yesterday looking for an old friend. I need to find her."

"Why?"

Pack lowered his voice, as if he were embarrassed. "I'm her dad. She was hurt a couple of months ago. Near Tallil. And now she wanders and gets lost—she forgets where she is, how to get home. I've been looking for her since last night and I'm worried sick." Pack surprised himself by how much he meant what he was saying.

The woman in the shower cap didn't seem as impressed. He wondered why; it was a pretty good story. She crossed her arms. "Yeah?"

"Have you seen her?"

"I don't think so. Why didn't you go to Records, see if they can figure out who else from her unit or whatever might be here? Sure beats asking random people."

Pack nodded sagely. "You're right, but I already did. They haven't been able to help me."

"Look, I've got to work. Give me your name and phone

number and I'll see what I can do."

Pack nodded and took a card out of his wallet. It had nothing but his home phone number and *"PACK"* written on it. He'd had them made up for his limo customers; it was all the information they needed.

The woman peered at it. "Pack? What's that?"

"Me," Pack answered.

"That's it?"

"That's my name."

"Okay. I'll call you if I hear anything." She slipped the card into her pocket.

"Thanks. Appreciate it."

"Don't thank me yet."

Janet watched Pack leave the cafeteria. When he was gone, she shook her head. "Pack. Who's called Pack?" She hadn't taken to him. With his dirty black suit and that nasty patch of hair under his lip. There was no way she was telling him about seeing that poor girl. And there was no way "Pack" was her father. She could tell he was lying when he went into that whole song and dance about her not knowing where she was, etc.

She remembered the young girl as soon as he started describing her. She'd been sitting with John Dax, the medic. She didn't look lost. She knew who Dax was. She was the one he'd gotten a cup of coffee for, the one who'd wanted sugar. Dax had said she'd been wounded in-country, and when Janet cleared a nearby table a few minutes later, she saw the angry scar running down the girl's cheek.

Dax seemed happy to see her, and he was a good guy, definitely on the up-and-up. And so good-looking. He reminded her of a boyfriend she'd had a long time ago, worked construction. She'd been crazy about him. Turned out he was a shit, but you couldn't blame that on Dax. Had nothing to do with him.

No, she wouldn't tell this creep Pack anything about the girl. Instead, she'd keep the phone number and give it to Dax. Let him decide what to do about Pack.

CHAPTER 22

The first person Millie thought of was Manny Duarte. Manny was a homicide detective in Albany who owed her a favor. It was an old favor, so he actually owed her old self, Mitch, but it had to be worth some information.

Five years before, Mitch had given Manny a heads-up when he saw the detective's sixteen-year-old daughter in a Hudson bar in the company of a thirty-year-old slimebag. The man had his tongue in her ear and Mitch had recognized the girl because he'd met her with Manny and his wife at the Columbia County Fair one week earlier.

He hadn't thought twice about ratting the girl out. She was underage and her date was married and had been picked up twice for domestic disputes, the second one ending with his wife's arm in a cast. The wife hadn't pressed charges so there was nothing on the books, but the guy was a bottom feeder, no question.

Millie hadn't spoken to the detective in a while. The first thing she did was ask about the girl: she had to remind Manny about the favor and soften him up for the questions.

Instead of answering, the detective said, "What's up, Mitch?"

Millie didn't expect Manny or any of the Albany police force to be aware of her change in lifestyle, about the emergence of Millie and the shelving of Mitch. She wasn't about to tell him now.

"Nothing much. Just got a favor to ask of you, Manny."

"Anything I can do," was the answer, which meant he would do it if it was legal and didn't upset any applecart of his own.

"Do you know anything about the murder of a woman in Delmar? She was found in her home today."

"What's your interest? I heard you were retired."

Which meant he'd heard more than that. He'd heard about Millie.

"Lady was a friend of a friend, and I'd like to give any update directly, instead of waiting for the press. Which, as you know, may or may not give a follow-up."

He heard silence of the other end.

"You still there?"

"I was just thinking, about the Delmar woman. It's not my case, but my partner lives near her and has an interest so I'm hearing some of the details. Turns out she was tied up and bludgeoned with something heavy. I'm not telling you anything I'm not supposed to, but don't go calling WNYT."

"They got a suspect?"

"Not yet, but they want to talk to a young woman, was staying with her for a week or so. Someone saw her leaving the house at a run."

"What time?"

"The witness couldn't say exactly. Sometime around lunch-time maybe."

"Anything missing from the house?"

"They don't know. It doesn't look like the vic had much to start with."

"Could it have been a random thing, a stranger passing through?"

"Unlikely. Word is, it was ugly and personal. Papers strewn around, closets dumped. The killer was looking for something. When she didn't find it, she got really pissed off."

"She, huh? Did the killing take a certain amount of strength?"

"What d'you mean?"

"I mean, are you sure it could have been done by a small woman?"

Now there was a longer pause. "Why d'you say small? You know something I should know?"

"No, no, I swear. I'm just trying to put a picture together of the girl running off, the woman in the house. I'm trying to make it real."

"That sounds like total bullshit, Mitch. If you have information—"

"I tell you, if I hear anything or learn anything, I'll call you. I give you my word, Manny. I gotta go. Give my best to your daughter. She okay?"

"She's given me four grandbabies, if you call that okay. And she's not yet twenty-two."

"Well," Millie said, looking for a silver lining, "at least they're all healthy, right?"

"One of them's a crack addict, just like his mother."

"Shit, Manny, I'm sorry, I shouldn't have asked."

Manny laughed. "Just pulling your chain. She's fine. No kids yet. She's studying Jurisprudence at John Jay. Hey, maybe I have you to thank for that. Stay in touch, okay? And don't keep any secrets."

CHAPTER 23

Shelley Gustafson pulled on a jacket and put her new cell phone in her pocket. They'd had a snowfall the night before, but it was only a couple of inches and she'd shoveled the front walk first thing that morning. She and Bill paid special attention to the path and steps, sweeping light snow, shoveling anything heavier, and salting any frozen snowmelt. They didn't want it to be slippery in case Vida came home in the middle of the night.

She crossed the street at an angle and headed left. At the end of the block, she stopped in front of the last house. In the evening light, she moved cautiously, knowing they weren't as careful here about clearing their walkway.

However, it was a good time to come. She knew Marci's mother, a bridge player, would be out, and she needed to have some time alone with the girl. She rang the bell.

Marci and Vida had become friends at the end of second grade, during Bill's first year with the railroad. Marci had her feet well-planted on the ground, a kind girl and the best sort of friend for Vida, who was full of dreams and ideas. They made a good pair. Marci now worked at the local bank and was studying computer programming part-time at the community college.

Vida's friend came to the door wearing a dark skirt with a white blouse partially untucked, as if she'd been about to change. She had a string of large fake pearls around her neck and her stockinged feet were bare. Marci had played basketball in high school and was tall and thick-limbed; her hair was a reddish-brown and fine, her skin rosy and clear. Dressed like that, she looked like a girl in a high school play playing the part of a middle-aged matron.

"Mrs. Gustafson! What's up?" Her expression showed concerned. "Is everything okay?"

"Hi, Marci. Can I come in? I need to talk to you."

"Sure, of course."

She followed Marci inside the cluttered little house. Marci's mother worked at a hotel downtown, and sold cleaning products over the Internet in her spare time. The living room was her office, boxes of brochures on the furniture and samples in untidy piles on the floor.

Marci stood in the middle of the room, as if trying to figure out where they could sit. She picked up a blanket from the couch and put it on the back of a chair, punched the couch cushions a few times, and gestured. "Here's a seat."

"Thanks, honey." Shelley thought Marci looked nervous. Maybe she was just worried there was bad news about Vida. She sat down at one end of the couch, Marci at the other. They were turned toward each other.

"Marci," she began, "Vida never rejoined her unit."

Marci looked shocked. "You're kidding!"

Shelley waited, but Marci didn't seem to have anything else to say. "You knew she was going to take off, didn't you?"

Marci's tone became more guarded. "Why do you say that? I didn't know anything about it."

Shelley wanted to shake her. "Come on, Marci, she's in trouble. I need to know if you've been in touch with her."

"No, I haven't." Marci held out for about ten seconds before adding: "She told me she'd be out of reach."

Shelley stood, as if the cushions were too hot to sit on. "You knew what she was planning to do."

Marci looked at her and said pleadingly: "I'm really sorry, I am, but she made me swear I wouldn't say anything. She said it was for your own good, she didn't want you to have to lie to her commanding officer."

"Damn it, Marci, it's been close to two weeks! You should have come to me. I've been worried sick. Where is she?"

Marci put her hands between her knees. She looked as if she were going to cry. "I swear, I don't know. All she said is that she was going east to find her family, and together they were going to get proof that someone killed Haley. Because she knew where to find it."

"What did she mean by proof? What was she talking about?"

Marci shook her head. "I don't know exactly. I don't think she really knew. Maybe it was something that Haley or the killer left behind."

Shelley groaned. "Oh, god, she told you that too? How come she didn't trust *me?*"

Marci looked frantic. "I swear, she wanted to, but she thought you'd never let her go! I tried to stop her, I swear."

Shelley sat down again. She took off her glasses and rubbed her eyes, suddenly overwhelmed. "I'm so afraid for her. I should call her CO and explain everything. Maybe they'll excuse her on some kind of mental grounds. A breakdown, or something."

Agitated, Marci shook her head. "You can't do that. She says it'll go on her record and she'll end up being discharged from the Army."

Vida's mother laughed bitterly. "I'd love that. She could go to college and have a real life."

"No, she wants to finish her time, maybe even stay in. She likes being a soldier. I know, it seems really weird to me, but she loved what she was doing."

Shelley sighed and shook her head. "Okay." Then she looked

at the younger woman. "But you and I need to take care of something. We need to put together a list and then send everyone on it an email. And you, you get to help me write it. Okay?"

"Yup, Mrs. Gustafson."

"Call me Shelley, for chrissake. The Mrs. days are over."

CHAPTER 24

Dax was halfway through his sandwich and Carla, the nurse, was telling him about a patient, a Korean War vet who'd been scratched by the family cat. By the time he came in, she said, his hand was so swollen it was like he was wearing a red boxing glove. Describing it, she was laughing so hard tears moistened her eyes.

Dax stared at her. What a turnoff. Disgusting thing to talk about while he was eating. And anyway, what was so damned funny about some old guy being scratched by his wife's cat? He tried not to listen as she droned on stupidly. Talk about pus. Her mouth was like a boil. He realized she had a bad voice, too, way too nasal. How was it he'd never noticed before? She sounded like his fucking mother, when she was on a tear, or bitching about the neighbors.

"I need coffee," he said, interrupting her. He stood up and made his way through the cafeteria tables. He filled a large Styrofoam cup, grabbed a lid off the stack, and went back to the table.

Carla, put out by his abruptness, said: "You could've brought me some."

He looked at her, his eyes cold, his mind on other things.

Carla blew air out of her nose, dissatisfied. She shot a look of irritation at something or someone behind his back just as he felt a touch on his shoulder. He turned. It was his pal Janet, the cafeteria lady.

"Hey, hon, I've been waitin' to see you," she said.

He liked Janet. She reminded him of his grandmother, his father's mother. He'd always felt she cared about him, unlike his own mother. He gave her a wide, friendly grin. "Yeah? And why's that, sweetheart?"

"Someone was in here, lookin' for you." She raised her eyebrows meaningfully.

"Oh, yeah?" He stood up and winked at Carla. "Well, maybe you should tell me about it in private. Excuse us, Carla."

Carla watched them move away, her mouth twisted. Why was he acting so weird? She pushed back her chair and hesitated, hoping he would stop her. But when he didn't, she sat back down and kept her eye on them, trying to hear what was going on.

Dax noticed none of it. He was watching Janet, who was going through her pockets looking for something. "Here it is." She handed the crumpled card to him.

He glanced at it. All it said was *Pack,* and a local number.

He looked at her. "What's 'Pack'?" His knee started jiggling impatiently as he waited for her to answer.

Janet ran her thumb and forefinger down the sides of her mouth, pulling her slack lower lip away from her teeth. Dax averted his eyes.

"That's his name, hon. There was something off about him. He was wearing a real beat-up suit, had this messy, crazy white hair up around his head. He was asking about a young girl— you know—the one that came in here the other day to see you. He wanted to know who she came here to talk to."

Dax stopped moving. "How did you know he was looking for her?"

"Because he described her. Scar, limp, said she was small. Had to be her."

Without trying to hide the impatience in his voice, he said:

"What did you tell him?"

Janet, sensing a change in his manner, said, "Nothing. Nothing important."

"What do you mean, nothing important?" He wanted to grab her arms and squeeze, but forced himself to keep his hands at his sides.

She pulled herself up, offended. "Hey, I'm on your side, remember? I told him I never saw her. That's it. I just thought you'd want to know."

Dax slid the card into his pocket. "You're right, I'm sorry. You're a doll." He patted her on the shoulder. "I'll give him a call and find out what's up. Thanks."

Janet, mollified, said: "Yeah, well, he seemed like a weird duck to me. Be careful. He even claimed to be the girl's dad."

Dax's eyes fixed on hers. "That's what he said?"

"Yeah, but he was lying."

"How d'you know?"

"I just do. Have good instincts. Anyway, if he is, how come she's running away from him? Something weird about that guy. Watch out."

He smiled broadly. "Aw, you're looking out for me. I love that."

Satisfied, she nodded and returned to her station. Dax put his hand in pocket and touched the card, making sure it was still there.

CHAPTER 25

Vida was sitting at a corner table in the noisy student cafeteria, her back to the wall, eating a cheeseburger and drinking a cup of hot coffee. It was a cavernous room, poor acoustics, the sounds of plates and voices crashing and echoing around her. She'd found a campus newspaper in a rack near the entrance and had it open in front of her, pretending to read it as she ate, hoping it'd work as a deterrent to anyone who might want to join her.

The college kids flowed around her, occasionally standing still, mostly chattering, moving, the boys' clothes loose and oversized, the girls' tight and short, exposing tattoos and bellies. They all seemed to know where they were headed and what they were going to do when they got there. Not that different from high school, Vida thought. Her sense of being an outsider was the same, too.

She wished she could check her email or find a way to call home. Maybe if she reached Marci, she could give her friend the password and get her to check Vida's mail for her. In case there was anything important. Maybe she could buy a disposable phone somewhere. Maybe even on campus. She'd taken four hundred dollars in cash out of her bank account before leaving home, but she was getting low. She should've taken more, but she'd never expected things to turn out this way.

At a table about ten feet away, two girls were talking intensely. They spoke, overlapping each other's sentences, nodding, eyes unfocused on anything but each other and the subject at hand.

Both their cells phones rested neatly on the table next to them. One girl was wearing a faded pink t-shirt with *SAN JOSE* printed on it. Her phone was turquoise.

Vida took another bite of her burger, eyeing the turquoise phone. If the girl was from San Jose, there was a good chance she had a number with a California area code.

A group of friends came up to the two girls, crowding around them, teasing the one in pink about something she had done. She denied it, and one of the guys started rifling through her bag, pretending to look for something. Vida could see the San Jose girl was getting more and more upset (*You're an asshole, Josh, you know that?*) until she suddenly stood up so hard her chair teetered and fell over. The crash stopped the guy from what he was doing, but by then it was too late: San Jose was seriously pissed. She turned her back to the group and started talking and gesticulating to her original tablemate.

For a moment, the cluster of kids was completely focused on its own little drama and the turquoise phone lay alone on the table, unprotected. Vida got to her feet, hung her backpack on both shoulders so she'd have more mobility, and walked up to the group, slowing down just enough. She kept her eyes on the exit in case anyone was watching her.

She was just about to reach between two bodies and scoop up the cell phone, when one of the two moved and blocked her access. The moment was gone. Vida kept zigzagging between the tables and toward the double doors.

Outside, it was dark and quite a bit colder. At first she didn't feel it, because her heart was beating fast. Damn, she'd been close. What if she'd been caught red-handed? How would she have explained it?

But it made her realize something. Here she was, on a campus of hundreds, no, thousands of students. It shouldn't be a problem to make a call or write an email. She just didn't know the system yet. She had to figure it out—and keep her head.

She pulled her thin jacket around her. Seven-thirty in the evening, and she had nowhere to go. She noticed students entering and leaving a large building on the left side of the quad. The light spilling out of the glass doors was inviting, and she wondered if she could find a place there to sit, keep warm, and stay out of the way. She walked toward it.

It was the library. It looked welcoming—but there was a guard at the front door, and students were walking through a turnstile and swiping their IDs.

Vida turned away. She wished she knew someone here, but Albany wasn't a common college destination for Alaskans.

And then she remembered the guy from the bus depot, Tom Frost. He was having a party, right? It was cold and she needed a place to spend the night. Preferably somewhere where there were other women, so a dorm was good. Were dorms co-ed? She had no idea. Either way, she could take care of herself. She also liked the idea of a place where the kids were drinking, because she'd have easier access to money, credit cards, and phones.

Yes, she could do it. She was the right age, looked the part. She just had to relax and feel like a student. She smiled ruefully to herself. Maybe she should pick a major.

She walked toward the library. A girl and a guy emerged, talking, books in hand. "Can you tell me where Indian is?" Vida asked them.

Without breaking his stride, the man turned around, walking backwards, and pointed to the closest tower.

"Thanks," she said, as he turned back and kept going.

As she neared the entrance to the dorm, she slowed down, looking for problems. She saw a group of people walking toward the entrance and speeded up, pacing herself with them, making sure to arrive at the concrete steps just a few feet behind the last one, a boxy guy in a red t-shirt, and shorts that reached mid-calf.

The lead man opened the door and the other two filed in behind him. Vida caught the door from Boxy Guy, who glanced automatically over his shoulder at her and kept his hand on the door, holding it open.

"Thanks," she said, and followed them in.

Done.

CHAPTER 26

Pack woke up at six the next morning. He lay in bed with his eyes closed, letting his thoughts drift and swing around in his head. He saw himself again on Birchwood Lane in Delmar, watching the man unroll the crime scene tape. He thought of the train station. He was drifting over it, looking, not trying to understand anything, just seeing it all. He thought of the Pakistani at the newspaper kiosk, and from there he remembered the young woman selling tickets at the bus depot. Which made him think of the two cops. Heavy equipment on their belts, their shirts a little too tight. Their squad car, already there when he drove up, with nothing but one car between his car and them.

He tried to remember the car. Small, wasn't it? And then he saw it—a dirty blue Jetta, Wisconsin plates (when was the last time he'd seen one of those?) a SUNYAlbany sticker on the back window, pulling away from the curb. Students, back from a weekend away. Maybe a concert in New York or Boston. He remembered two people in the front seat. And wasn't there at least one silhouette in the back?

Pack swiveled his feet onto the floor. He sat on the edge of his bed, hands on his knees. Thinking. That could be it. She could have been standing there, waiting for her bus. The cops pull up, she gets spooked and hitches a ride from the blue Jetta. She would've gotten in a car with someone, anyone, just to get out of there. And that Jetta was probably on its way to the

SUNY campus. Bingo. And what better place for a twenty-year-old to lose herself?

Pack stood up and went looking for a clean white shirt and unstained tie.

He was on the road within half an hour, wearing his black suit, over which he'd passed a damp cloth in an effort to remove the dust and lint.

Forty minutes later, he turned off the highway at the SUNY exit. He left his car in the visitor's parking lot and followed signs to the admissions office. He'd only been on campus a couple of times when he had to drop off a visiting lecturer or prospective student; his impression was of modern archways, gray cement, and grass. It looked practical, like you could hose it down after a big party. He wondered if he was on the right track, if Vida was here. If she was, he'd find her. He wouldn't leave, he'd sit in the fucking fountain and wait, if he had to. But he'd find her.

He asked a young woman behind the first desk he came to, where he could find a map of the campus. She pointed out a wall of fliers.

As he walked back to his car, he studied the small map. Pretty straightforward. There seemed to be a dedicated parking lot for each of the dormitories. So if he found the Jetta in the Dutch lot, the owner might well be housed in the Dutch dorm.

For the next two hours, he cruised through the crowded lots of the university, carefully checking each car. He found six blue Jettas, but no Wisconsin plates. He began to wonder if he'd made a mistake about the state—maybe it was Wyoming, or Indiana. He decided to finish one round of the student lots and, if he hadn't found the vehicle, he'd widen the parameters of his search. He refused to even consider the possibility that he was wasting time on a bad hunch. He'd committed to the course, and he'd plow on through. If he didn't find her, then he'd try one of the other campuses in Albany.

Finally, in the last lot, the one called Indian, brazenly parked in a handicapped spot, he found the Jetta. Blue, Wisconsin plates, SUNYAlbany sticker. Just as he'd remembered it.

Pack pulled his car into a spot nearby and walked back to examine it. The inside was thick with crap—cups, papers, junk food wrappers, wiring, sneakers, textbooks, socks, gym clothes. The ashtray in the front seat was overflowing, and the inspection sticker was peeling off. No handicapped tag hanging from the mirror. Not that he'd expected one.

He tried all the doors. Locked. How come a slob like this remembered to lock his vehicle? He wished he had some kind of a tool for breaking into the little shit machine. If he could look in the glove compartment, he'd have the kid's name. It was obviously a guy, given the size of the sneakers.

He kept circling the car, looking for something to help him. Eventually he found it: an orange notebook, its cover bent and frayed. With a name scrawled on it in black magic marker. The lettering was sloppy, and Pack had to crane and twist to see it. But he finally had it. Cohen. First name, Richard.

Back in his car, he studied the map again. He turned it around to orient himself. Satisfied, he got out, locked his car, and followed a concrete path through a leafless clump of trees toward the dorm named Indian.

CHAPTER 27

Dax lived in a small, one-bedroom rental in a block of apartments called The Heritage Residence on a side street in Albany. A large number of his neighbors—nurses, residents, technicians—were employed by the area hospitals. Most were single and worked long hours.

For now, it suited Dax fine. The truth was, the building gave him a community not all that different from the one he'd left behind in Iraq, except at Heritage he had more privacy and his own bathroom.

Carla had come by about twenty minutes earlier. Lying on the bed, face down and naked, she waited for him. Dax was sitting in the living room, reading the newspaper. Today, he'd ignore her until she gave up and got dressed. Then he'd stop her from leaving, fuck her on the floor of the living room, on the scratchy carpeting. She'd get to work late, with her ass on fire.

But his heart wasn't in it. He was too busy thinking about Vida. He'd let her get away from him twice now: once at the hospital, and a second time at Haley's house.

Now he had to find her. A problem, because he didn't know that much about her.

Haley's mother was dead, so she was no use to him. He knew he'd gotten way too rough with her, but she was everything he despised in a woman: fat, sloppy, and ugly. Bizarre, though, how the old bitch had accused him of always trying to control everything. Told him he was selfish and cruel. She'd stuttered it out, half blubbering, half defiant, and it had almost sounded rehearsed, as if she'd thought it through. Which kind of freaked him out.

Then, when she said that he'd always told Haley what to wear, he really lost it. How did she know about that? Haley must've told her. Not that Haley could dress in civvies, but he did tell her what underwear to put on, or when not to wear any at all.

And how did she know about the friends? Him telling her who she could hang out with? Jesus, Haley must've written details and everything. Even though he found the few letters Haley'd sent home, and they were so tame and full of lies, he could've left them right there.

The funny thing was, when he first rang her doorbell, the mother had acted like she didn't know him from a hole in the wall, like Haley had never mentioned him even once. But once he'd strapped her to the chair, she'd started babbling all that other shit.

He'd just let his short fuse get the better of him, which was a mistake. If only he had controlled his temper, he could have dragged all the information he wanted out of her, and gotten his hands on Vida, too.

Dax was still offended by the stuff she said. He was a decent guy—or he would be, as soon as he got his life back on track. Bottom line was, the old woman had no idea what he had had to put up with from her crazy daughter—the tantrums and threats. Hell, Haley had jumped on him and tried to rip his eyes out.

And when that hadn't worked, when he'd shaken her off like a rabid animal, she'd smiled and said to him, her voice like a sliver of broken glass, that her father was a powerful man, a very dangerous man and she was going to call him and he would reach out anywhere in the world and he'd have Dax *erased.* She said she could do that, have him *erased,* and she kept repeating it like that, over and over, hissing the ess, a little white glob of spit on her lower lip. She said his body would never be found. All she had to do was tell her father what Dax had done to her.

Dax knew she was full of shit, but it pissed him off, her all bug-eyed and voodoo, trying to scare him. To be on the safe side, after she died, he'd gone through all Haley's stuff to see if she had any addresses or letters lying around. But he didn't find anything. And he certainly hadn't found a journal.

He dug in his pocket and pulled out the card Janet from the cafeteria had given him. "Pack." Who was Pack? And what was his interest in Vida? He claimed he was her father. Could he be an investigator, hired by the family? He'd have to call and find out, but he'd need to be super careful. You never know how talking to someone like that could backfire. And he didn't want this Pack to know he'd gotten his number from old Janet, or he'd trace him back to the VA. So he'd just have to pretend to be someone else.

He tried to think how to get information without giving it. The damn phones gave away so much these days, thanks to caller ID. And if you used a public phone, it probably specified that too. Which was fine, unless you were pretending the call was official. So should he call from a business, act like he was selling something? He could go into a store, buy things, then ask to use the phone. Nah, too much. Too complicated.

Dax had to fight the urge to rip the piece of paper into tiny shreds. What a fucking waste of time.

Sometimes Dax couldn't tell what he wanted. He let other people get in the way, *their* needs, *their* feelings. It wasn't right. He just had to keep going in a straight line, no detours. So, unless Buttinsky Pack could give him information about Vida, he was just a detour. He had to be, because if Pack knew where

Vida was, he wouldn't be looking for her, would he? No.

And then it came to him. Simple. Just call the guy and ask for Vida. Pretend *he* was looking for Vida. Or better yet, say he had information about Vida, but they needed to meet up. And then, when the guy showed up, *erase* him. Dax had to smile. Of course, he wouldn't do that, he didn't believe in violence without provocation.

Still, there was something satisfying about the word. Erase. Dax, The Eraser.

CHAPTER 28

If the cement walkway to the dorm was a main artery, then the paths through the grass on either side of it were the veins, shortcuts to places unknown, worn down to the bare earth by countless feet. Pack sidestepped a coiled, used condom on the concrete.

The double doors to the dorm were inside a small arched quadrangle, the cement slab under it dingy and stained. A faint smell of beer permeated the space, undefeated by the fresh breeze that blew through the columns. An emergency light was mounted between the doors, with a security phone and alarm halfway below it. Both doors were locked.

Pack waited.

About six minutes later, two young women appeared inside the lobby, headed out the glass door. The one in front hesitated when she saw him, but only for a second. Having a friend with her must have given her confidence, because she pushed through. Both girls were wearing spandex shorts and running shoes and had their hair tied back, iPods attached to their waists.

Pack held the door for them.

"Can we help you?" the first one said, an edge of hostility in her voice.

"Yes, you can," Pack said, still holding the door open, ready to go in. "I'm looking for a Richard Cohen. Do you know him?"

The girls looked at each other. The taller one hesitated, then said, "I think he rooms with Tom, Tom Frost."

Her friend wasn't giving in so easily. "Why do you want to know?"

Pack pulled out a card from the limo service where he worked. "I've been hired by his parents to pick him up. It's a surprise. They're over at the Desmond, and they want to treat him to breakfast."

The second girl rolled her eyes dismissively.

"That's pretty cool," said the tall one. "Seventh floor, last room at the end. I'm pretty sure. But his name'll be on the door."

"Thanks so much. Enjoy your run," Pack said, giving a courteous bow of his head. Like the perfect butler or valet. If only his other clients could see him. They'd be struck dumb.

Inside, Pack's victory was short lived. There was a handwritten note stuck on the elevator door, announcing: OUT OF ORDER! Again! Just for the hell of it, Pack pushed the call button, but nothing happened, no stirring sound from the shaft. With a deep sigh, he followed the signs for the stairs and started up.

The air in the stairwell was old and used up. He could smell pizza and beer, or maybe it was Chinese take-out and beer. The only sure thing was the beer. His feet clanged on each metal-edged tread, the sound echoing up the high, empty space.

By the third floor, he was sweating heavily. He stopped and took off his suit jacket and leaned on the wall. He had to get in shape, this was terrible. He thought bitterly of the two girls. Why the hell go for a run, when they could just walk up and down the stairs a few times?

By the sixth floor, his pace had slowed to a crawl. He sat down on the top step and listened to his heart as it tried to bust out of his chest and gallop away.

When it had slowed down enough so he could hear himself think, he stood up and trudged up the last flight. He pulled open the door that led out onto the floor.

Two narrow hallways branched off at right angles to each other. He picked one and followed it to the end. No Cohen. Just Najimi and Bartolotta, written in block letters on a piece of typing paper and stuck to the door with tape. He went back the other way. His legs felt weak and jittery from the long climb.

He found the room on the second try. Cohen and Frost. Their names were surrounded with messages written in various handwritings and inks: *Where the hell are you guys?!? Gimme my fucking notes dickwad. I am the walrus.* There was also a drawing of two penises wearing what looked like backwards baseball caps. Obviously, compared to dullards Najimi and Bartolotta, these guys were fun magnets.

Without hesitating, Pack turned the doorknob, and went inside.

And nearly wished he hadn't.

The blackout blinds were pulled down, with only an inch or so of daylight visible, so Pack had to stand in the doorway while his eyes adjusted to the dark. The smell from the room was overpowering—of stale cigarette breath and feet, with an overlay of marijuana. From what he could see, Pack figured the room was a small cubicle, maybe twelve by ten, cement block walls. There were metal bunk beds against the left wall, what looked like two small desks to the right, and two closets, one on either side of the door. Those were the things that would have been on the official description. The reality was that the room was an explosion of clothes, food, cans, and bedding. And he'd thought Cohen's car was bad.

Pack picked his way over the floor, hoping no one was lying there. He pulled the blind down until it escaped his grip and disappeared noisily into the roll at the top of the window frame. Oops. Light flooded the room. He cranked the window open, knocking an ashtray onto the floor, the contents spilling into a cloud of gray ash.

Someone groaned. The body on the top bunk, obviously disturbed by the noise or the light, rolled away to face the wall.

The body on the lower bunk didn't stir, though Pack could hear him snoring lightly.

Pack found a dinner knife on the ground, probably lifted from the cafeteria. He began to bang it against the bed frame, hard. It made a harsh clanging.

The guy up above groaned and rolled back toward Pack. He had brown hair and was unshaven. He opened one puffy eye. "Hey, man, who the fuck are you?"

"I'm the terminator, dude, and I've come to find my daughter. So you should get your sorry ass out of bed right now, before I kill you."

The young guy looked somewhat concerned, which was the best he could do, given his condition. He sat up on an elbow. The bedding fell away from his thin bare chest. "Hey, I don't know what you're talking about. I don't know any daughter."

Pack pointed the knife at him. "Frost or Cohen?"

"Frost."

"Okay, Frost. I think you do. Did your friend Cohen drive to the bus station yesterday? Or did you do it? I know one of you did."

"He did, he came to pick me up. So what?" Frost was sitting up now, sounding a little more defiant, though it was hard to be too defiant sitting naked on a bunk bed.

"You gave a ride to a girl yesterday, right?"

"So?"

"Where did you take her?"

He stuttered. "Look, we didn't do anything to her. We gave her a ride to campus and said goodbye. That's it."

Pack felt a wave of relief. Finally. He was close.

He hit the knife against the bed frame once more. "Don't lie to me, Frost. I need to know where she is. Now. It's important."

Frost scrambled off the foot of the bed, letting himself down clumsily to the ground. He kept as far away from Pack as he could. He was wearing yellow boxers with happy faces on them. "You're psycho, you know that? Why should I tell you anything about her? For all I know, you're a killer."

Pack saw he was losing his advantage. "Listen, she's in trouble, she needs my help. You better tell me when you last saw her, or I'll cut off your roommate's nuts."

Just then, the guy in question groaned and moved. Frost, now pulling on a pair of jeans, snapped: "Hey, fuck you, I'm going to call security."

The blankets on the lower bunk were thrown off and Pack looked down.

There was Vida, squinting up at him.

"You're here!" he said, stating the obvious.

"So are you. How come?" she said sleepily.

"What d'ya think? Get up, let's go."

To his surprise, Vida didn't give him an argument. She sat up and pulled her backpack from the dark corner of the bed where she must've wedged it earlier. She looked around under the covers until she found her sweatshirt and jeans and took her time getting them on. Then she stood up and hoisted the pack onto her shoulder.

"Thanks for the help, Tom," she said to the half-dressed man who'd spent the night above her. She hesitated, then gave him a hug.

Irritated, Pack said: "Come on, come on."

"Lighten up, okay?" She led the way out the door. "I've got to pee."

Pack waited in the hall while she went to the bathroom. A young man came out of the same swing door, hair wet, and naked but for a towel wrapped around his waist. He nodded incuriously at Pack as he walked by. Pack wanted to kick his bony ass.

Vida followed him down the stairs. "Why'd you come find me?"

Pack didn't pause. "Because Mitch told me to." Even to his own ears he sounded sullen.

Neither of them spoke until they were in the parking lot. Pack noticed how pale she was. He felt bad and said, as he opened the driver's door, "Your mother's going nuts—she's worried sick. The situation's hairy. You know about the woman you were staying with, right?"

Vida turned on him. "So? I didn't do it."

"I never said you did, but the police are looking for you. You've got some questions to answer."

"Great. Now you think I'm a killer."

"Shh!" he said, looking around the empty lot. "Not so loud."

Vida shrugged and gave a shake of her head, as if he was being unreasonable, which was irritating.

They got into the car in silence. Once they started moving, the only sound was a rattle coming from somewhere on the console. Pack tried to find it. "Goddamn!" he said, eyes on the road, groping in the general area.

Vida watched him without helping. "Where're we going?"

"To my cousin's house."

More silence. They turned onto the highway. Suddenly, Vida said, "Why did you leave us, Pack? When I was a kid?"

Pack groaned. "You're kidding, right?"

She sat back and put her feet up on the dash. "Might as well tell me. We've got nothing else to talk about."

"Take your feet down, okay?"

"Were you an alcoholic?"

"No, I wasn't an alcoholic." His grip tightened on the steering wheel.

144

"So was it drugs? I bet it was drugs, right? Were you dealing?"

"God, no. Why do you say that?"

"You drove a semi from one end of the country to another. You could've carried whole shipments."

"Well I didn't. Jeez."

"But you smoked a lot of pot."

"Too much, yeah. But that wasn't it. What did your mother tell you?"

"Nothing much, just that it didn't work out. Were you having an affair?"

"No. Can you take your feet down? You're messing up my car."

"Come on, what happened? Were you tired of my mother?"

"No."

"Was I a terrible kid?"

He shook his head. "No, no. You were great."

"I was?"

"Yes, sure. You were great."

Her voice became sharper. "Then why?"

"No good reason."

The rattle on the console became more pronounced.

Vida shrugged. "There must've been something. You don't just disappear one day for no reason at all."

"For Christ's sake, take your feet off the fucking dash!" Without signaling, Pack pulled onto the shoulder of the highway and jammed on the brakes. They both lurched forward and slammed back into their seats.

Pack turned in his seat to face Vida. His face was red. "I was a shitty father, okay? That's it."

Vida put her feet on the floor of the car. "This is upsetting you, obviously. What do you mean, you were a shitty father?" She looked at him, and then something terrible slowly occurred

145

to her. "My god, you abused me."

Pack frowned, not understanding. Then the penny dropped. "What? No, never. I would never. God, that's disgusting."

Vida read his face, believed him, and moved on. "That's a relief. That would've been a hard one to get past, you know? Then what was it?"

Pack gave a monumental sigh. "I couldn't do it. That's all. I felt like I was going to die."

She blinked. "What?"

"Yeah, I know, it sounds ridiculous. But I'm not lying. I felt suffocated. No, I was suffocating. Literally. When I was home, I'd wake up in the night not being able to breathe. I'd be gasping for air."

"Only when you were home?"

Pack rubbed his face, as if washing it clean. "Yeah. When I was on the road, I was fine. But within hours of coming home I'd feel sick to my stomach, have a constant headache, couldn't sleep."

"Great. Sounds like you had an allergy. To us."

He didn't deny it. "Maybe. I'd get up and walk around the house while you and your mother were sleeping. Didn't matter how tired I was. There were times I'd leave the house and walk, sometimes for two, three hours. It started when you were about six months old, went on for five more years. Somewhere in there I ended up resenting your mother, like she was forcing me to be there, sucking the air out of me."

"Was she?"

The lines on Pack's face deepened. "I think she just wanted us to be a regular family, for me to find a job that didn't take me away so much."

"That must've scared the shit out of you."

He stared at the road, as if he was looking at a different landscape than the highway in front of them.

"And me, did you resent me too?"

"I loved you so much. You were funny, sweet."

"But you resented me."

"No! No. I don't know. Maybe."

"So you disappeared."

"No, I didn't just disappear."

"That's what it felt like to me."

"Shelley and I separated for a while. I rented a shitty little apartment, and while I was there I was fine. So we tried it again. I moved back in and it all came back. At that point your mother thought a clean break was better. She moved to California, where she met your stepdad."

"Hmm."

"See what I mean? Not much to tell. I was a lousy father."

He pulled into Millie's driveway. He figured he'd let his cousin do the questioning and the sorting out of information and he'd take a back seat on this one. He had done what he set out to do—find the girl—and now he could deal with her mother with a clear conscience. He was still feeling shaken by their conversation. If that's what it was. God, he'd sounded like a spineless jerk. Well, call a spade a spade, right?

He turned off the engine.

Vida reached for the door handle.

He stopped her. "Hold on," Pack said. "You remember my cousin, you used to call him Uncle Mitch?"

Vida looked at him questioningly. "Not much. Mom said he was a good guy. A cop, right?"

Pack nodded. "Yep. But there's more. I just want to prepare you."

Vida waited. "Okay."

Pack shut his eyes as if he wanted to avoid looking at her while he spoke. "He's a good man and a good friend. But now

147

he dresses like a woman."

Vida started laughing, a big guffaw. "You're kidding, right?"

Pack's face tightened up angrily. "No, I'm not kidding. That's what he needs to do, so I go along with it and support it."

Vida looked at him with something like pity. "It's not such a big deal, you know. You shouldn't take it so seriously."

"I don't, okay? I just wanted to let you know."

"One of my two best friends in ninth grade was a cross-dresser."

"Yeah? What happened to him?"

"It was bad. His parents ended up sending him to military school."

"I assume that didn't work out."

"No, it didn't. He was miserable, he tried to commit suicide twice. I wanted to go with him, I figured I could take care of him and I wanted to be a soldier anyway, but with my parents it was like, never in a million years. Anyway, he lives in San Francisco now. Hasn't spoken to his folks since graduation."

Pack sat there, looking at her, suddenly and unexpectedly proud of her. "Jeez."

"So come on, let's go inside. I'm hungry."

"His name's Millie now."

Vida's grin spread again. "Millie. I like that. Do I call him Aunt Millie?"

Pack opened the door and put his left foot out on the ground. "Ask him. Just be respectful, okay?"

"Oh, please."

They walked up the steps. Pack pointed at the doormat and wiped his feet to set the example, even though they'd just been sitting in the car. The front door was unlocked, and a breeze blew in the house with them, swirling the lace curtains.

Pack called out: "Millie? You here?"

"In the kitchen," Millie yelled back.

Pack glanced once at Vida, and led the way. Millie was doing something at the counter. Her back was to them, the red wig in place on her head. A pot of water was boiling on the stove, hissing and spitting out from under the lid. A smaller pot bubbled next to it. Pack could smell burnt tomatoes.

"Hey, look what I found," Pack said.

Millie glanced over her shoulder, her face a scowl of disturbed concentration. "I'm screwing up the—" she said, and then she saw Vida. She put down the knife she was holding and turned to look at the young woman standing there, expression wary. "Well, I'll be damned. Hello, Vida."

Vida smiled, her mouth only going up on one side, uncommitted. "Hi."

Pack went to the stove and turned off both burners. The surface of the stove was covered in pools of blackened tomato sauce. "You're burning everything, Millie. Christ."

"Shut the hell up. I know what I'm doing. I'm making spaghetti and meatballs. For the church shelter."

"They won't want it," Pack said, gesturing at the stove with his chin. "It's all burnt."

"Sure they'll want it. But you know what? They're not going to get it. Vida, you hungry?"

The girl nodded.

"Good. Pack, why don't you set the table and we'll have some supper."

"Now?"

"Just set the table, okay? Vida, you come over here and help me. Put your stuff down over there somewhere. Let me look at you. Are you crying? You're laughing? Aw, come on, sweetie, don't cry. You're just hungry. Let me give you a hug."

Chapter 29

Before they sat down to eat, Pack gave his phone to Vida and told her to call her mother. She took it out in the hall and they could hear the murmur of her voice, rising and falling, punctuated by silences. When she came back into the kitchen, her eyes were red, but she looked more relaxed.

It felt good to sit down and eat together, Pack thought. Family. And the spaghetti sauce wasn't that bad after all. "Just tastes a little smoky, like barbeque," Pack said generously.

"I think it's good," Vida said, looking at Millie. Pack smiled cynically and shook his head: suck-up. Vida narrowed her eyes at him.

Millie ignored the not-so-subtle exchange and ate on, muscled forearms on the table. "So, what's the next step, Vida?" she said, her expression thoughtful.

Pack watched Vida, curious to hear what she'd say.

She wiped her mouth with a paper napkin. "I'm thinking I should turn myself in. I can get in touch with the nearest JAG, see what they say."

Pack shook his head. "It's too late for that. There's a dead body in the morgue in Albany and the cops think you—"

"That's why," Vida interrupted. "Hey, I had nothing to do with it, I just found her. I freaked out and ran, when I should have stayed there and faced the cops. Maybe I can even help them figure out who did it."

"That's bullshit," Pack said. "They're not going to want your help."

"Hey, you can call it bullshit, but Haley and her mom, what happened to them is connected, I know it."

"Okay, how?" Pack sat back in his chair and crossed his arms.

"I saw her. She'd been tied up and tortured. Hit and beaten. It was seriously horrible, vicious. And deliberate. So either the guy who did it was a sadist or else he wanted information from her. Except she didn't know anything. I mean, I talked to her a lot, she was a sweet, sad lady, but she hadn't a clue, you know? So maybe they came for me. Because of something I know. Something I don't *know* I know."

"Yeah, but what's the connection to Haley?"

"You're not listening! Me! I was there when Haley died."

"Why couldn't it be because Haley's mom had something the bad guys wanted?"

"Like what?"

"Money. Jewelry. Stuff—they're greedy, right?—and stuff seems to work fine for most criminals."

"Okay. You just don't want to see what's right in front of you." She stood up from the table and started clearing the dishes.

Millie, now cleaning her teeth with a toothpick, said: "Hey, you need a shower?"

Vida looked at her, surprised. "Yeah. That'd be great."

"Pack, take her upstairs and get her a clean towel from the closet at the top of the stairs. Shake it out, in case there's ear-wigs, okay? Go on, honey, we can get this. We'll talk more a little later. Time for another list, I think."

CHAPTER 30

Dax stood on the street at a pay phone near his apartment.

He dialed the number from Pack's card. He'd let the bitch Vida get away a second time, and now he was stuck following this weird little lead that Janet from the cafeteria had given him. Probably a dead end. He listened to the ring, pretty sure no one would pick up. Middle of the afternoon, who's home? Anyway, he'd be fine leaving a message. But the rings kept on going. Just as he was about to give up, a machine finally picked up: "Reynolds Packard here. I'm out on a run. Leave a message." And then the beep. Dax hung up and wrote the name on the card. Hmm. Reynolds Packard.

He stood there, thinking, his knee locking and unlocking, his right hand fanning Pack's card back and forth against the fingers of his left hand. Reynolds Packard. He had the name now and with a little easy work with a phone book, he could find out where the man lived.

And Packard—that was Vida's last name. So the guy wasn't an investigator, he was a relative. Maybe her father, after all. Much better. Because it meant he wasn't a professional, and he'd make stupid decisions based on his feelings, and not on experience. But the best part was that, if he was family, sooner or later Vida would go whining home to him.

Energized, Dax walked quickly back to his apartment.

The first thing he did when he got upstairs was get online and try the reverse directory trick with the phone number, but nothing came up. No problem, it was the Internet age; he'd find him. He changed the last two digits to zeros—those kinds of numbers were often taken by restaurants or retail businesses, entities that liked to be found. Sure enough, a florist popped up in New Canaan, New York. He repeated the experiment, just to be on the safe side, changing the last digits again. Again, New Canaan appeared. He looked it up on a map and found that it was about forty minutes southeast of Albany. That made sense.

He thought for a minute, then looked up the address of the New Canaan Post Office. Good place to start. He found a plain envelope, folded a blank piece of paper into it, sealed it, and wrote:

Reynolds Packard, 131 Water Street, New Canaan, NY.

All small towns had a Water Street, and if New Canaan was the exception, it didn't matter.

An hour later, he drove out of the parking lot. His black Corvette gleamed, just the way he liked it; his GPS was set for the New Canaan, New York, post office. He didn't need it, the directions were simple, but the clipped British accent reminded him of James Bond's secretary, whatever her name was. Which made him an agent, naturally.

On a mission.

Thirty-one minutes later, he turned off the well-traveled state road that went east toward Massachusetts, and pulled into one of the three parking spaces outside the New Canaan Post Office. It was housed in a small white frame building and shared space with a local utilities company. A blue mailbox was anchored to the cement walkway.

Dax pulled open the wooden door. The single room was empty. To his right was a wall of numbered boxes and to his left, a bulletin board. He glanced at the faces on the Wanted posters. Losers.

On the opposite side of the room from where he stood was a small customer window. He went over to it and peered in. The window was made for shorter people and he had to hunch over. A slim, dark-haired woman was sitting at a desk, tallying something on a calculator. He waited a moment then cleared his throat.

She looked up, startled. "Oh, I didn't hear you come in."

"Sorry if I made you jump," he smiled.

She laughed as she stood up and came toward him. "I'm used to it, working here. It's so slow that I jump every time someone comes in. What can I do for you?" She spoke with a slight accent. Maybe Eastern European.

"Well," he began, and hesitated, as if uncertain how to continue. "I've got a bit of a problem."

She waited, head cocked, willing to be helpful.

"I've got a check here for a man who's done some work for me—Reynolds Packard. In fact, I know he's waiting anxiously for it. But the only address I have for him is this—" and here he took the envelope out of his pocket and peered at the address on it: "131 Water Street, New Canaan. I sent it but it was returned—address unknown. Can you give me the correct one?"

The woman looked sympathetic but slowly shook her head. "I'm so sorry, but I can't do that. Can I see that?"

She took the envelope from him and examined it. "This hasn't been mailed."

Caught out in a lie, he said: "No, right, well, it was all scribbled on. This is a new one, obviously."

"I see. Look, I'll keep this and put it with his mail. I won't even charge you for a stamp, since you already sent it once." She turned and put the envelope on a counter off to his right.

"I was hoping to take it to him. He doesn't have mail delivered?"

Her expression hardened imperceptibly. He understood he'd

gone too far. Who hand delivers checks to their creditors? "I'm sorry, no. But if you leave the envelope in my care, I'll be sure it gets to him."

He pretended to hesitate. "You know, I'll call him and get him to stop by." He held out his hand.

She picked it up and handed it back. "Whatever you prefer."

He had to stop himself from snatching the letter out of her hand. He knew and she knew that he was lying. He could feel himself beginning to blush, heat running up his neck and into his face. He made sure to turn away quickly, before she could see the rush of color.

The heat cooked him into anger. Ignorant, small-town whore. From some two-bit country in the middle of nowhere, defending her little piece of turf. Without looking back at her, he walked to the door. "You've been very helpful," he said as he left.

In the Corvette, he waited until his cheeks had cooled and his breathing had settled down before pulling out onto the road. He'd handled that badly. He'd have to find some other way. This Packard must have friends; maybe he was a volunteer firefighter. Or a member of the fucking Elks. He had to belong to something. This time Dax would be more careful.

CHAPTER 31

The water was hot and Vida stood under it, eyes closed, as it beat down on her head and shoulders and streamed onto her face and into her mouth. Aaah.

She reached for the shampoo. The bathroom was a sweet little-old-lady bathroom, with dried flowers and hand towels with initials embroidered into them. Nothing like back home. It was pretty clean, too, which surprised Vida, seeing how her father lived. Now that was a house she wouldn't want to shower in. Worse than the dorm. At least that had been new dirt; Pack's filth was old and deep.

She wished her father had a little more belief in her. I mean, why did he take it for granted she was full of shit? It made her angry. She was trying to look at it all rationally, but it wasn't easy. She was a fugitive who'd found the beaten corpse of a kind, harmless woman. What should she do now? And what was the deal with these two crazy old men? How could they possibly help her?

She massaged the shampoo into her scalp. She thought of Haley, whose greatest fantasy had involved taking a hot shower every day: no waiting in line, no water rationing, no dirty clothes when you were done. Haley would've loved this bathroom, doilies and all.

Her mind drifted gently into the past as she rinsed the lather from her hair.

★ ★ ★ ★ ★

It had begun with a banging on the door. Someone was smacking it flat handed. Startled, Vida jumped off her bed. But before she could get to it, the door swung wide open. A woman stood there, one duffel bag slung over her shoulder, the other dragging on the ground behind her. Like everyone else, she was in pale, gray-green camo ACUs; she had blonde hair tied back in a ponytail and was pretty in a fragile way, her bones delicate under her clear skin. When she saw Vida, she let go of her stuff and stood straight. She was a lot taller than Vida, maybe five foot nine.

She said in a slightly raspy voice, her smile tired. "Hey, you got anything to drink here? I've been traveling for three days with a bunch of dumb ol' boys, I need to take the edge off."

Vida smiled back. "Nope, sorry. Haven't found a source yet."

"We'll work on that. Specialist Flynn, 88 Hotel. But you can call me Haley," and held out her hand.

Vida shook it. "Specialist Packard, 88 Mike. Vida."

"Match made in heaven."

And that was how she met Haley. Their specialties were similar—Vida was a driver and Haley was a Cargo Specialist, and they'd become friends quickly, the way you do when there's not a lot of time for dancing around. They were both in the motor pool, and though they went their separate ways during the long working hours, at the end of the day, if they were both free, they hung out.

Haley was funny. She could imitate anyone perfectly—the way they walked, the way they sounded. Her voice would change, her slender body would realign itself, and she'd become someone else. She imitated the platoon sergeant, a pie-faced woman with a powdery, high-pitched voice and a way of patting one cupped hand softly inside the other when she was making a point. But usually it was the men around them, even the ones she liked, that Haley made fun of. She could make Vida laugh so hard, she'd double over and beg her to stop.

Haley was protective, too. Vida remembered one day she was on her way to chow when Pascoe stopped her, looking to harass her about something, she couldn't even remember what it was. But before she could say anything, Haley appeared behind her.

"What's going on?"

Pascoe glanced at the blonde, his eyes taking her in from top to bottom. He smiled intimately at her and said: "None of your sweet business, sugar tits." He'd learned his tough guy dialogue from bad movies, it seemed.

This was Pascoe's way, and most of the women ignored him as much as they could. But Flynn looked hard at him and said softly, seriously: "If you fuck with me or my friends, you'll be sorry."

Pascoe let out a guffaw. "I'm so scared."

"No, I mean it," she went on, her voice casual, as if she were talking about laundry. "I will come into your room at night and stab you deep in the left eye, you hear? And if you get sent home before I get round to it, then I'll put your name and address in an email to some very bad people I know, and they will hunt you down in whatever little shit hole of a town you come from and pull your skin off in long, thin strips. It's what they like to do."

Pascoe looked confused, like a Chihuahua'd just bitten him hard on the throat.

"Come on, we'll miss our chance to eat," Haley continued, the tone of her voice unchanged, her eyes still on Pascoe.

Vida had followed her, laughing, looking back at Pascoe's face. "Whoa, you are one badass. He's gonna hate you from now on," she said. But when she glanced at Haley, she was surprised to see her friend was glassy-eyed and trembling. "Are you okay?"

"I hate that guy. I'm going to kill him one of these days, I swear."

Vida was surprised. "Pascoe's just an asshole. You can't let him get to you or you'll go nuts. This place is brimming with assholes."

Haley took a deep, shuddering breath, as her shoulders seemed to let go of some of the rage. She shut her eyes, nodded once: "You're right. I can't let some hick make me crazy."

"He's harmless. He just needles people to get a reaction. Ignore him and he'll go away."

"Like the clap, right?" Haley said, looking at her.

"You need penicillin for that."

"So. Brimming with assholes, is it?"

"The law of averages. A lot of males, a high percentage of assholes. Unavoidable."

Vida thought of that as she dried off. Men. And here she was again, outnumbered. By two weird old men.

CHAPTER 32

When Vida came downstairs, Pack was sitting at the kitchen table but Millie was nowhere in sight. Pack said: "Where's my gun?"

Vida shrugged her shoulders apologetically. "I was afraid the cops would pick me up and find it on me, so I threw it down a storm drain. I'm truly sorry, Pack."

He looked at her, trying to read her, then shook his head. "Bull. Let's see the backpack." He held out his hand.

Vida kept hold of it and said, her voice rising: "What are you saying?"

"I'll show you. Here, gimme the bag."

Millie appeared in the doorway that led to the dining room. She stood, her bulky body filling the entry. She crossed her arms and listened.

Vida huffed. "Jeez. Talk about trust." Then, after a pause: "Okay. But why can't I keep it? I need the protection."

"It's my gun. You shoot someone with my gun, I'm gonna get in trouble."

"He's right," Millie said. "And it's dangerous."

"Oh, please."

"Why don't you clean it for your dad?" she said, pleased with herself, as if she were suggesting baking brownies. "I've got to clean my Browning, we can work together."

"Yippee," Vida said. She put the backpack on the table angrily.

"Hey! Hey! Easy there," said Pack. "Don't go banging it around."

Ten minutes later they were sitting at the dining room table, the lacquered surface protected by sheets of newspaper. Vida and Millie were across from each other, breaking down the two handguns. Between them were the supplies—an orange bottle of Hoppe's solvent, a spray can of oil, brushes, and patches. Pack sat at the head of the table, a pad of clean paper in front of him. He tapped a pen against it.

Vida frowned. "God, Pack, this gun is bad. When's the last time you cleaned it?"

"Hey, I don't know. A couple of years ago."

"More like fifteen. Do you ever go to the range?"

"Believe it or not, I'm not like Millie here, a gun-crazy redneck."

Vida glanced at him. "So how come you have a handgun?"

"I got held up one night by some backwoods tweaker. My fault—I felt sorry for him and gave him a ride from the train station. Quarter of a mile out of Hudson, he pulled out a .45. All I had was twenty bucks and a cheap radio so he got a tad pissed. I thought the little shit was going to shoot me. That's when she," he pointed at Millie with his chin, "made me get a permit and a gun. I haven't used it once."

"You should keep it in the car," Vida said.

"What if the car gets stolen?" he shook his head. "Now, can we get down to business? We need to figure out what we're going to do here."

Millie said, eyes on her work: "Vida's right, you should go to the range, brush up on your skills."

"I don't have any skills, okay?"

"I'm just saying."

"For chrissake, can we do some work here? What do we have so far? Come on."

Vida looked up. "Haley and I knew this guy, Pascoe. He was

with the Rangers. A real turd. Maybe he killed her."

They both stared at her.

"Any reason for him to do so, that you know of?" Pack asked.

"No, but he was a mean, woman-hating dick and I think he'd have enjoyed it."

Pack and Millie looked at her.

Pack wrote "PASCOE" on the top of his pad of paper. "Okay. Good. What else?"

"All I know is that Haley Flynn was murdered. Then Mrs. Flynn was murdered." She looked defiantly at her father and his cousin, daring them to contradict her.

Pack scratched his chin. "Let's start with the first one. With Haley."

"Okay."

"If she was killed by a fellow soldier, then it's about money. Or passion."

"How d'you know that?"

"By passion, you mean it was a relationship that went bad?" said Millie.

"Yeah, you know, a crime of passion. Something to do with love. Gone wrong."

"Well, then it wasn't Pascoe," Vida said. "He sure as hell didn't love her. But you know what? I saw her fiancé the other day. He told me they were all set to get married. Maybe she had someone else on the side, someone who got jealous."

"You're kidding. When did you meet him?" Pack asked.

"I went to the VA hospital and found him. Wasn't that hard."

"I went there too, looking for you. I couldn't find anyone who'd seen you."

"You can't have looked too hard, I sat in the cafeteria with him. Had coffee. I even met a couple of the nurses."

"Huh. I was down in the cafeteria. I talked to one of the women who worked there, but she had no memory of you."

"The guy I'd been looking for made a big song and dance about getting me a cup of coffee, you'd think they'd all remember. He was flirting with some old lady and acting like a rock star. Honestly, he's kind of a jerk."

"Did the old lady work there?"

"Yeah. She got him some sugar."

"I think I talked to her. Or someone like her. And why's he a jerk? It sounds like every guy you went to war with was some kind of a shit."

"Not true. There were plenty of decent guys. But they aren't as relevant right now."

"I wonder why that old lady didn't tell me about you?"

"Maybe she thought you looked sketchy. You do, you know. No offense."

"I don't look sketchy. Christ."

Millie cleared her throat. "Enough. Can we go back, just for a moment, to the question about Iraq, and what reasons someone might have had for killing Haley? Pack, you said money . . . or passion."

Pack sat back. "Yeah, take jealousy. She's going out with some guy, or gal, someone else gets involved, feelings run high, it's a macho world, men with guns, and all that. That's one scenario."

"What else? Vida?" Millie looked at her.

"I'm trying to think about the money idea. I mean, everyone's making the same amount of money. So how do soldiers fight over money?"

Millie: "Gambling debts? Drugs?"

Pack: "Were there a lot of drugs at the base?"

"I don't know. Some, I'm sure. You hear stuff, but it wasn't my scene so I kept out of it."

"But drugs would've been something to fight over, and killing over drugs is nothing new." Millie pointed at Pack's list.

"You writing this all down? Okay, what else?"

"Is there a black market, Vida? You know, food, alcohol?"

"I don't know. I just bought the usual crap at the shopette."

Pack sneered. "Shopette? What the hell's a shopette?"

Millie sighed. "Whadya think? It's a small shop, moron."

"Sounds ridiculous."

Millie shook her head at him.

Pack continued. "What about her love life, Vida? Do you think this guy you saw at the VA is legit? I mean, his claim about his relationship with Haley?"

Vida sighed. "I don't know. I don't remember them being an item, but Haley and I had drifted apart in the last month. She was out a lot at night, and when she was around, she seemed pretty shut down. I was relieved, honestly. But I thought she and this guy were just buds. Or maybe a little more—" she squinted, as if trying to see into the past. "Whatever. I certainly don't remember any engagement."

"So if we believe what you saw, that Haley was murdered, then this guy could be a contender. He could have killed her. What was his job?"

"Medic."

"That fits. He'd be one of the first at the ambush site, right? Looking for the wounded."

"True. I hadn't thought of that. Creepy. I just thought he knew us both, so he'd help me remember."

"What else did you talk about with him?"

"Well, I asked him if he remembered Haley writing in a journal."

"Did she?"

"I don't know. I just remember her lying on her bed, writing. Could be a journal."

"What did he say?"

"It seemed to get him all fired up. He told me I was making

him look bad, if the woman he was going to marry kept a journal and he hadn't known about it."

Pack leaned forward. "Good. Let's pretend this is the guy who killed her. If he is, then this talk about a journal is going to really get him going. He's got to assume that it's going to have some stuff in it he won't want anyone to read about. Maybe one of them had an affair with someone else, or maybe he hit her—"

Millie nodded. "Yeah, which would explain why, the next day, he goes to the mother's house. He's looking for the journal."

"But there was no journal!" Vida said, distressed.

"I thought you said there might have been?" Pack said, puzzled.

"Yes, there might have been, but Mrs. F. didn't have it. All she had from Haley were a few emails. Full of lies, about church and her good works with little Iraqi kids. No journal."

"But that doesn't mean the killer believed her."

"Oh, shit. You mean, he might have done it because I mentioned a diary?" Vida's face paled and there was fear in her eyes when she looked at her father.

Pack wanted to help her, but it would do no good to lie to her. "That might have set him off."

Millie shook her head. "Come on, come on, let's get back to facts here."

"But why? Why would he do all this?" Vida's gaze drifted around the table, as if the answer were written in the newsprint that covered it. "I just kind of made it up. She used to write, but it was letters, I think."

Pack shrugged. "Who knows? Maybe he didn't. But let's pretend, okay?"

Vida chewed on the corner of her thumb. "Okay. He killed Haley's mom, looking for the journal. Didn't find it, because it doesn't exist. Now what's he gonna do?"

Pack turned to Millie. "Maybe you should contact your detective pal in Albany, give him a name. What's this medic called, anyway?"

"John Dax."

"Too risky," Millie said. "We don't know for sure that he's the guy. And how do we tell the cops without mentioning Vida? Or do we just say we saw his name in a dream?"

Vida held up a hand. "I have an idea."

Her two relatives looked at her. Millie said: "Let's hear it."

"Pascoe. So maybe he didn't do it, but he's a real douche, and he knew Haley and Dax. Maybe he knew what was really going on. What was really going down with them."

"Okay. Where do we find him?"

"I don't know. But it shouldn't be too hard to track him down."

CHAPTER 33

To Dax, the town of New Canaan was laughable. It was a drive-through, just a couple of ugly little strip malls surrounded by rolling countryside. There was a small supermarket, the fire station—called the Protective Association—one liquor store, the library, a pizza place, and two empty restaurants. He figured he'd be able to crack this nut easily.

He parked in front of the Protective Association, turned on the charm, and knocked on the side door. No one answered. He tried the handle, but it was locked. "How the hell are they protecting anyone?" he said to himself, returning to the car.

The gift store was a few doors further down. A bell over the door tinkled as he opened it, and the smell of candles enveloped him as he stepped inside. The place was empty, and the stock on the shelves threadbare, as if good intentions hadn't been enough to bring in customers. He walked around, pretending to look interested. Trinkets, decorations, little stuffed animals, cards, candles, arrangements, goodies, jokes. Useless shit. He had the urge to slide his hand along the shelves, wiping it all to the ground.

A large woman was kneeling in front of a box of something pink. She saw him and stood up slowly. "Yes?" she said hopefully, eyebrows raised to her hairline.

Dax smiled warmly at her. "I'm looking for an old friend of mine who lives here in town. I was hoping you might be able to point me in his direction."

Her eyebrows dropped in disappointment. "Oh. Who's your friend?"

"Reynolds Packard. His friends call him Pack? White hair, in his fifties or so?"

She shook her head. "No, no. Doesn't ring a bell. You should go to the post office, they're your best bet."

"The post office? How come I never thought of that? Well, sorry to have bothered you."

"Uh huh," she said, turning back to her boxes. She groaned as she lowered herself back to her knees. He was already forgotten.

Two hundred yards further down the road, Dax tried the diner. A waitress said she'd get the owner, who eventually came through the swing doors of the kitchen. He was speaking in a foreign language, probably Greek, to someone behind him. A small, sharp-featured man with short black hair. He raised his chin at Dax in question. "Yes?"

Dax tried to turn on the charm, but the man just stared coldly at him. He shook his head. "No sir, don't know him."

"A man in his fifties, white hair, lives here in New Canaan?"

"No, I can't help you. Go to the police, down there," he pointed toward Massachusetts. "On your right."

"Good idea, thanks." Right, the police. Not likely. Outside, he looked back. The owner was watching him. Suspicious son-of-a-bitch. He'd love to toss a brick through his window one night. That'd fix him.

Dax was running out of ideas. He drove to a smaller strip mall across the road and parked in front of the little super-market. Only one of the two registers was open. The cashier was a woman in her sixties, short and wide, wearing a high crowned cowboy hat with what looked like three large turkey feathers stuck in the band.

After listening to him explain his interest in Pack, she shook her head. Thinking there was something wrong with her, he repeated his question. She said: "I heard you the first time, sonny. Don't know 'im. Wouldn't tell you if I did."

Dax went to his car, furious. "Fucking people deserve to live and die in this hole-in-the-ground," he said aloud as he climbed back into his now dusty Corvette. Pulling violently out of the mall, he cut in front of a pick-up. He drove past the library. "Forget it," he shouted at the small building, as if it had begged him to stop by.

He was a mile out of town when he saw a sign by the side of the road that read Top Notch Fuel. It was hanging in front of a small gray house that had once been a single-family home. In the parking lot behind it he could see a couple of pick-ups, a white van, and a long fuel delivery truck.

On impulse, Dax turned into the driveway of the gray building. He pulled up next to the delivery truck.

The paint on the house was peeling and the porch to the door marked OFFICE was sloping unevenly, as if the posts that held it up were rotting at different speeds.

The area open to customers was tiny, separated from the rest of the interior by brown paneling and a chipped gray metal desk. A middle-aged woman, ash blonde hair in a bun, tanning-booth-brown skin, sat at the desk tallying figures on a calculator.

Across the desk from her sat a big man, probably in his upper forties. He had thin gray hair curled in baby waves around the sides of his head. Deep grooves were carved around his downward-turned mouth. He wore a stained denim work jacket and heavy work boots.

When Dax walked in, the man looked up. The woman kept adding, her long red nails clicking on the plastic numbers.

The man stood and said: "Okay, you tell him that I'm waitin' to hear."

The space was narrow, so Dax had to move to the side to let him out. The fellow edged by him without making eye contact. He left a smell of oil in his wake.

"How can I help you?" the blonde said, but she wasn't interested in the answer. He knew by her expression she'd be no use to him—neither curious enough to retain details about her customers, nor crooked enough to pass them on to him.

He snapped his fingers and said: "I just remembered something. I'll be right back."

Outside, the man was about to climb up into the cab of the high tanker truck.

"Excuse me, sir," Dax called out.

The man looked at him. "Me?"

Dax nodded. He approached the driver, glancing back at the building to make sure the woman wasn't watching from the window. The man shifted his weight impatiently. "Yeah?"

Dax reached into his pocket and pulled out a roll of bills. He lowered his voice. "I need to find someone, he's an old friend and he lives in New Canaan." He flipped through the bills and pulled out four twenties. "You think you can help me?"

The man's eyes darted quickly toward the office door, then back to Dax. "Who're you looking for?"

"His name is Reynolds Packard. In his fifties, white hair."

"Never met him."

Dax wanted to groan aloud in disappointment. He couldn't believe his lousy luck. "Never?"

"Never once."

"Shit."

The man lowered his voice. "But I deliver to his house. He's just never around when I do. So I've never actually met him."

Dax smiled. "Excellent." He peeled off another twenty. "Do you think you can tell me where he lives?"

The man looked at the bills in Dax's hands. He swallowed. "I think so."

Dax's smile got wider. "How 'bout a map? Can you draw me a map?"

CHAPTER 34

Vida did a little online research, and found Pascoe in Birmingham, Alabama, working in the public affairs office. "Public Affairs? Pascoe? That's a joke," she said as she read it. "No wonder the military has a bad rap. Okay, let's go get him," she said, looking up from the computer.

"There's no *us*. You can't go," Millie said, shaking her head.

"Why not? I know how to talk to him, I'll—"

"Vida, Vida, easy. You can't get on a plane, remember? You can't show your ID anywhere, and it's too risky to drive. Sorry, kiddo, but this trip is not for you."

The next morning, Pack and Millie drove to the Albany airport. They had a ten-fifteen flight to Birmingham via Charlotte. The red wig stayed at home along with the blue eye shadow; an army base was no place for Millie.

After Vida had gotten over her disappointment at not going with them, she had some parting advice: "The best way to get him to meet you off-post is to tell him you have money for him. Hey, try this, 'General Abizaid says he owes you fifty bucks and when he heard I'd be passing through, he asked me to give it to you.' "

"He won't fall for that," Pack said.

"Trust me. He's dumb and greedy. He will."

"Okay. We'll come up with something."

CHAPTER 35

Dax found the deliveryman's directions easy to follow.

He made it up to Pack's in twenty minutes, and drove slowly by, keeping one eye on the dried ruts in front of him. There was no car in the short driveway and he could see that the door was half-open into the below-ground garage. It was just as the man had described it, though Dax found it hard to believe that anyone would live in such a dump. No one, he amended, other than some welfare mother with six kids by five different fathers. To someone like that, this house might make sense. But not to a man alone. A man alone should have some pride.

All it meant was that he was dealing with a loser, and losers were halfway in the hole. You didn't have so far to push them. He imagined "Pack" in his ugly black suit and white hair, holding onto the edge of a deep abyss, his knuckles bloodless with strain, face a mask of desperation. "Please, please, help me!"

Dax had to smile at his own lively imagination.

He drove past the house until he found a widening in the dirt road and pulled over and parked. He locked his car, frowning at the coating of dust on its smooth, black flanks.

At the house, he rang the bell. He heard nothing, no distant chime, so he had to believe it didn't work. He knocked hard on the door. It would be perfect if Vida opened the door. But no one answered and there was no sound of movement from inside.

He had to wade through waist-high nettles to get to the back of the house, his hands already starting to burn by the time he got to the raised deck. Irritatingly, the steps were rotted and fallen away, forcing him to boost himself up onto the raised platform. As he did so, he caught his right knee on a nail and felt the stab of pain just as he heard his jeans tear.

By the time he was standing on the warped planks of the patio, he was furious. On the blotchy red palm of one hand a thick brown sliver of rotting wood had dug into the flesh. He checked the hole in his pants, but the nail had barely broken his skin. Luckily his tetanus shots were up to date.

"Fucking deadbeat," he said, cursing Pack. He pulled most of the splinter out, though a little speck of black remained embedded in his hand. Then, brushing his hands gently on the seat of his pants, Dax went to the glass door and tried it. He was hoping it'd be locked—he was in the mood to bust some glass. But instead it slid bumpily open.

CHAPTER 36

By lunchtime, Vida was going stir crazy. She had to get out. She walked down the road to the Dairy Queen, the sky overcast with patches of black in the gray clouds. Ordering a cheeseburger, she ate it outside sitting on a picnic table, her feet on the bench. She was the only customer in the windswept area.

Back at Millie's house, she prowled through the rooms, looking in drawers, opening cupboards. In one closet, she found a little A-line wool coat with a moth-eaten fur collar; shirtwaist dresses in dark colors; little felt hats. Opening another, she came across large shiny dresses, oversized sensible pumps, one pair of hefty red sandals. She shut the closet guiltily, ashamed to be prying into her dad's cousin's life.

She went outside again. Pack had left his mud-splattered Town Car in Millie's driveway. She looked inside it for the key, but it wasn't there. She searched the front hall table, hoping he'd left it. She called him on his cell phone.

"Yeah?" he answered.

"Where are you?"

"We're just leaving the airport, heading to the base."

"Where are your car keys?"

"Why?"

"I need to go for a drive. I'm going nuts sitting around here."

"Too bad. You can't drive. If you get pulled over and they check your license, you're screwed. Just watch TV or something. Clean the bathroom."

Vida hung up on him. Douche.

She was rifling through a drawer in the front room when the phone rang. She picked it up. "Yes?"

"Millie says there's a bike in the shed behind the house. Knock yourself out, she says. Oh, and stop looking for the keys, I've got 'em right here."

The small shed was neat and orderly, tools oiled and shelved, clear jars of nails lined up on the wall, extension cords coiled and hanging on hooks. An old black bicycle was upside-down in a corner.

Vida turned the pedals. They whirred around smoothly, the sound rich and well-oiled. She lifted the bike and turned it over, then pushed it out of the shed.

CHAPTER 37

Dax went methodically through the house. He wore his driving gloves, partly for the fingerprints, but mainly because of the filth. How could anyone live like this? Obviously, this guy had never been a soldier, or he'd have learned better habits.

He went through every drawer, every box, every filing cabinet. He found out where Pack worked, he discovered how much he earned, and he copied out his bank details. To his disappointment, he didn't find that wealth of information, a computer. And no sign that Pack owned one and had taken it with him, either. No desk area, no passwords or secret numbers.

But he did find a pad of paper next to the phone, with the names Millie and Mitch on it, circled and underlined. As if the man had been doodling as he spoke to them. Must be friends, maybe a couple Pack was close to.

There was no trace of Vida, so Dax assumed she'd never been there. But he did find old letters from her mother, information about the divorce, a few baby pictures. So he was her father. That made sense.

He wondered if Pack was an alcoholic, though he saw no hard liquor in the house, just a few beers in the fridge. The condition of the house interested him. This guy was definitely on the skids. Reminded him of his dad—broke and a deadbeat. What was his story? What was his weakness? He found an old yearbook from a high school in the Berkshires. But little else, other than a record of Pack freelancing for a local limo company.

Perfect: no commitments, no ties, always on the move. His dad had worked as a deliveryman, when he bothered to work at all. Same kind of guy.

He also managed to find out that Mitch's last name was Jedd, was Pack's cousin, and lived in Goose Creek. Dax wrote down the address. No mention of Millie.

He was about to leave when he saw the tape deck on the dining room table. What did this guy listen to? Probably some tired old heavy metal band. He turned on the machine and held down the play button. No music, just talk. It took him a second to figure out what it was, but when he did, he laughed out loud. The voice belonged to a self-help idiot, droning on about inner battles, etc. So not only was the guy a loser, he was a sorry loser trying to improve himself. A double loser.

He left, feeling like he had the edge. Other than a sore hand and a dirty car, the trip had been worthwhile. The sting of the nettles had worn off and he'd learned a lot.

When he got down to the county road he turned left, toward Goose Creek. Time to check out Mr. Mitch Jedd.

CHAPTER 38

Once she was on the road, Vida pedaled north, toward Bantam. It felt good to be outside. The air was chilly, but it cut through the boredom and anxiety she'd been feeling, and within minutes she began to warm up.

It was about two and a half miles to Bantam, and soon Vida began to wish she'd worn gloves. By the time she drove down the long, tree-lined avenue that led into the village, her body was sweating but her fingers were numb with cold.

In Bantam the road split, the left fork crossing the railroad tracks and becoming a slow, narrow Main Street, the original heart of the town—with department store, movie theater, clock tower, and storefronts. The right fork led north and east into Massachusetts.

Vida bumped across the railroad tracks and rode onto Main Street. She was thirsty. Across the street she saw a sign for Victor's Café so she pedaled over and leaned her bike on the side of the building.

Inside, the café was a single room with counters straight ahead and to the right. The place was empty except for one woman on the customer side, leaning against the counter, back to the door. A small, dark-haired man stood behind the counter. They were obviously talking but when Vida walked in they stopped and both looked at her, the woman staying where she was but twisting her head around.

"What can I get for you?" the man asked. He was wearing an

apron over a t-shirt. Even features, short beard, and watchful eyes. He measured her, then gave her a businesslike smile. She guessed he was the Victor of the sign.

"Hot tea and a glass of water, please."

"One hot tea, coming up. What kind do you like? All the choices are over here. Abby, get out of the way and let the young lady choose."

The woman, attractive in a careless way, pushed herself off the counter. She went to one of the tables, pulled out a chair, and sat down sideways. She put one elbow on the table and stretched her long legs out in front of her. Vida chose her tea and after she'd paid, she took her cup and water and went to a small corner table.

"Abby, you want your dressing on the side?" Victor called out.

"Whatever. Sure." And then, after a short pause: "But you know what really pisses me off? He didn't give me any warning whatsoever. I mean, nothing. Not a day, not even an hour."

Vida wondered if she was talking about a boyfriend.

Victor put a Styrofoam box on the counter and started ringing something up on the cash register. "You'll figure it out. That'll be $7.49, m'dear."

She looked dissatisfied with the response. Standing up, she dug in her pocket, found a crumpled bill, went over to the counter, and laid it on the counter, smoothing it out. Change in hand, she picked up her food. "Never again, I swear. I'll hire a Seeing Eye dog first."

Okay, maybe not a boyfriend.

The man laughed. "Don't bet on it. Wait till the next big weekend rolls around. Any warm body'll do."

"I hope not. What a waste." She turned and walked out the door.

When Vida was done, she took her cup back to the counter.

Victor had disappeared into the kitchen and a young girl with a ring through her nose and her hair dyed a dull black was wiping down the counters.

Outside, Vida pulled down her sleeves to cover her hands for the drive home. Once on the road, she pedaled hard to warm up, which was probably why the return trip seemed faster than the outgoing one. The cars and pick-up trucks that passed her gave her a wide berth. She didn't pay much mind when a black Corvette passed her, going too fast on the isolated curve between Bantam and the Goose Creek cemetery.

Chapter 39

Dax slowed down as he looked for the house numbers along the main stretch of Goose Creek. The village seemed to be nothing more than a gathering of buildings along a road that led somewhere else. He passed the Dairy Queen and nearly missed the house he was looking for. There was no number on it, but there was on the house beyond it. He slowed down to a crawl and peered out the passenger window.

It was Dax's idea of a nightmare. Fussy and old-fashioned, it looked like a doll's house, lacy curtains and all. An old black Town Car was parked in the driveway. No one in sight.

He turned away from it onto a side street. Engine rumbling, he drove into the empty parking lot of a municipal building on the corner and parked, facing the house. He turned off the car and slid down in his seat.

From where he sat, he could see the place perfectly. He looked it over carefully, keeping an eye on both upstairs and downstairs windows. He waited. Something had to happen. It was just a matter of being patient. His right leg jiggled.

He didn't have to wait long. Within five minutes, someone on a black bicycle pulled into the driveway. Dax felt a rush of excitement. The rider dismounted, walking the bike past the Town Car to the backyard. He kept very still, watching, hoping. Even without seeing the person from the front he knew she was female, small, and dark-haired. Had to be Vida.

Luckily for Dax, she didn't go inside through a back door

but returned to the front of the house, ran lightly up the steps, opened the door, and disappeared inside. He got a good look at her. He smiled. It was her.

He reached for the handle and opened the door, excitement propelling him. As he put his foot on the asphalt he stopped himself. Whoa, he couldn't just go charging in there. What if there were other people in the house? No, he had to think this through.

He pulled his leg back in and shut the door.

See? he said to himself, I can show restraint. I can plan.

So, if this was Mitch's house, who was Mitch? What was he to Vida? And what was she doing in Goose Creek? Who was she going to see? And why hadn't she been driving if there was a car sitting in the driveway?

He also had to decide what he wanted to do about her. He could threaten her, warn her that if she talked about anything, he'd come after her. But he dismissed that idea before it was even fully formed in his head. Like Haley, she wasn't the kind of girl who scared easy. Look at her, tracking him to the VA center. Hell, she was a U.S. soldier, he thought with back-handed pride. If and when she remembered him, she'd start screaming bloody murder, no matter how much he threatened her.

If he hadn't accidentally killed the old lady, he could have let it go, hoping that whatever Vida remembered would be viewed as the post-traumatic ravings of a non-combatant caught in her first firefight. But the old lady was dead—he hadn't known his own strength—and because of that, his situation was much more precarious than it should be. He had to make sure that nothing and no one connected him to either Haley or her mother.

It looked like Vida was the only real link.

He watched the gingerbread house, imagining Vida inside,

like an ant in a nest, hidden from view. She felt safe in there, but her safety was up to him. If he wanted to get her, he would. He felt a pulse of excitement. She had no idea who she was up against.

He knew her power would come as soon as she remembered any of the events in Tallil. When she did, he knew she'd start filling in any gaps and exaggerating and guessing at the rest. And then she'd start making those calls to the Army and the police, accusing him. They'd believe her, because they always believed people like her, and they always assumed people like him were liars. And because of her, he'd lose everything.

As he imagined the future according to Vida, he began to feel exactly as he had on the day he'd been fired from the battery company. His temperature rose and he started to boil at the thought of the shame Vida would soon be raining down on him.

Quickly, the hot pulsing in his face turned to rage. If only he had his rifle. He still missed it, like a shadow limb. If he had his weapon right now, he'd wait until dark, rest it on the hood of his car, take aim, and shoot her right between the eyes, through the front window, through the little lace curtains. Bam.

That's what she deserved. This little bitch who was endeavoring to fuck up everything he'd worked for and get him sent to prison for the rest of his life. Just like Haley.

Dax took a deep breath and sat back, forcing his hands to unclench from the steering wheel.

The funny thing was, he was an honorable guy. He wasn't a spy or a traitor. He loved his country. But he also believed that life is what you make of it. It's exactly what his mother said the day she left; after a casual pat on the head, she said, "Life is what you make of it, little man. I gotta go." And she did, abandoning him to his dad's unique parenting skills—mostly neglect, with a dash of brutality to spice things up. Dax was barely eight years old.

But he'd soon learned she was right. You can't just lie down and take whatever gets dished out to you. You have to protect yourself from those who would do you harm, and you have to think to the future.

When he first joined up, he figured that was it, his future was taken care of. And he liked being a soldier just fine. But after a while he thought, this Army talks the talk, but what happens if he got his arms blown off, and he couldn't lift a shovel or work a computer? The fucking military won't look out for him then, hell no. Give him a shitass little VA disability check for a few years, and then cut him loose. No, he had to look out for himself. He had to be practical.

And now, once again, some little bitch that he had thought was out of commission was trying to grab him by the balls and twist. He didn't look for trouble, but it certainly came looking for him, and usually it was female. He loved women, he really did, ask anyone, but they kept trying to beat him down.

No, he had no choice. He couldn't risk her giving up his name. He had to defend himself, like any good soldier. It was the right thing to do.

His lips lifted in a slight smile. He'd have to kill her.

So now, the important decision was how to do it. Not in daylight, that's for sure. At night, what were his choices? Could he make it look like a suicide? Break in there and shoot her in the temple or hang her from a chandelier? Gotta be a chandelier in *that* house. It could work. Patriotic young woman, depressed by her disfigurement in the war, takes her own life. He didn't hate the idea. It felt a little like television, though. And it meant going in the house. He'd be at a disadvantage in a house he didn't know.

Or he could grab her, kill her, and hide the body. It would look as if she'd taken off. And when a mangy old deadbeat dad or family friend or whoever told the police that she had no reason to run away, the cops would assume he was lying. Cops never believe the relatives.

He had to play this one cool, go home, and think about it. If he hung around anymore, someone might remember him. I mean, how many beautiful black Corvettes did these hicks see, right?

An hour later, he pulled into the clean, uncluttered parking area of his apartment building. He was relieved to be back in the city. Albany was poky and one day he'd move back to Los Angeles, or maybe a city like Dallas, big and new and sprawling, but for now he was relieved to be out of the boonies. Everything was always rotting and falling apart in the country. Like Pack's house. Filthy and alone and rotting, decomposing under your very eyes.

Thanks to Pack, when he opened his own door he took special pleasure in the soothing sparseness of the place, the cleanliness.

After making himself a cold drink he stripped down to his briefs and sat at his computer. He logged onto his email and began deleting form letters and advertising, letting his mind wander to the Vida problem. Halfway down the inbox was an email from a fellow soldier, one of these bleeding hearts eager to help every Iraqi brat with a scab on his knee. The subject line was enough to make Dax toss it: Fw: Fw: Fw: OUR MUTUAL FRIEND NEEDS HELP. He knew what it was going to say. Send this on to twelve people and you'll receive the answer to your prayers, or some such crap. He deleted it, hitting the key with force.

And then he wondered. He went into his deleted list, and opened it. Lo and behold—it was, in fact, the answer to his prayers.

He checked the date. It had been sent out twenty-four hours

earlier by an old school friend of Vida's, someone called Marci. It looked like she'd emailed a group of close friends. The circle had obviously widened quickly as the note was forwarded to others. By the morning it had reached the box of someone from the same high school in Alaska, who'd joined up two years before Vida. She had sent it to, among others, an NCO who'd been in Iraq when Haley was killed.

The NCO was the one who sent it on to Dax, maybe because he remembered that he knew Haley. The message itself was short and somewhat cryptic, but to Dax it revealed quite a bit.

hey friends, i'm on the lookout for vida so if she gets in touch with you tell her to write me or call her mom, it's important! but just don't call Big Brother he's already pissed.

A number was included. Dax wondered who Marci meant by Big Brother. Her father? And then, of course, it came to him. Vida wasn't just running from him, she was running from everyone. No one was in touch with her. Which meant, she probably hadn't been discharged or released from duty. If so, Big Brother could very well be the government. The Army.

Now it made sense. Vida was AWOL.

Dax sat still, thinking. It made all the difference knowing what was really going on. Suddenly, the option of making it appear as if she'd disappeared fit like a glove. She was already scared and jumping at shadows. It would make perfect sense for her to take off one night without telling anyone. People would assume she'd made a run for Canada.

It was a sweet idea. No one would know she was dead, so there'd be no investigation, no evidence to worry about, none of that. All he had to do was figure out the how. The rest would fall into place.

CHAPTER 40

That night, Pack and Millie caught the last flight out of Birmingham that connected to Albany. They were both tired, but for the first leg of the trip Pack restlessly stared out the window as Millie slept. In Baltimore, they got hot dogs and waited until their connection was called. They spoke very little and anyone watching them might think they'd just come from, or were on their way to, a funeral.

It was only during the last half hour of their second flight that Pack said: "Do we have to tell her?"

Millie just shot him a look. "What do you think?"

It was one A.M. by the time they pulled into Millie's driveway in Goose Creek. For a moment they just sat, too exhausted to get out of the truck. "You better spend the night here so we can talk to her in the morning," Millie said softly.

Pack shook his head. "Nah, I should head home."

Millie opened the door and started to climb out of the cab. "No way. You're spending the night here."

Defeated, Pack followed her into the house.

The next morning the sun was shining and Vida woke up feeling hopeful, something she hadn't felt in some time. She wasn't sure why she felt that way, but she liked it. She wondered if she could have pancakes for breakfast.

She'd awakened briefly during the night when Pack and Millie arrived home. When they came upstairs, one of them had bumped into a piece of furniture and followed it with a whimpered *Goddamn!*. She heard them creaking heavily as they crossed the landing outside her door; she heard as each of them flushed the toilet, ran water, and finally shut their bedroom doors. Eventually she'd drifted back to sleep.

She pulled on her clothes and went quietly down, socks padding silently on the polished wooden floors.

In the kitchen, she found Pack reading the paper.

"You're up. 'Morning," Vida said.

He looked up. "Hey there. Sleep well?"

"Pretty well. Other than the elephants on the stairs at about one A.M."

If she expected to get a rise out of him, she was disappointed. He just smiled vaguely and nodded.

"Millie sleeping?"

Pack pointed with his chin in the general direction of the street. "Grocery store."

Vida poured herself a mug of coffee. "So. Tell me everything. Did you find Pascoe?" She sat down across from him.

"Yup."

Vida raised her eyebrows in encouragement. "And?"

"It's a long story," Pack said, shifting in his chair, avoiding her gaze. "Let's wait for Millie, she'll explain it better."

"Explain what?"

Pack folded the paper carefully and looked at the door, as if Millie would materialize if he concentrated hard enough. "Stuff, you know. This and that. There was a lot of information, Vida. It's hard to know where to start."

Vida kept her eyes on him as she drank. "Try, Pack. What happened?"

He rubbed a hand hard around the top of his head, as if massaging some anxiety away. He managed to activate his hair to new heights. His expression was beginning to look desperate.

"Look, this Pascoe, I don't know if he's reliable. One of those muscle-headed bullies who'll say anything to make people look bad."

"I know he's an idiot. I worked with him, remember? But what did he say? Come on, Dad, spit it out."

Pack was about to say something, and then he heard what she'd called him, and looked at her, thunderstruck. She'd called him Dad. He had no words.

"Pack? Hello? What did Pascoe say?"

Pulling himself back into the moment, he took a breath before speaking. "I'm sorry, Vida, you're not going to like this. What I have to say." He cast a last desperate look in the general direction of the front door.

"What're you talking about?"

"It's what he claimed. And he's probably full of shit."

"Are you going to tell me what he said?"

"It's just malicious talk."

"Goddamn it. Say it."

He cleared his throat. "He said your friend Haley was hooking. Selling sex to soldiers."

Vida burst out laughing. But when he didn't join in, she looked confused. "You're kidding, right?"

"No. And John Dax, her fiancé? Pascoe claimed he was her pimp."

Vida shook her head. "What do you mean?"

Just then, Millie walked into the kitchen, red wig on her head, a plastic shopping bag hanging from each hand. "Good morning," she said.

Vida looked at her, then back at Pack. "That's disgusting," she said. "I don't believe it."

Millie didn't move. She looked at Pack's unhappy expression and back at Vida. She put the bags down on the counter. "Vida, honey. This is a hard one, but we'll tell you everything Pascoe told us."

Vida stood up and shook her head. "You shouldn't have talked to that scumbag. He's a lying pig and you should've killed him for spewing that kind of shit." She walked out of the kitchen.

They heard her slam the front door and saw her run around the side of the house. A minute later, she pushed the bike out of the shed, climbed on, and wobbled out the driveway. She looked very young and small.

The cousins stood at the window, watching her leave.

CHAPTER 41

Without giving it a second thought, Vida headed back the way she gone the day before, toward Bantam. She pedaled hard, using her feet to shove away the images Pack had thrown at her in the kitchen. She didn't know it, but she was grunting with each thrust of her foot.

She couldn't believe the two of them had gone all the way to Alabama and come back with such a crock of shit strapped to their backs. How the hell could they buy it? The answer was simple—they didn't know Pascoe. They didn't know what a hate-mongering, lying bitch he was. It was totally clear to anyone who knew him for more than five minutes. Vida couldn't believe she'd ever considered him harmless.

As she tore along, she thought back to that episode in the corridor, when Haley'd threatened Pascoe. No wonder he talked trash about her. Haley had his number—hadn't hesitated to put him down and he'd never gotten over it. Still trying to get back at her, even after she was dead.

She pedaled on, oblivious of the cold.

As her heart rate and the distance from the house increased, Vida began to calm down. She was a fair-minded person and, even though she didn't want to, she had to admit that, at the time, she'd wondered just why Haley had gotten so bent out of shape that day. The way she'd gone off on him had seemed out of all proportion.

A thread of doubt began to present itself to her. Was Haley

really just being protective? Or was it something else? What if Pascoe had said something offensive, that Vida missed? Or had they, in fact, had more going on between them than she'd been aware of? The idea made her skin crawl.

She thought of Haley, in tears that night she'd woken Vida up. What had really happened?

She pedaled harder, angry at herself for even considering Pascoe might be telling the truth. Wasn't that what guys said about women they couldn't get into bed? That they were sluts? He was just taking it a couple of steps further.

By the time she reached Bantam, Vida was beginning to feel badly about having stormed out on Pack and Millie. She should have listened to what they had to say and kept an open mind. Didn't mean she had to believe whatever that lying sack of shit in Alabama put forward, but she should have heard them out. They'd gone a long way to talk to him.

Victor's Café was busy. People were waiting in line to order, and all the tables were full. She got a coffee and went back outside. The sun had gone in and it was cold, but she sat at one of the sidewalk tables, hands around the cup, drawing warmth from the hot liquid.

When she was done, she biked down Main Street, delaying the inevitable return to a conversation she didn't want to have. Suddenly, she heard shouting. Looking for the source of the noise, she saw two people, standing facing each other. The guy was going at it, yelling at the woman, pointing at the building behind her, a free-standing three-story brick wrapped in ornate porches. The sign over its front door read: "The InnBetween."

"Yeah, well, and I happen to disagree," he was saying, his head tilted, indignation in every line of his body. "And working like a slave for you sucks, okay?"

Vida recognized the woman from the day before. Abby, Victor had called her. Curious, Vida slowed down to watch.

Abby spoke in a much lower tone. "Boo hoo. Goodbye. Get lost. And don't come back."

The guy strode away from Abby, toward Main Street. Abby turned back to the restaurant. But the man wasn't done. He swiveled and shouted: "Hey!" When Abby looked back, he held up his middle finger.

Abby returned the gesture. Only when he'd lowered his arm did she do the same. She disappeared into the building through a side door, slamming it hard behind her.

CHAPTER 42

It was early afternoon when Vida sat down with Pack and Millie. She was calm and ready to explain to the two men why Pascoe was lying. "Start at the beginning. I swear, I won't jump all over you."

They were sitting around the dining room table. Pack was eating a ham sandwich and Millie was gluing the handle back onto a delicate china tea cup.

"Okay, well," Pack started, "we met him at a diner a mile or so from the base."

"Yeah," Millie said, a laugh in her voice, "we told him we had a present for him, from a *lady.*"

"That must've got him running," Vida said darkly. "Creep."

"Hey, he didn't seem so bad to me. Just a country boy," Millie said.

"That's 'cause you're not a woman," Vida snapped, and then looked confused. "Sorry, I mean—"

"Shh, shh. Anyway, we came clean after he'd been there for a while."

"What'd you say?"

"We told him we're looking for you and we want to know what went down the last days and weeks you were in-country."

"And?"

"He said, not much. He was doing a lot of convoy escorting, his and your paths didn't cross much."

Pack said: "He didn't look alive until we mentioned Haley.

Then he got worried. Scared is my guess."

"Scared? That's great. Maybe he's the one I saw . . . maybe he's the guy."

Millie shook her head. "Nah. What d'you think, Pack?"

"I don't know. He's definitely not an upstanding kind of guy. But I don't know if he's a killer. But then again, he's a soldier, right? Aren't they all supposed to be killers?"

Vida sighed heavily, annoyed. "Yeah, yeah. So what next? What else did you ask him?"

Pack shrugged. "We asked him about John Dax. That's when he got this funny grin, like he had some smart-ass secret."

Vida shuddered. "Yeah, I can see it. What did he say?"

"At first nothing, and then he goes all confidential and excited. *'Can I tell you guys something, you won't report it to my CO?'* We said, hey, us? No way. Then he backtracks a little, hems and haws, and then, pow, he lets it all out."

Vida stiffened, imagining them huddled over the table about to tell and listen to lies about a woman who wasn't there to defend herself. Vida felt a wall of maleness suffocating her, made up of all the boys she'd known in school, the soldiers she'd lived and trained with, all the good guys and the fools, and now her own new-found family. "What exactly did he say?"

To their credit, neither Pack nor Millie was enjoying this. Millie sat back, deferring to her cousin.

Pack said: "He claimed that John Dax first approached him about it one night when they were out together, doing guard duty. Pascoe says he was bitching about the females, that none of them were putting out for him," he continued, glancing apologetically at Vida.

"I wonder why," she said.

Pack kept going. "That's when Dax told him he knew someone very hot, but she was pricey. Pascoe got curious, because he assumed Dax had somehow tapped into a ring of lo-

cal prostitutes, maybe through the support staff or kitchen workers. He'd heard rumors of that. But Dax said, '*no way, my friend,
I'm talking beautiful blonde American GI. But only for guys willing
to spend real money.*' "

"After hearing some more,"—here Millie looked down at the
table and Pack scratched his ear—"he was psyched. When Dax
told him how much, though, he was shocked. But what the hell,
he figured, he was making decent pay and his expenses back
home were low."

"How much did he say Dax wanted?" Vida asked.

"Eight hundred bucks."

"Jesus, I can't believe this. So does Pascoe claim they did it?"

Pack sighed and nodded. "Dax told him to get rid of his
roommate for a couple of hours. He did, and she came over."

Vida sat there, motionless. "Dax forced her, obviously. Maybe
blackmailed her."

"According to Pascoe, she was willing . . . and very able."

Vida made a face of disgust. "He would say that."

Pack and Millie said they'd insisted on going over Pascoe's
story in detail. He seemed very happy to provide them with
intimate descriptions of his meetings with Haley. According to
him, she'd been happy, no, eager to do anything he wanted.
When they asked why he'd stopped seeing her, he had the grace
to look uncomfortable. His wife, he explained sheepishly, was
watching their bank balance and starting to ask questions.
Nonetheless, he planned to see Haley once more before his tour
ended. But she was killed before he had a chance to.

"Jesus, how am I supposed to believe this, Pack?" Vida asked.

He shook his head. "I don't know."

Millie, who'd so far not said much, now spoke up. "Look, I
sat and listened to your friend Pascoe for two hours. He's a
Neanderthal, but I think he's telling the truth. I think she did it,
and it sounds as if she did it willingly. Could've been for a

number of reasons. I mean, people have secret needs that drive them, you know? Maybe she enjoyed it in some way. There's power in sex. You've got to at least consider that possibility, Vida."

"Maybe she needed the money." Vida rubbed her forehead.

"Exactly."

"Were there other women involved?" Vida said, steeling herself.

Millie shook her head. "Maybe a few more. He didn't know."

"Did he ever talk about the money with Haley? It could be that she didn't know Dax was pimping her out."

Pack shook his head. "Nah. The second and third times, he paid her directly. Before they got down to business."

That evening, nobody felt like cooking. They ordered pizza and sat where they'd been all afternoon, around the formal dining table, eating off paper plates and drinking beer from cans. Vida waited until she'd finished eating, while Pack and Millie were still chewing, to announce, "I've got a job."

Pack said a muffled: "What?" and Millie, her cheeks bulging, grunted in surprise.

She leaned back in her chair and stretched her arms over her head. "You don't have to worry, it's safe."

Swallowing dryly, Pack said: "What d'you mean, it's safe?"

"She needed a waitress, but I said I didn't like working with the public, I couldn't work with the public—I pointed at my scar—so she's letting me do dishes."

"Letting you do dishes? Who's she?" Millie said, wiping her hands on the small paper napkin till it became nothing but a ball.

"Abby, the woman who runs the InnBetween."

"In Bantam? Vida, there's too many people in and out of that place. That's a bad idea," Millie said, leaning forward.

Pack: "Shit, Vida, you can't work in a restaurant."

"Why not? They seem like okay people."

Millie: "Because you can't. Too much exposure."

Pack: "Anyway, you already have a job. Remember, Uncle Sam?"

Millie: "He's right. And what about getting paid?"

"All taken care of. I told her it'd have to be off the books."

Pack: "Great. Now she knows for sure something fishy's going on."

Millie: "What'd she say?"

" 'Fine. No problem. Happens all the time.' "

Pack: "But—"

"You guys, I can't sit here hour after hour, waiting around. I need to do something."

"But—" Pack said.

Millie put a restraining hand on Pack's arm. "Okay. We'll shut up, and you can tell us about it."

Vida let the silence settle before starting. "Nothing much to tell. I knew she'd just fired a guy, so I went in and offered my services."

Pack's eyes narrowed. "Did she make you fill out applications and give your social security number, stuff like that?"

Vida shrugged. "Yeah, but it was one page and I made up a social. She's never going to check it."

Pack sighed, the sound full of dismay, as if this were the beginning of the end.

Vida leaned forward. "It's okay. I'll be extremely careful, Pack."

"Yeah. Well, we'll see. Your mother's going to kill me."

"Good thing she's in Alaska, then, right?"

Millie put a finger under her wig and scratched her head. "When do you start?"

Vida looked at her watch. "In about twenty minutes. Anyone feel like giving me a ride? Or better yet, lending me a car?"

CHAPTER 43

Dax chose to be a medic because he figured it'd be less dangerous than infantry, and he could use it as leverage to get into medical school when he got out. The fact that med school required a college degree and transcripts was of little concern to him. He considered himself a problem solver, able to cross any bridge when he came to it. He could already see the vanity plates on his Corvette: DOCDAX.

Once he was overseas, he looked around for a way to use the system to produce a little extra for himself. It went back to the revelation he'd had after he was betrayed by Carol, the wife at the online battery company. He'd discovered during that time that not only was he unburdened by guilt or a strong code of ethics, but he enjoyed looking for an angle. Puzzle solving, without the restraints imposed by everyday dos and don'ts.

It didn't take him long at the base to start getting ideas. One in particular struck him as solid, and soon he had a working plan.

It all came together with Trisha, an average-looking, curly-haired girl from Washington State. She didn't seem to have many female friends, but word was she'd have sex with any soldier who'd give her the time of day. Sounded perfect.

The first time he saw Trisha without anyone else nearby, she was walking across the flat sandy expanse near vehicle parking. The midday sun in a pale, burnt-out blue sky was cooking the world, while the distant horizon line danced and shifted in the haze. He called out to her; she stopped and waited for him to catch up. She was covered in a sheen of sweat. He asked her if he could walk with her, and she nodded, smiling a little, as if she knew what he was after.

It took two days to accomplish what he set out to do. The first phase took place in his room while his roommate was out. When it was over he did up his fly and pulled her onto the bed next to him.

"You're a beautiful woman," he said, stroking her hair, his voice sad.

She responded immediately to the warmth in his voice. "No I'm not," she said, begging for more.

"Yes, you are. And you're an amazing lover, too. You have a real gift. But you know that, don't you?"

She looked away.

He turned her face gently back to him and looked in her eyes. "You don't believe me, but it's true. It's your generosity that makes you so special. But you know that. In your heart, you know that."

"Really?"

"Come on—" for a moment he forgot her name "—Trisha. A woman like you, with your sexuality, I mean, you're like an electric current, any man who sees you is on fire for you. But you know that, right?"

"Oh, stop."

"But I think what you're doing is a crime."

"What're you talking about?" She tried to twist away from him, suddenly leery of him.

He kept hold of her, rolled her onto her back, and kissed her. "You were made for sex," he whispered. "But you know what you're doing wrong?"

She shook her head.

"You're letting yourself be *used* by the guys here. These idiots you go with? They're taking advantage of you."

"You're wrong. No way. Nobody makes me do anything I don't want to do," she said, and as if to prove it, she tried to push him off.

But Dax didn't move until she stopped struggling, and then he rolled off her and pulled her to her feet. He straightened her shirt, smoothed her hair, and took her hands. "I know that's what you think, baby. But you're giving away something that is very special and in great demand. You could be doing exactly what you're doing, and getting paid a lot of money for it."

She stepped back, shocked. He was still holding her hands, so it looked like they were about to dance. "What're you saying?"

He pulled her back close to him. "Everyone says you're a slut." She flinched, as if he'd hit her. He spoke softly, soothingly. "You and I know that's not true, but that's the word. You can't tell me you don't know that. So all I'm saying is, you should quit being a slut and become a professional. Get paid for what you do best, what you're giving away. Make a nest egg for yourself. Get your self-esteem back."

"Who says I have no self-esteem?" Her tone was belligerent, but her eyes filled with tears.

He stroked her cheek. "I say. And it's wrong. So just think about it. If you're interested, come and find me. I'd take care of all the arrangements, and for that, I'd take a small percentage. All you'd have to do is keep doing what you're doing, enjoy it, and deposit the cash."

The way Dax looked at it was this: wherever there was an army, there were whores. Fact of life. Look at Nam. His Dad was a vet, he'd told him about the bar girls. If it weren't for the U.S. Army, they'd have been picking rice in a paddy somewhere, covered in leeches. Instead, they made money, wore nice clothes, partied with Americans. They loved being whores.

But Iraq was different. No one was allowed out off base. Yeah, there was some smuggling of prostitutes onto camps, women and girls pretending to be kitchen workers. Some from the Philippines, Bangladesh, other parts of the Middle East. Hell, Dax had a theory they came into the country as a family and split off at the border: men to join the insurgency, women to sell themselves. He liked to say, *this way we get fucked by them all, no matter what.*

But, seriously, he was an American; he wasn't interested in Syrian pussy. So why smuggle something in, when you had what you needed right in your own backyard?

That was his master plan. Work up a stable of good, healthy American girls looking to make some extra cash, and healthy American boys looking to let off a little steam. No one else need apply.

Within a few days, Trisha came to see him. Her biggest obstacle was her belief, her illusion, that she was a nice girl. She didn't want to lose that. Dax reassured her that nothing she did in Iraq had to follow her home; that she'd always be the sweet girl her grandma made cookies for. But now she'd be a sweet girl with a fat bank account.

Haley was his second recruit. And first mistake. He should never have taken her on.

They knew each other to say hi to, but she was aloof and spent most of her free time with her roommate, Vida. Since she was extremely hot, many of the guys came on to her, but she showed no interest in any of them. The natural conclusion was that she was a dyke. Had to be.

Then, one day, she sat next to him at chow and told him she'd been talking to Trisha. He waited for some feminist rant, brimming with anger and disgust. But all she did was ask in a businesslike tone, "She making good money?"

He nodded, not wanting to commit himself. Not only was he taken aback but for all he knew, she was setting him up somehow. But then she said, "I'd like to get in on that."

He looked at her. She was tall but delicate. Blonde. Very different from Trisha. He was tempted to agree because she was sexy, but she had a tension about her that made him uncomfortable. She wouldn't be as easy to handle as Trisha, and he didn't want any divas. "No openings right now. Sorry."

"I need the cash." She looked at him, assessing him. "I'll get you to change your mind, and you won't regret it."

She was right. Whenever she was around him, she'd make a point of flirting—touching guys, smiling at them. He could see how fired up they'd get. Eventually, he lost sight of why he'd said no to her in the first place. He set up the first date.

The night in question, she came to see him before she went to the guy's room. She was wired, like she was on speed, her eyes bright and her movements jerky. He expected her to be nervous, but not like this. He asked her if she wanted out but she said, no, she wanted to do it, she couldn't wait. So he walked her over and nodded goodbye at the door. That was it.

The next day, the guy approached him and said she was crazy. Dax cursed himself for being played. He shook his head, thinking he was going to have to apologize and give the fool some of his money back, when the soldier asked how soon he could get with her again.

Later, when he asked Haley what the hell she'd done to the guy, she raised her eyebrows suggestively. "Just a little something my daddy taught me." She was kidding, he was sure, but it was still a nasty thing to say. He didn't allow his curiosity to show again.

She seemed to love doing it. What she actually said was: "I love doing them." She was funny. She'd occasionally volunteer details—what they liked or disliked, if they had any hidden birthmarks or surprising piercings or tattoos. He kept all the information in his head, just in case he needed it.

After each date, she asked about the next one. Sometimes when he saw her at chow he went over and sat at her table. He expected their relationship to be different, but she still treated him as an acquaintance. He knew that sooner or later they'd have sex, but every time the opportunity arose, Haley had something else to do.

And then, one night, it started to get ugly.

Haley had been away for a few days with her unit in Baghdad. He knew she was due back that evening, but he hadn't seen her. He was dirty and tired from a long day out. Just as he was opening his door, his other girl, Trisha, showed up. She had come by to show him her picture in *Stars and Stripes*. They'd done a story on deployed women and she was mentioned in it. She was proud of it and running around showing anyone who would bother looking.

She was all bouncy and excited, and he planned to get her to go down on him, to celebrate, when Haley walked around the corner. She paused when she first saw Trisha, and then she kept coming. Her timing was irritating. He didn't want her to screw up the moment for him.

"Haley, how're you doing, babe?" he said.

"Look at this," Trisha said, shaking her magazine. She held it up for Haley to see. "Look, I'm in fuckin' *Stars and Stripes*. Pretty cool, huh?"

"Don't swear when you talk about our flag." Haley looked at her like she was dirt.

"But I didn't—"

Ignoring her, Haley said to Dax: "I need to talk to you. Alone."

Her tone turned the gas on a pilot light that was always lit in his brain. He felt a pop of anger followed by a rush of heat to his face. How dare she talk to him like that, the whore? "Get lost. Trisha and I are busy." He smiled at the girl with the magazine. "Right?"

Trisha, her brown curls bobbing as she glanced from him to Haley, hesitated. "Um, yeah, I guess," she said.

Haley's nostrils flared slightly, but she didn't say a word. She turned on her heels and walked away. Dax felt a vicious satisfaction.

For the next few days, Haley was again out on an assignment. When she got back, they didn't run in to each other. Dax figured she was avoiding him. He had a date for her so he went to her room.

She opened the door when he knocked. "Yes?" She looked at him as if she'd never seen him before.

"I've got you a visit. Can you handle it?"

Her smile had a mean edge to it. "What d'you think?"

He gave her the soldier's room number, and the time.

"This is it. The last one, okay? After this I'm done," she said. Without waiting for a response she shut the door on him and he heard the lock turn. Bitch! He wanted to kick the door in, kick her face in, stomp on her. But he didn't. He remembered the battery company and Carol, with her false accusations of rape.

That night, when Haley came out of the soldier's room he was waiting for her.

"You come for your money?" she asked, voice flat, eyes hard.

"I've come to make peace," he said. He held up two airplane-sized bottles of Jack Daniel's. "Friends? I got more where these came from."

She looked at the liquor then at him, taking her time, as if she couldn't quite decide. Bitch, he thought again, but he kept a grin on his face.

Finally, she shrugged. "Sure. Friends. Anyway, I need

something strong to wash the cum out of my mouth."

Tacky, he thought. "Come on, baby. Let's go somewhere we can talk. I have something to give you."

They walked outside.

"Where're we going?"

"Someplace we won't get busted," he said. He led the way to a deserted building, pockmarked with shell holes, that had once housed Saddam Hussein's troops. Their feet crunched on the gravel and dirt.

It was dark in the building. Moonlight cut through the windows. He handed her one of the bottles and without talking, they both drank. When they were done, he put his bottle in a pocket and reached for her hand. He kissed the palm.

To his surprise, she pulled her hand away. Okay, not yet. He could play along with that. He looked her in the eyes. "Listen, Haley. You know Trisha needs a lot more handling than you do."

"You're kidding, right? She's a fat little idiot. Should be easy for you to push around."

Dax laughed. "Come on now." Now he knew where he stood. She sounded jealous.

He got two more little bottles out of his pocket and gave one to her. When they finished their second bottles, Dax moved in on her, putting his hands on the sides of her head and pulling her toward him, pressing his lips onto hers. He felt her respond, and he slid his tongue into her mouth.

Suddenly, she put her hands up between his and knocked them apart, away from her. "Get off, Dax. I'm not interested—" she said, making a disgusted face.

"You're kidding," he said. It was all he could come up with at short notice.

"No, I'm not kidding. You want it, you pay for it like everyone else." And she started to turn away.

He felt a rush of blood to his face and a pulse thudded in his neck. How dare she? The stupid whore. He grabbed her and spun her back.

Haley swung her arm at him. Dax slapped her hard and she stumbled, off-balance, and went down on one knee. He hit her again and shoved her over onto the ground. Before she could recover, he started ripping at her uniform, the Velcro closings on the ACUs the only sound over both their panting. She bucked furiously and tried to push him off her, all her energy going into the fight, but he had the advantage. With one hand he held her by her hair, and with the other he hit her until she stopped fighting him.

When he was done, he rolled off her. Then he went through her pockets and took all her cash.

Slowly, she stood up, pulling her clothes around her.

He watched her.

When she was dressed she went to the entrance. She looked at him. "I'm going to see that you go down for this, that you are crucified for this, that everyone in the world knows what you've done."

Dax watched her warily. "You better not."

"I'll kill you!" She moved quickly back from the door and launched herself at him, hitting and punching.

Dax had just enough time to put his hands up to protect his face.

When he finally got back to his room, he locked his door before going to bed.

He woke up some time later and started to worry. Haley wasn't Trisha, easy to manipulate. He'd made a mistake jumping her, even though it felt right at the time. She could very well file a complaint with her CO, and then he'd be screwed. And even if the charges didn't stick, it'd be a problem. He thought of the way he'd beat on her. Shit, he shouldn't have done that. It was short-sighted.

At last he got out of bed, went to her room, and knocked softly. After a few minutes, she came to the door. She looked so bruised and vulnerable he had a moment of genuine affection for her.

He reached out and touched her swollen cheek. "I'm so sorry, baby, I don't know what got into me."

She just stared at him, saying nothing. He could see her breasts rise and fall with each breath.

"I shouldn't have drunk that booze, it was a shitty day and it hit me hard. I took it out on you, and I'm so sorry. I really love you."

She stepped out of the room and shut the door. She took his face in her hands and brought it to hers, kissed him, and took his lower lip in her teeth. She bit down just a little, then harder. He flinched, tasting the blood. She released him.

She said: "Just so you know, I'm going to take pictures of the bruises and write a detailed description of what happened here, okay? If you do anything like that again, I'll report you, swear to god. I'll make your life hell. Oh, and I want you to dump Trisha, okay? From now on, it's just you and me."

After that, he had no a choice. When her Humvee hit the IED, and he was first on the scene, he knew what he had to do. But there was a loose end: her account of the rape. He'd looked for it amongst her stuff, but hadn't found anything. So it had to be in the journal that Vida mentioned.

Oh, and Vida. Vida was the other loose end.

CHAPTER 44

Dax couldn't have asked for a better night.

It was overcast and there was a northerly wind gusting hard enough to rattle street signs and send fingers of cold damp air shooting up and around people's collars and sleeves. No one was going to linger outside on a night like this, they'd head for warmth, however and wherever they found it. Which was one of the things Dax was counting on.

He had been watching the Goose Creek household for a couple of nights. Not an easy thing in a small town. The first night back he pulled in where he had parked before, across the road. This time he was driving Carla's little blue-green Hyundai, a cheap piece of crap but perfect for what he was doing. Nobody looked twice at a car like that, and even if they did, they'd never remember it.

At about five-thirty Vida came out of the house, followed by Pack, the guy with white hair. He got behind the wheel of the Town Car and she hopped in the passenger side. They took a right out of the driveway.

Dax waited till he saw them accelerate out of town before following them. It was dusk so their headlights were on, which made them easier to track.

They drove north toward Bantam and stopped at the single traffic light on the edge of town. He was three cars behind them and couldn't see if they had a turn signal on, but he wasn't worried. They were comfortably within his sights and he felt calm and in control. They wouldn't get away from him.

In the village, they took the left fork and crossed the railroad tracks onto Main Street. The two cars between them veered off to the right, so Dax had no buffer and was forced to slow down.

At the end of Main Street, they drove around the circle. Dax was so far back he nearly missed it when they turned off the roundabout onto a side street. They came to a stop and Vida got quickly out, slamming the door behind her.

Dax was just in time to see her open a door into the building they were parked next to, and go inside. The Town Car pulled away and continued on down the side street.

Dax didn't care about Pack at this point. Good riddance, in fact. He just wanted to know what Vida was up to. He found a parking place and walked back to the small bakery on the corner. He paused at the entrance. From where he stood, he could see Vida's building. It had porches on each floor, and a sign over the front entrance that read *The InnBetween*. A string of white lights had been draped over the sign and, as he watched, they pulsed rhythmically. He pulled open the door to the bakery.

The place was empty of customers except for a single woman sitting alone. She was wearing a bright red sweatshirt. Dax went to the counter and ordered coffee and a sandwich to go. While she was making it, he said to the young waitress, "Maybe you can help me. I need to take my mother-in-law out for dinner, and I just noticed the place across the street. How is it? Appropriate for an older lady?"

"I think so." She handed him his coffee and gestured to the lone customer. "But you're in luck. She used to work there. Hey Reena, tell the man about the InnBetween!"

The woman had frizzy black hair and smudged makeup. The sweatshirt read: *Masseuses d*—but the rest was hidden by the tabletop. She was holding a large cup of something between two hands, and as she drank she sucked it in noisily. The sound set Dax's teeth on edge—he wanted to tell her to shut the fuck up. Instead, he moved politely closer to her so he wouldn't need to shout. "How's the food over there?"

"Eh." She shrugged.

"Who's the chef?"

"George. He knows what he's doing, more or less."

"George? Is he there every night?"

"He was when I worked there. Which wasn't long." She sounded as if she had an axe to grind, but he had no interest in getting her started.

"So, if I wanted to check it out, I just go in there, through that side door?"

She looked at him as if he was simple-minded. "No, that's the staff entrance! Go in the front. Under the sign. Can't you see the sign?"

He felt a slow burn in his cheeks and turned away. Cow.

When his sandwich was ready he paid for it and went back to his car. He moved the Hyundai to a small parking lot on Main Street, property of the bank. The lot backed onto the side street that Pack had used, so Dax had a close view of the restaurant's side door.

His only problem arose when he had to urinate. It was eight-thirty, the restaurant was fairly busy, though the rest of Main Street was quiet. He guessed he had plenty more time to wait. When he was sure no one was around to see him he stood behind a large SUV, in the darkest corner of the parking lot, and pissed long and hard on a small bed of weeds.

Then he sat in his car and catnapped. By ten-thirty, when Pack pulled up just forty feet away from him, he was awake and watchful. A few minutes later, Vida emerged from the side door and got into the passenger seat. Dax watched them drive away.

Satisfied, he headed back to Albany.

The following night, he was in place in the bank parking lot by a few minutes before ten. Pack appeared again at ten-thirty, but the girl didn't come out as quickly. She must've been held up doing something, but Pack sat waiting patiently. It was almost eleven before she came out of the restaurant.

Good. Vida's erratic schedule was going to work well for Dax.

The next day, Dax rented a Town Car. It wasn't easy to find a similar older model, but he got lucky with a limo rental company. That afternoon he drove it on the back roads near Pack's house. By the time he was done, the lower half was covered in a thin crust of dirt and the wheel wells and fenders were caked with dried mud. No question, it looked like the dad's shabby car.

Dax had made a paper license plate, a rough copy of Pack's original. It didn't have to last or look genuine, it just had to satisfy someone who might glance at it on the darkened street.

He arrived in Bantam at the InnBetween at ten-fifteen and parked about thirty feet from the restaurant, on the same side. He taped the paper license plate over the real one and stepped back to take it in. Not bad. Luckily, by ten P.M. most of the nearby house lights were turned off, and the closest street light was back by the restaurant. He checked his watch. Eight more minutes and his plan should get underway.

Forty minutes earlier, he had called Pack's cell phone and when Vida's father answered, Dax said: "Hi. You Pack? This is George, the cook at the InnBetween."

"Oh, right," Pack answered. "Everything okay?"

"Everything's fine, but Vida asked me to tell you to pick her up at eleven-thirty instead of ten-thirty. We have a really big party in tonight, and we need her for an extra hour."

"Oh. Yeah, okay. No problem. Mind if I have a word with her?"

Dax was expecting that. "No, sorry, man, she's crazy busy right now. I'll have her call you if she can break away, but no promises. Hey, I gotta get back to work—don't forget, eleven-thirty, okay?"

"Eleven-thirty, got it. Thanks."

"Sure."

Dax breathed out. That seemed to have gone pretty well. He didn't know what Vida did at the restaurant, so he'd been forced to keep it general. But Pack seemed to have gone for it.

So here it was, the moment he'd been waiting for. He was nervous about the two things he had with him. He'd have preferred just one, but his plan entailed them both. It was the best he could come up with. He should've practiced on someone. He should've practiced on Carla, he thought, with a jolt of sexual arousal.

The wind gusted, sending a shiver down his back. He double-checked the doors on the car, to make they sure they were unlocked. The girl had to be able to get in quickly out of the cold, without giving it a second thought. One possibility bothered him. If Pack had phoned Vida and spoken to her, Dax was screwed. But so far so good, no sign of Pack.

Leaving the engine running, he got out of the car.

He crossed the street and moved into the shadowed area of the bank parking lot and waited.

CHAPTER 45

Vida looked at her watch. Ten-fifteen. Nearly time to call it a day. Her hands were sweating in the thick rubber gloves, and her front was soaked through, apron and all. She was tired, no question, but she kind of liked working in a restaurant. Or at least, this restaurant. The only other one had been a diner in Talkeetna, summer of her junior year of high school. She'd done it to help pay for a class trip to Hawaii but it hadn't mattered anyway—she'd come down with the flu and missed the whole thing.

Just then Bailey, the head dishwasher, came up the backstairs carrying the mop and bucket. He was huge, about six foot six, head as big as a drum and mean little bullet eyes. He didn't say much, but she had a feeling that was a good thing—she wouldn't want to know what he was thinking. He was a brutal farter, too. She worked next to him occasionally and the last time he let one loose, he did it with a smirk on his face. Lucky for her, most of the time he was in the kitchen doing pots, and she was in the prep kitchen running the machine.

"Vida," said Abby from the doorway, "finish up what you're doing and get out of here. Dining room's closed and we're all set up for tomorrow. You're done. Go."

" 'Kay." Vida put the last plate in the commercial washer, pulled down the handle to close the case, and pressed the start button. She could feel and hear the force of the water as it crashed against the walls of the machine.

"Anything else, Bailey?" she yelled over the noise.

He looked at her and, for a second, she thought he was going to say something obscene—he had that look in his eye—but he just shook his head. "Nah. You're good. See ya tomorrow."

Vida threw her apron in the dirty laundry, and hung up her gloves. She stuck her head into the dining room. Abby was sitting at one of the tables, a stack of checks in front of her, writing in a ledger.

"Bye, Abby."

Abby looked up. "Hey. Thanks, Vida. Tomorrow?"

"Yup."

"Great." She went back to what she was doing.

Vida was just about to let herself out the side door when the bartender, Henry, came out of the kitchen. "Wait. I was looking for you. Don't leave yet. Let me buy you a drink."

Vida was tempted. Henry was cute, with a thick, dark ponytail and a sexy smile. And he didn't seem to notice her scar. It made her hope for the day when she could stop looking over her shoulder. But it wasn't going to work. "I can't. My father's waiting."

"Maybe he isn't here yet."

Vida pulled open the side door and looked out. At first she didn't see Pack's car, but then she spotted it further up the street. She wondered briefly why he'd parked that far away. "No, he's here."

Henry looked disappointed. "Maybe tomorrow."

"Yeah. Maybe tomorrow night I'll ask him to come a little later." She was pleased Henry hadn't given up too easily.

She stepped outside and the cold was a relief after the thick, humid air of the kitchen, with its smells of food and grease and cleaning chemicals. She took a deep breath.

But her relief didn't last longer than a few steps. The cold wind quickly chilled the warm moisture of her t-shirt and jeans, and she shivered. She ran down the sidewalk to Pack's car. She could hear the engine rumbling, and hoped he had the heat up high.

As she approached, she saw her father wasn't in the driver's seat, which surprised her. She scrambled inside, slammed the door, and tossed her backpack onto the rear seat. She noticed that the car smelled different. Maybe he'd had it cleaned, though she didn't like the new smell—it was cloying, like cheap air freshener. She looked for the overhead light. But when she tried the switch, it didn't work.

Just then the driver's door opened. All she could see of Pack was his black pants. He threw a magazine in her lap. She looked down at it. It was a big fat fashion magazine, and it felt like he'd just dropped a brick on her thighs. She looked at the cover, puzzled. Weird, to give her this. But pretty sweet, at the same time. He probably figured it's what girls like.

Pack lowered himself into the driver's seat, rear first, his body turned away from her. The door shut with a heavy clunk.

"This a hint? Tired of the way I dress?" she asked, hands on the magazine, eyes on the cover.

He turned toward her, head down, and before she could take in what was happening, she felt a grip on her arm, followed by a quick pinch.

"Hey," she said, annoyed, pulling her arm away, glancing at him.

But it wasn't Pack.

In that first split second she thought two things: first, that John Dax's pupils looked yellow, like a dog's; and second, that she had to get away from him.

She lunged for the door handle. At the same moment, he smacked her hard on the temple. Dazed, she heard a tearing sound, and before she could react he pushed her head back hard and wrapped something around her neck, smoothing it down, tying her to the headrest. She tried to get free by throwing herself forward. The band around her neck tightened, strangling her. Her head was still foggy, but she tried to get a grip on the tape, to get it off her. She couldn't find where it began or ended. More tearing, and before she could do anything, he pressed a length of tape onto her mouth. She punched wildly at him, but he grabbed her arms and held them down. She bucked, trying to throw him off her. She twisted and doubled her body up, trying to kick at him, her head always anchored to the neck rest, but he kept within the radius of her feet, his arms wrapped around hers.

Finally, she stopped, exhausted, panting, barely able to breathe. She had to get out of the car before he drove away with her. When she felt his grip relax, she broke free from his hold and began clawing at him and swinging in the direction of his face.

"What the fuck—" he said, surprised.

She tried to punch at him, but her movements now were getting slower and more labored.

He leaned back onto his seat, watching her, not even swatting her away. He laughed. " 'Nighty 'night, baby."

She remembered that laugh, but his name was disappearing from her mind; it was on the tip of her tongue, and then it was gone. Maybe it didn't matter. It occurred to her, briefly, that she was drugged. Not good. She tried to look at him in the half-light from the street, but her eyelids lowered, then closed.

She drifted away.

Chapter 46

Forty minutes later, at eleven-twenty-five, Pack pulled up in front of the restaurant. He was an early riser and Vida's restaurant hours didn't suit him. He was tired, and after he turned off the engine he put his head back and shut his eyes. He dozed off.

He awoke, cold. The car clock said it was a quarter to twelve. Where the hell was she? The temperature in the vehicle had dropped quickly, so he turned the key to warm it up again. It didn't engage right away, just whined and strained. He turned it off and tried a second time. It started.

Why the frig make a plan for eleven-thirty if you're not going to stick to it, he thought grumpily. Ten more minutes, then he'd go in and drag her out by her hair.

Just then the side door to the restaurant opened. "Finally!" he said out loud.

But it wasn't her. It was a young woman, but this one was taller than Vida, and older, probably in her early thirties. She bundled her coat around her body and crossed the street behind his car, heading toward Main Street.

Quickly, before she could get away, Pack opened the door. "Hey, miss!" he called out.

The street was empty and quiet. She turned her head. "Me?"

"Yeah," he answered. "How much longer is Vida going to be in there?"

"Vida?"

What was she, deaf? "Vida, yeah. I was told to be here at eleven-thirty."

"She's gone. Left at the end of her shift. About an hour ago."

"No, she didn't, I'm her ride and some guy told me to pick her up now. Well, not now, eleven-thirty."

The woman shrugged. "I saw her leave a few minutes before ten-thirty. She said goodbye and took off."

"How's that possible? George called me and told me to get her now."

The woman shook her head. "George? Our George? Why would he say that?"

"How should I know! Because there was a big group tonight and you were really busy and needed her to stay late."

"Not true. We were pretty quiet tonight. You must've misunderstood."

"I didn't—"

"Anyway, George is the chef. He wouldn't call for the dishwasher. Doesn't make sense."

"I want to look inside."

"There's no one there. Just Bailey."

"Who's Bailey?"

"The main dishwasher."

"Then I need to talk to him, don't I?"

She sighed. "Okay, sure."

She pulled open the side door.

"How come this doesn't lock?"

She pointed at the brick that was blocking the door from closing. "So we can come and go."

"That's dumb," Pack said, fear twisting his throat.

Inside, the bright fluorescent strips made Pack squint after the dark night. They found Bailey mopping the kitchen floor. Guns N' Roses was playing, loud, on the tape deck. "Bailey!" the woman shouted.

The big man paused and looked up. "Wha'?"

She pointed at the source of the music and made a slicing gesture across her throat.

He leaned the mop against the stove and did what she asked. He moved slowly and Pack wondered if he was handicapped or doing it deliberately.

When silence finally descended on the room, Pack could hear water dripping from one of the faucets, and the pilot lights hissing on the stove top. The smell of disinfectant was overpowering.

"What's up? Miss me already?"

She ignored his gibe. "Did Vida leave at the end of her shift?"

"How the fuck should I know?"

Abby tightened her eyes. Pack saw her jaw slide outward. "Bailey," she said, her tone a warning, "I'm not kidding."

The man raised a hand, as if in surrender.

"Did she leave right away?"

"Looked like it, but I only saw her leavin' the kitchen, I didn't see her walk out the door. I don't make it my business to keep track of all your kiddies."

Pack wanted to take out a gun and shoot the guy through the heart. He stepped forward. "If she's in trouble and you know something, I'll come back and cut your nuts off. I swear to that."

Bailey stared at Pack, measuring him, enjoying the break. "Oh, yeah?"

Abby turned on Pack. "Hey, you, back off. Bailey, this is serious. We don't know where she is."

Bailey looked away from Pack, losing interest. He held his finger over the tape deck. "I'm telling you, I don't know nothin' about the girl. But you should ask lover boy from the bar. He was sniffin' around her. Maybe they took off together."

He pushed down the on button. Heavy metal took over again,

making speech impossible. Bailey moved back to his mop and Abby herded Pack out of the kitchen.

In the dining room, she picked up the phone, dialed and waited. "Henry, it's Abby, call me back on my cell. I need to know where Vida is. It's important."

Pack started to say something, but she held up a finger. She dialed another number. This time, she got a live answer. "George?"

Pack could hear a murmur on the other end of the line.

"Sorry, sorry, I know, but I have a question. Vida's dad's here—" A pause, then: "Vida, the new kid on dishes, the one who replaced Dimwit. Right. Did you call him today—no, Vida's father—and tell him to pick her up an hour later? Yeah, yeah. I know. Wait, you talk to him."

She handed Pack the phone.

One minute later, he'd hung up. He shook his head. "Nope, not him." His expression grew blacker.

Abby looked at him. "Hey, I'm sorry. I bet Henry talked her into going to a bar with him. He knows all the after-hours places."

Pack shook his head. "I don't think so. I'm not saying she wouldn't do it, but she'd call me first. No, something's wrong. I got to go."

She nodded. "Give me your phone number. When I hear from Henry I'll call you, okay?"

"Yeah, thanks. Okay. Christ."

Pack sat in his car, engine running, brain a blank. Where did she go? What happened to her? He dialed Millie's number.

His cousin answered after four rings, her deep voice groggy with sleep. "Yeah?"

"Mitch, she's gone."

"Wha' d'ya mean? Wha' d'ya talking about?"

"Vida. I came to pick her up and she's gone. She left an hour ago."

"Hold on." He heard rustling and grunting. Millie sitting up and shaking herself awake. She came back on the line. "I thought some guy from the restaurant called you, told you to come in later?"

"Turns out it was a scam. The cook had nothing to do with it."

"Christ. Where d'you think she went?"

"No idea. Maybe Canada?"

"She'd have told us."

"That's what I say."

"The guy who called you, what'd he sound like?"

Pack shrugged, frustrated. "I don't know, like some guy. He told me his name, George."

"Is that the cook's name?"

"Yeah."

"Pretty easy to find that out."

"Right."

"Anything open around there, anyone see anything?"

"It's midnight in Bantam, Mitch. It's a morgue."

"Long shot. So come on back. I'll put on the coffee and we'll figure this out."

When Pack walked into the little house, he could hear Millie banging around in the kitchen. He followed the sound and found her taking something out of a cupboard.

"What're you up to?"

"I'm making sandwiches, in case we have to drive to Canada."

Pack pulled out a kitchen chair and sat down heavily. "Why would she just take off like that?"

Millie stopped what she was doing and turned, pointing a peanut butter-smeared knife at him. "I've been thinking."

Pack looked at her, his eyes tired and defeated.

Millie kept going. "You were right the first time. She wouldn't take off like that. We shouldn't even consider it."

"Then why'd she go?"

Millie shook her head impatiently. "Come on, don't be a dumbass. There are two possibilities here. Either she went of her own free will, which is extremely unlikely because she'd have told us, or somebody took her."

"Jesus, Mitch, what the hell—"

"Pack, Pack, think about it."

"Okay, okay. Who? Who took her? How do we find her? What the hell are we going to do? Do we call the cops?"

Just then, the room was filled with a tinny version of Johnny B. Goode. It was Pack's cell phone, ringing in his pocket. He yanked it out, ripping the lining of his pocket as he did. "Yes?"

"This is Abby, from the InnBetween."

"Great, great. Did you speak to your guy?"

"Henry called me back—he's at the Dutch Inn in Kinder-hook. He says yes, he invited Vida to come down to the bar and have a drink with him while he was closing up, but she said she couldn't, she was being picked up. But she said she could maybe do it tomorrow, she'd get her ride to pick her up later. Then she left."

Pack felt a weight settle in his chest. "That's it?"

"That's it."

"Do you believe him?"

"He has no reason to lie."

"Did he see her leave?"

Abby hesitated. "Let me ask him. I'll call you back."

Pack closed the phone and rested it on the table in front of him. "She's going to ask him and call me back."

Millie nodded, dropped the knife into the sink, pulled out the chair opposite him, and sat down.

They waited. The house creaked and sighed around them. Millie coughed once.

The phone burst into song again. Pack picked it up. "And?"

"He said they both looked out the door, to see if the car was there yet. You know, in case there was time for a drink. It was, so they couldn't."

"What was?"

"The car. It was there."

"Impossible."

"But that's what he said. What he said *she* said. 'My dad's here.' "

Pack looked at Millie. "The bartender says they looked outside and the car was there." He spoke into the phone. "And this was ten-thirty?"

"Yup."

"Did he see what kind of car it was?"

"Henry said it was dark, and the car was up the street so it was hard to see, but it looked like a Lincoln. You know, a limo. Black. But he couldn't see a driver."

Pack stared at Millie. "Thanks." He refolded the phone. "It was my car. My car came to pick her up. That's how they took her."

CHAPTER 47

Vida was shaken awake by the motion of the car. Her tongue was stuck to the tape that covered her mouth—she unstuck it and swallowed.

Disoriented by the movement and the pitch blackness around her, she tried to put her hand out, but her wrists were bound together in front of her. Her panic grew, tightening her throat and making her breathing start to race. She remembered what had happened—Dax had jumped her in the car and she'd tried to fight him, but he'd overpowered her like she was nothing.

The vehicle she was in was bouncing up and down, as if they were going fast over potholes. She was on her side, knees bent, and when she tried to straighten her legs, her feet hit a curved wall. When she attempted to maneuver herself upright, she slammed her head. She was in the trunk.

Vida felt a wave of nausea threaten her, brought on by the closed-up smell, the ride, the taste in her mouth, and the fear clutching her gut. Before it could overwhelm her, she told herself to cut it out, stop whining—she was trapped in a metal box with her mouth sealed shut and if she threw up she'd suffocate. She closed her eyes and forced herself to breathe carefully through her nose. In and out. Again. After a while, she felt the steel bands in her stomach loosen just a fraction and the nausea recede.

The road grew even bumpier, and finally, after a sharp right turn, they came to a stop. The engine died. Then nothing, until she felt the car bounce as the driver moved around. Then one of the doors opened, more bouncing, slam. Finally, the trunk opened, and with it came a rush of cold, fresh air.

Dax stood over her, looking down. She could barely see him in the dark. She wondered despairingly what he had in store for her.

He reached into the trunk and grabbed her by an arm and began to pull her out. She didn't fight him, but scrambled to get her legs in place. She wanted out. But at the edge of the trunk he let go and she fell heavily onto dirt and gravel.

He watched, as she tried to right herself. "Get up." He yanked her quickly to her feet, turning her, dragging her when she stumbled. The headlights of the car were on, bathing them both in harsh blinding whiteness. Their two shadows, linked together, moved like a giant spider against the building in front of them. Vida saw a short flight of steps leading up to a door.

It was night, the light was harsh, and she wasn't thinking clearly, but she knew she'd been there before—and then she wondered if she'd dreamed it. She thought she recognized the garage to her right, down an incline, darkness visible under the half-open door. She had a moment of confusion, trying to sort out the information, followed by a sickening sense of betrayal.

She knew this house. It was Pack's house, her father's house.

Was her dad involved in this? With Dax? He had to be, if his house was being used, his car being driven. Had he really allowed this man to kidnap her? She moaned, the sound muffled by the tape over her mouth.

At the front door, Dax turned the handle and opened it, as if he were expected. Vida could see that the interior was dark, no lights on. Where was Pack?

She suddenly realized she was about to step over the threshold with Dax. She mustn't let that happen, she mustn't go inside with him. She tried to twist out of his grip, and for a second broke free. But only for a second. He shoved her from behind and she landed face down on the dirty linoleum, her tied hands the only thing to cushion her fall.

CHAPTER 48

The first person they had to find was the medic, John Dax. He was the only lead they had, and the only person with any reason to wish her harm. He worked at the hospital, therefore he lived somewhere in or around Albany. Probably not in the phone book; he was too new to the area. They started with directory information. But there was no record of him, listed or not.

"No one has a listing any more because there are no more land lines," Millie said, shaking her head, as if she were mourning the loss of the horse-drawn carriage.

"Maybe the hospital has residences or something nearby. Places for people like him. New hires, you know."

"Good idea. Let's get my computer, look around, see if we find anything."

Millie put her laptop on the dining room table. The cousins sat next to each other, peering at the small machine, as Pack hunted and pecked, trying to find access to the information. The hospital websites seemed to offer no housing, but he found a few links that led to brokers. He kept digging. Finally he found an apartment building that claimed to be one of the few in the area that was within walking distance of the hospitals. Another selling point was its sizeable garage space.

"This sounds possible, right?" Millie said, touching the screen with a thick finger as she pointed at the website.

"Yeah." Pack copied the information down onto a piece of paper. "It's a start. I'm going up there—I've got to do something. I'll go to the VA hospital, and see if I can shake any information loose. Maybe if I show them this address, I can get them to confirm it—or if it's wrong, give me the right one." He stood up, jamming the small square of paper into his pocket.

Millie nodded and patted him on the shoulder. "I'll be here in case she calls. Or comes home."

"Let me know—about anything, okay?"

"Yup. And you keep me posted, Pack."

"Will do."

CHAPTER 49

On his way up to Albany, Pack stopped at the Hess station. He filled up and went inside for a cup of Rusty's brew. Rusty was the night-shift manager, a slender, born-again Christian who lived about a mile and a half from Pack in a small kit house he built himself. His wife, tired of living in the woods, had left him a few years before. She'd taken their twelve-year-old daughter with her, but left their overactive nine-year-old son for his dad. Rusty was content, even though he missed his girl. The boy could now use a chainsaw, ride a motorcycle, and hunt, though his grades were nothing to boast about. "Hey, boss. Late fare?" asked Rusty.

"Well, I'm not sure. But I hope so," Pack said, putting his money on the counter. "See ya, Rusty."

He got in the car and sipped the hot liquid before pulling out of the parking lot. His plan was vague. He would go to the VA hospital and say John Dax was a friend of his daughter's and she was sick so he, Pack, needed to reach him. He had an address for Dax—here he'd produce the one he and Millie had found on the Internet—but he'd been to the apartment in question and there was no sign Dax lived there. Maybe he, Reynolds Packard, Special Forces veteran, had got the apartment number wrong by a digit or two. Was there anything they could do to help him? Maybe, with luck, he'd be able to convince a tired staff member to give him the real address. It was a convoluted and unreliable plan, but he couldn't think of a better one.

It was two A.M. by the time he parked in the cold and lonely lot of the hospital. The few yellow lights created pools of emptiness on the black tarmac. He sat for a while, trying to straighten out his thoughts.

In his mind's eye, he could picture the lobby, the rows of mostly empty seats, all the old men gone for the night, just an occasional nurse or orderly walking through. Depressing. He sighed. On impulse, he pulled the address of the apartment building out of his pocket and thought, what the hell? Why not go there directly? It wouldn't take long to read the names on the mailboxes, would it? Back in a flash. For some reason, that option hadn't crossed his mind. He shook his head. "Gettin' old, gettin' stupid," he said to himself, relieved to get back on the road.

The drive was short, not much more than a minute or two. Good sign. It was on the intersection of two main thoroughfares, with its own well-lit row of garages lining one side of the parking area. He pulled his car near the front of the building, and climbed the few steps to the entrance.

Inside a small vestibule he was met by a bank of mailboxes and an intercom. He read each nameplate, hoping for Dax, but at least half of them were nameless—the apartments either empty or occupied by folks who preferred anonymity.

He saw the name *Camillucci* and thought, what the hell, good Italian last name; he'd had a friend in grade school called Camillucci. He rang the buzzer and waited. No answer. So much for old school friends. He tried another name—*Margolis*—and after a two-minute wait, he got an answer. The crackle of the intercom barely hid the man's anger: "What? What's goin' on?"

"Hi, is that you, Dax? John Dax?" Pack tried.

"Huh? D'you know what time it is?"

"Sorry, man."

He didn't know what else to do, couldn't think of another

good plan, so he stopped pressing randomly. Beginning with the top buzzer, he started to work his way down, asking for Dax. Most didn't answer. A few raged. One woman simply sounded afraid.

Halfway down the second row a woman answered, her voice tentative. "Yes?" There was no name on the buzzer.

"Hi, I'm sorry to bother you at this hour," Pack said loudly, trying to project sincerity into the tinny box, "but I'm looking for a friend of mine, it's an emergency. His name is John Dax. Does he live there?"

Silence at the other end. Maybe she hadn't heard him.

"Hello?" he said.

"Emergency?"

"You know him?"

"Uh huh."

Staticky silence.

"Hello? My daughter. It's about my daughter."

"Who's your daughter?" Crackle, crackle, bzzz.

"Her name is Vida, Vida Packard."

"Oh, her." And then it sounded as if she said something else.

"What? You met her?"

"No."

"She's missing and I'm worried," he yelled into the small grating. "Let me come up, please, so we can talk face to face."

"Okay. But just for a minute. 2F," she said. He heard a faint, wavering buzz from the door. He grabbed the handle before she changed her mind.

The lobby was dark gray, lit by three wall sconces shaped like orange slices that threw triangles of overlapping yellow light onto the upper walls and ceiling. The staircase was against the left wall, wide and gloomy, and he trudged up the two flights, head down, his footsteps a rhythmic echo in the empty stairwell.

The second floor hallway was covered in blue patterned

wallpaper with silver trim, as if the landlord had been recycling old gift wrap. The apartment doors were black. He read each number, looking for 2F, when he heard locks turning. A door at the end of the hall opened.

A young woman in a chenille robe, blonde hair sticking out untidily from her head, stepped into the hall. Even in the poor light he could see she was pretty, with wide-set eyes and small, neat features. When he reached her he held out his right hand. "Hi, thanks for talking to me, I'm Reynolds Packard."

She ignored his hand, didn't reciprocate with her name, and went to the door of her apartment and held it, gesturing for him to enter. Pack hesitated only for a moment. Before closing the door she gave a glance up the hallway as if making sure none of her neighbors had seen them.

"Start again," she instructed. "I didn't understand much of what you were saying, that intercom is like talking through a dead man's ass."

He was taken aback. She saw his reaction, and he thought he detected a glint of satisfaction in her eye. But mostly her expression was sour.

"Is there anyplace we can sit down?" he said. "I'm beat. If I don't get off my feet, I may have to fall over."

She stared at him suspiciously. "Are you drunk?"

"No. It's close to three A.M. and way past my bedtime."

"Okay, follow me. But take off your shoes, the old hag downstairs complains if I so much as drop a tissue up here."

She led the way to the right and threw a light switch. An overhead dome flooded the room with fluorescence. They were in the kitchen. "There," she said, gesturing to a chair.

Shoeless and blinking, he sat down.

She leaned against the sink and cocked her head. "I'm listening."

Pack cleared his throat. "I don't have much. My daughter

was in Iraq with Dax. She's been working a part-time job at a local restaurant and I went to pick her up—"

"She doesn't drive?"

Annoyed, he said: "She doesn't have a car at the moment. I drop her off and pick her up."

The woman nodded.

"What's your name?" he asked, feeling at a disadvantage.

She paused. "Carla. Okay?"

"Carla what?"

She puckered her lips, as if she were considering not saying another word. Then she shrugged. "Veltos."

Pack nodded. "Okay, Carla. Tonight I went to pick Vida up at work, and she'd left an hour earlier, gotten into a car just like mine, and disappeared. She was abducted."

"Oh, come on."

"Yes, she was."

"Even so, what does this have to do with Dax?"

"I don't know," Pack lied. "See, she doesn't know anyone around here except for him. It's a long shot, but he might know something . . ."

"Overseas—were they together?"

"Same base in Iraq."

"I mean, were they an item?"

"You mean lovers? No, just friends."

"I doubt that."

"Why?"

Carla rolled her eyes as if he were being slow-witted.

Pack asked: "How do you know him?"

"The VA hospital. I'm a nurse."

"I get it."

She frowned slightly. "You get what?" she said, sounding defensive.

"Nothing. Just, I get it, that's how you know each other. The hospital."

"That's it."

"So you're not dating him or anything?"

"So what if I am? Look"—she pushed herself off the sink—"it's very late and I have to be at work in a few hours. I don't see how I can help you."

"Where can I find him?"

"I can't give you his information," she said.

"Carla, please. I need to talk to him, I need his help. He saw Vida, he spoke to her. She must've looked him up for a reason. Maybe she told him what was on her mind."

"I don't know," she said. But she seemed to be wavering.

"Fine. I can wait until tomorrow and go through channels." He pulled out his VA card and put it on the table. "I warn you, I don't know how much John Dax will appreciate me bringing him into a police investigation. But if I don't get a chance to talk to him, I'm going to have to do that."

He saw a flicker of nervousness cross her face. Carla glanced at the card but didn't touch it. She chewed the inside of her bottom lip, thinking. "He has an apartment a few blocks away. I'll write out his address for you, okay? Then you have to go."

"And his phone number."

"You can't tell him I gave it to you, okay? He'll get pissed at me."

"He will? Why? I'm Vida's father, for Christ's sake, I'm looking for my kid. Why would he be upset?"

"He's very private is all. So just don't tell him I told you."

"I won't."

"Promise."

"Yes, yes, I promise." He hesitated, then asked, "Listen, is everything alright with you?"

"Yeah, I'm terrific. Why wouldn't I be?"

Pack stood up. "I'll just give you my card in case you need to reach me."

He pulled one out of his wallet and put it on the table, picking up his VA card. Carla walked out of the kitchen and he followed her.

As he was about to leave, he paused. "Does every tenant get the use of a garage?"

"Yes. So?"

"Nothing. It's just a nice perk. Do you use yours?"

"Of course I do. But I don't use it for my car, I store things."

"What kind of car d'you have?"

His questions were obviously irritating her. "Why?"

He smiled placatingly. "Just curious."

"A Hyundai Elantra, if you must know."

"Can I ask what color?"

Carla gave him a curious glance, then, "Aqua."

"What about Dax? What does he drive?"

"None of your business."

"I bet it's black and slick, right?"

"So?"

"A Miata, right?"

"Kidding, right? Dax wouldn't be caught dead in a Miata."

"How come?"

"It's not, I don't know, American."

"Okay. So what it is, a Ford Probe?"

She laughed meanly. "Why, 'cause he's a medic?"

Pack ignored the crack and kept thinking. He snapped his fingers. "I know, it's a Mustang."

"Wrong." She laughed again, for a brief moment caught up in the game. "Try a Corvette."

Pack grinned. "Mustang wasn't so far off. I was right about the black, wasn't I?"

"Big deal."

At the door, he tried to thank her but she brushed it off, irritated again. "Go, go. Goodnight." He was barely out the door before she closed it behind him. He heard the locks turning.

In the parking lot, Pack found the Hyundai in a space two cars down from his. He peered in the windows, but there was nothing that struck him as interesting or relevant. Except that she wasn't parked in her garage space. Maybe she was storing her stuff . . . or maybe the black Corvette. Most of the garages had their doors down. He jotted down the license plate number of the Hyundai, for lack of anything else to do.

CHAPTER 50

Carla Veltos went back into her kitchen and picked up the card. She recognized it. It was just like the one Janet, from the cafeteria, had given Dax. She'd seen it in his pocket later that day. Which meant that this guy had been looking for Dax for a few days at least, *before* his daughter disappeared.

Carla felt a wave of anxiety as she walked back to her bedroom. Without taking off her robe, she climbed back into her cold bed. She didn't know what was going on, but she didn't like it. She wondered if she should call Dax and warn him.

Where was he, anyway? He'd been away a lot these last nights. Even though it was kind of a relief not to see him, she still missed him when he didn't come by. Love is so painful, she thought, her small lush mouth turning down in sadness.

While Pack was outside looking through her car windows, Carla lay in bed, her stomach in a knot, trying to decide what to do.

Because the truth had just struck her. The girl's father could tell himself whatever he wanted about his daughter, that she'd run off to join the circus or been abducted by aliens but she, Carla, knew what had really happened.

The little monster had stolen Dax.

Carla had seen them together that first day, when Vida found him in the cafeteria, when she'd sniffed him out like a bitch in heat, smiling and hugging. Carla wasn't an idiot, she'd seen the chemistry; that was no bond between soldiers. She'd seen how

Dax had invited Vida to join them, had pretended they were "old friends."

Sure. Old friends. She'd stood in the entrance of the cafeteria, unseen by the two of them. She'd seen him get the girl coffee, she'd seen him leaning in to her, salivating. Not that Carla could understand why. That was some scar she had. But maybe it turned him on—some men were into deformities, and Dax certainly had his quirks.

Carla turned onto her side, staring unseeing at the wall. She wondered where they were, and began to visualize them together, her agitation increasing with each escalating image.

She shut her eyes, trying to close out the pictures. But like a Peeping Tom, she couldn't stop. Somewhere, they were all over each other, sweating and panting. The images tortured her and turned her on, all at the same time. Liars! Cheaters! When she forced herself to erase some of the more pornographic scenes, others appeared in their place.

She got out of bed and started pacing.

Until Vida appeared a few days ago, Dax had been hers. But now Vida had stolen him away. At last her misery became so absorbing, so acute, that she cried out and crumpled onto her bedroom floor. She lay there, wailing. Sobbing for her lost love.

Which is why at first she didn't hear the steady din. Eventually, however, each blow resonated through her body and she began to pay attention.

She sat up, her face streaked and blotchy.

Bam! Bam! Bam!

It took her a moment to locate and identify the sounds but when she did, her self-pity exploded into anger. The bitch downstairs! Carla was making too much noise for her, and Mrs. Stoller was banging on the ceiling!

"Arhh!" Carla cried out, slapping her hand hysterically against the floor. She wanted to keep slapping, she wanted to stomp on the floor, again and again. But she knew that as soon as she did, the old woman would run to the phone and call the super. Carla had fought not to put carpeting on the floor, she hated carpeting, but one more noise complaint and she'd be forced to comply.

She pulled herself together. "Die, you dried out old cockroach," she whispered, her mouth inches away from glossy parquet.

But Mrs. Stoller had broken the spell. Carla took a deep shuddering breath and slowly stood up. She had to do something. She couldn't just sit here feeling sorry for herself. She had to find them, and get him back. She knew if she could see Dax face to face, she'd be able to convince him Vida was a conniving whore who was just playing him.

But first she had to figure out where they'd gone.

Maybe she should just call him on his cell. But what could she say to convince him to tell her where they were? She could say the police were looking for him. But when he found out she'd lied, he'd be extremely angry with her. And Dax even mildly irritated was frightening.

Sitting on the side of her bed, she pulled out the bedside table's small drawer, dumping the contents. Taped to the bottom of the drawer were two keys on a ring. She pulled them off, and held them in her hand.

Dax had never offered her his keys, even though she'd given him a set to her place. When she finally got up the nerve to ask him, it was one night right after they'd made love. They were lying on her bed, naked and covered in sweat. She figured there wouldn't be a better time.

But he'd only chuckled. "Forget it, babe. I can't share my privacy with anyone. It's an army thing."

And he'd squeezed one of her buttocks, tightening his grip until she was forced to twist away from him.

She'd never asked again, but she hadn't forgotten. Just waited until the right moment to make it right. She somehow convinced herself it was what he would have wanted, if he hadn't erected such high walls around his heart; men like Dax were out of touch with their true feelings.

The right moment came along one morning. He'd just worked a double shift at the hospital, called her as he was leaving work, met her at the apartment, made them each a Bloody Mary, fucked her, and fallen asleep. She knew he'd sleep like the dead. In fact, she was surprised he let her stay.

She saw her chance and didn't hesitate. Taking his keys off the front hall table, she let herself out and went to the closest hardware store. She had the clerk make her two copies of each key—lobby and apartment—in case one of them didn't work; she knew she might never get another chance. On her way back, she stopped at a bakery and picked up some muffins, her excuse for going out, in case he was awake when she got back.

But he was still asleep, and she tried the keys out immediately. They worked perfectly. Satisfied, she left him a note, took her fresh muffins, and let herself out.

She hadn't used the keys before because, until now, she hadn't needed to. But tonight, things were different.

This was an emergency.

CHAPTER 51

Pack drove to Dax's address. The Heritage Residence was a much newer building than the one Carla lived in. Each unit had French doors giving onto a small balcony. He looked around the parking area. No Corvette of any color.

He sat in the car and called Millie.

"Hear anything?" he asked.

"Not yet."

"Shit. The good news is, I've found Dax's apartment."

"Good going. Is he there?"

"Don't know. I haven't tried. I don't want to spook him, you know, get his back up. Do you think there's any chance he has her here?"

"It's an apartment block?"

"Yeah. Kind of modern, little balconies, parking."

"Doubtful. Those places have thin walls and neighbors who can hear everything; elevators always have people in them. All in all, a bad idea; I wouldn't do it."

"But it's possible, right?"

"It's possible. You need to get in there and see for yourself."

"Any suggestions how?"

"You could ask nicely. But if he's not there, use gloves and a crowbar."

"Jesus, you're an officer of the law."

"Not anymore I'm not."

After he hung up, Pack looked in the trunk of his car for

some kind of a tool. He found a wrench and the handle of the car jack. He put on a pair of driving gloves.

The first set of glass doors at the Heritage led into a small, clean entryway, a well-lit area that housed nothing but a gleaming new intercom system. To the right of the intercom were the inner glass doors opening into the lobby itself.

Pack was relieved to see that Dax's name was clearly printed and inserted into the name slot by the buzzer for apartment number 4B. He wouldn't have to call all the neighbors. He pushed the buzzer, hard and long.

No answer.

He pushed it again and held it down. He wiggled the button in case he wasn't making a connection.

Still no response.

Now to convince someone in the building to let him into the lobby at this time of the morning so he could break into 4B.

He rang the top left bell and waited. While he did, he picked up a flyer and looked at it. There were several stacks of them deposited by the door. The one he'd chosen was for a car service; the others were menus.

Huh. Pack stood there, thinking it over.

He walked back to the car, threw the tools into the trunk. Sitting behind the wheel, he called Millie.

"Yeah?"

"Mitch, we know he used a Town Car, right? I mean, he conned Vida because he had one."

"Right."

"But this guy Dax doesn't drive a Town Car, I know it 'cause the girlfriend told me. He drives a black Corvette. Makes sense he'd drive something flashy, he sees himself as a serious chick magnet, right? A Lincoln's a geezer car."

"Hey, you said it, not me."

Pack paused, momentarily irritated. "I need mine, it's a limo.

My point is, if he wanted a Town Car, he'd have rented one."

"Makes sense."

"We need to find out from where."

"Good idea. A rental that handles Lincoln Town Cars. Older models. What year is yours? A '95? Can't be too many around here."

"True. Okay, I think I'll hold off breaking and entering until I hear from you."

"It's not the best time to call businesses."

He glanced at the brochure he was still holding. "Oh, and try Sun Valley Rentals. In Clifton Park."

"Is the Corvette there, in the parking lot?"

"Nope. But I wouldn't be surprised if he stashed it in his girlfriend's parking space."

CHAPTER 52

Millie was glad to have something to do, now that she was awake. She looked at her watch. Three-thirty in the morning. It was too early, or too late, to call most limo companies. To her surprise, a wan voice answered the Sun Valley Rental number. "Sun Valley, Len speaking, how may I help you?"

Millie could tell Len didn't really want to help. He'd much rather go back to sleep with his head on his desk.

Millie put on her best cop voice. "This is Sergeant Mitch Jedd. I'm trying to locate a vehicle you rented out sometime over the past couple of days."

"Yeah?" Len was uninterested. "You'll have to call back during business hours. I'm just here for a special group rental. Once I log the cars in, I'm gone."

"Len, I understand. The trouble is, I can't wait for business hours. This is an Amber Alert."

"Huh?"

"An Amber Alert, sir, is the emergency broadcast of the abduction of a child."

"Yeah, I know what it is. What happened? Who got abducted?"

"I'm not allowed to discuss the case with you, Len. However, any help you provide will be noted and greatly appreciated."

"I think I need to call my boss and ask him."

"No time. We're racing against the clock, and this is the first step to finding the missing child. We need the name of the customer who rented a Lincoln Town Car from you sometime during the last few days. We're talking an earlier model, say about 1995."

"Oh, jeez. Ninety-five? I'll look in the file." Millie heard the receiver being put down. She waited. Finally, the guy came back on the line. "Nah, we don't have any that old. No call for them."

Millie shut her eyes briefly in disappointment. "I see. Do you know of any other local company with older models in their fleet?"

There was silence at the other end.

"You still there, Len?"

"Yep, I'm just looking through our contacts. We have reciprocity with a few of them. Oh, here. These guys rent a lot of older cars, some are pretty cool—vintage, stuff like that. They might have an old Town Car."

Millie said goodbye to Len and hung up. She looked once more at her watch. It wasn't much closer to daylight than it had been before, but what the hell. She dialed the number for Glory Rides Unlimited. The phone rang and rang, but no one picked up. She put the receiver down and sat there, tapping her pencil against the phone book.

CHAPTER 53

As Pack waited for Millie's response, a car turned into the parking area, its brights catching him full in the face. He shut his eyes and put a hand up.

It pulled up next to Pack. It was the aqua Hyundai, with Carla at the wheel. Pack got out of his car and walked around to the driver's window. She rolled it down.

"So, what're you doing here?" he asked.

"He's my boyfriend. I come over a lot. What are *you* doing here?" she asked.

"I told you, I need to speak to the guy. You have a key?"

"So what?"

"I need to get in."

"No way."

"Just a quick glance, just to make sure my daughter isn't in there. Put the whole thing to rest."

She gave a burst of mirthless laughter. "Never in a million years. Dax would kill me."

"Okay then," he tried another tack. "I was just about to ring the doorbell, and if he isn't there, I was planning to wait. But you could at least save me waiting in the cold. You could let me into the lobby."

She rolled up the window. "Forget it," she mouthed through the glass.

She pulled into an empty space and got out.

He wondered if he should grab her and force her upstairs. Tempting.

Another car pulled into the lot and Pack knew his chance of strong-arming Carla was gone. She was already going up the steps. He followed her. "Wait, Carla!"

She turned, her expression fearful.

He slowed down and held his hands up, proof he intended her no harm. "All I ask is, when you're in there, keep an eye out for any sign of her, okay? Any items of her clothing, her backpack, any sign of a limo company he might have used—we think he rented a Town Car just like mine—anything you notice. Please."

She didn't answer, just turned away from him and pulled open the glass door. He watched her fit a key into the lock of the inner door. The resident who'd just driven in walked up the steps, and Pack moved aside to let him pass.

Frustrated, Pack went back to his car and sat in it, fingers clenching the lower part of the steering wheel. He'd wait her out, unless something happened at Millie's end. Trouble was, even if Carla discovered something, she'd probably clam up, refuse to give him any help, and be on her way. And that would be his one good lead, lost. He needed his gun, and he needed his cousin. Opening his cell phone, he dialed Millie.

"Hey. Listen, you doing anything important right now?"

"No. I wish I was."

"Okay, here it is. I need you to meet me, here, now, at Dax's apartment. His girlfriend's on her way up but she's not cooperating. We're going to have to get tough with her if we want to get in there. So I need you to bring my handgun. We don't have much time and I don't want to piss it away begging for favors."

"Gimme the address."

Satisfied, Pack leaned back in the seat. Thank god for Millie.

Even though she'd been a cop, she had her priorities straight.

He shut his eyes, just for a moment, and before he knew it he had fallen asleep.

CHAPTER 54

When they first entered the house, Dax cut the tape on Vida's wrists. Her heart lifted—there was no other way of describing it: she thought, for a second, that he was going to let her go. But before she could adjust to her new freedom, he yanked both arms behind her back and began retaping them, tighter than before. She struggled and tried to cry out through the gag over her mouth, but he ignored her. After pressing the tape down, he shoved her onto the couch where she lay, her shoulders burning, her breathing strained. When she felt the needle prick, she was nearly grateful; it was a relief when the drug took over and she fell back into a fitful sleep.

When she awoke it was still dark. She felt queasy, the dirty couch shifting under her and the room slowly revolving. When the motion stopped, she remembered what had happened, where she was.

She guessed she was going to die. The picture of Haley's mother, strapped to a chair, waxy and blood-covered, drifted into Vida's mind. The fear the image generated, once it was there, worked like too much caffeine. It started her nervous system jumping wildly, so that she couldn't think straight.

A sudden noise broke through her building panic. She listened, straining hard to hear something. Nothing. Maybe she imagined it. Maybe he'd gone out, at least for a while—or he was asleep. She shifted her hips until she was on her side, her back burning with the pain of changing positions. How long had she been lying here? When the ache lessened, she pulled her knees into her chest and maneuvered herself up so she was sitting on the sofa, arms behind her back. Gratefully, her feet rested on the ground. She felt better upright; having her feet flat on the floor was a little thing, but she felt less vulnerable, more hopeful.

There were no lights on in the room, but a fixture was on in the corridor behind her. So she could see enough to know the place looked much as it had the last time she was there. Dismal.

Suddenly, she remembered Pack's handgun. Had he brought it back? She'd cleaned it for him, and when she was done, he'd taken it away. She assumed he'd left it at Millie's, but when he came back to the house to get ready for Birmingham, maybe he'd brought it home. With dismay, she wondered if he'd put it right back in his bedside table.

She thought back to the night before. Why had Dax taken her? She knew, now that she was thinking more clearly, that Pack wasn't in this with Dax. That possibility simply wasn't worth contemplating. Maybe Pack had left the InnBetween to do something, and Dax happened by, saw her get in the car on the deserted street, and moved in on impulse. But she discarded that idea even as she came up with it. What were the chances that he was hanging around Bantam at that particular hour of the night?

She made herself think back to what she knew about John Dax. She thought of Millie and Pack, and the tale they brought back from Alabama, straight from Pascoe. That Dax, Haley's boyfriend from Iraq, had really been her pimp at the base. However much she discounted anything coming from Pascoe, something about it rang true. The trouble was, she couldn't sort out what he wanted from her. But she'd find out soon enough.

She heard a door open behind her, down the hall. Heavy footsteps, walking around. Maybe going to the bathroom. It had to be Dax. Yes, the bathroom. She heard him urinate noisily, then flush. His footsteps grew louder. He was walking into the living room.

Vida braced herself to see him. The gag on her mouth was causing her breath to whistle, her tongue was dry, and her shoulders throbbed as each breath she took expanded her chest and put pressure on her joints.

He was wiping his hands on his pants when he appeared in her field of vision. He stopped in his tracks when he saw her sitting up, held out his hands, and said, as if he and she were traveling companions sharing a motel room: "This place is a cesspool—I'm afraid to use the towels, y'know?"

CHAPTER 55

Four flights above the street, Carla was helping herself to a Valium from the bathroom cabinet. It was the least Dax could do for her, considering what he was putting her through.

Being alone in his domain was making her nervous. What if he and the girl suddenly showed up? The thought galvanized her into movement. She walked from the bathroom to the bedroom, looking around, trying to see what was different. But there was no sign of her, no rinsed-out panties hanging in the john, no overnight bag, nothing in the closet that didn't belong. Carla wanted to lie on the bed, sure she'd be able to smell another woman on the sheets, but was afraid to rumple the taut, inspection-ready bedding. He would know if she had. She settled for leaning down and very carefully putting her nose to the pillow. She sniffed, paused. Nothing, just Dax's aftershave, an expensive mixture of spices and mint.

She had to admit that the apartment looked as it usually did, smelled as it usually did, and made her feel as it usually did. There was no evidence another woman had been here—not recently, anyway.

She went to the doors that gave onto the balcony. Dawn still far off, though there was a lightening in the sky in the east, toward the river. She looked at her watch.

Four A.M.

She unlocked and slid one of the doors open. A cold breeze greeted her, sending a chill into the room. She stepped out onto the balcony and looked down into the parking lot. She could see the black limo below her. That man was still waiting for her, impatient to know where Dax had gone. Well, he wouldn't find out from her.

She stepped back inside and closed and locked the door. She looked around. To the right of the doors was Dax's desk.

"Yes," she said aloud.

His laptop wasn't shut down, and when she stroked the touchpad, it whirred then popped to life. She pulled up the chair and started looking.

She tried to get into his mail, but no good. Disappointing, because any plans he and the girl had would probably have been made online. She went to his browser and looked at his recent searches. She was so intent on looking for inns and resorts, that she nearly missed the references to the New Canaan Post Office.

When she saw the name, she sat back in the chair. New Canaan? Where the hell was that? She went to the map search. "Huh," she said. His last directions search was also for New Canaan, NY. So maybe this New Canaan was where he and Vida had planned to meet, or the location they'd picked to get to know each other better. Two-timing bastard. No, no, it was that whore who'd lured him away.

Yet, looking determinedly, she found no name of an inn or motel, no private address, no phone number.

It didn't take her long to decide what to do next. She'd would follow his tracks and go to the New Canaan Post Office. Little place like that, they'd help her figure it out.

She didn't need to print out the directions. They were pretty straightforward: south on the highway, take exit 11East to Massachusetts, go straight for twenty miles, turn into the post office on your right.

She grabbed her jacket off the sofa and looked around, making sure that everything was as she'd found it: bathroom cabinet closed, lights off, balcony door shut tight. At the last minute, she took four more Valium out of the bathroom, and stuck them in her pocket. Dax really did owe her.

Outside the apartment, she carefully locked both locks. She took a deep breath and walked to the elevator.

She should be nervous about what she was doing but, for some reason, she felt confident, strong. That meant it was the right move, obviously. What was that song? The elevator arrived and she got in.

CHAPTER 56

The short nap he'd allowed himself had helped Pack. He was tired but alert, his eyes on the front door of the apartment building. He hoped she had enough to occupy her upstairs; he didn't want her to be done before Millie arrived. But sure enough, sooner than he anticipated, she pushed open the glass and emerged. He climbed out of the car, as if he were going to meet her.

Carla looked in his direction and shook her head, held up her hands, empty, regret expressed in the tilt of her head. She had nothing for him.

Or so she wanted him to believe. Pack watched her. There was something lively and optimistic about the way she bounced down the steps to the asphalt. He swore to himself and pulled his cell phone out of his pocket.

"Yeah?" Millie answered.

"Where are you, man? She's heading for her car."

"I'm just turning off New Scotland Avenue. What d'you want me to do?"

Pack thought for a moment, watching her as she climbed into her car. "Turn around and pull over. Wait for a blue Hyundai to drive by you—she should be there in minutes. But don't let her see you. Follow her. She's got something going on, she knows something. Let's find out what. I'll wait here until I hear from you."

"I'm on it," Millie said.

The phone went dead.

Millie waited, slumped down in the seat of her red Dodge Ram pick-up, engine idling. She'd done a U-turn, and now was facing in the same direction Carla'd be going when she passed by. Millie wasn't sure how the whole thing should unfold, but the most important thing was not to lose her. The tricky part was that the streets were deserted, and Millie's pick-up was highly visible. It would be hard not to be spotted.

She looked in her rear-view mirror, and sure enough, the little Hyundai appeared at the end of the street. It was moving fast, drawing closer. Two blocks away, it barely slowed down at the four-way stop sign. Now it was one block away, then thirty yards. Millie braced herself, apologizing silently to her truck.

Just as Carla passed the last intersection, Millie pulled out from the curb, turned sharply alongside the nurse's car and, before the woman could react and pull away to the left, she drove into it.

There was a crash and tinkling of broken glass at impact. The jolt, however, wasn't enough to deploy either airbag, and as soon as her head stopped ringing, Millie climbed out of the cab. Carla had braked. Millie looked at the front of her truck. Not too bad. She glanced up and down the street. There was no one around.

Carla was just getting out, and she was spitting mad. "What the hell's wrong with you? You didn't look! Why didn't you look?"

Millie let her face wrinkle up with dismay. "Oh, blessed Jesus—I'm so sorry. I didn't see you. You were going so fast, you were tearing along the street and your car is so small, I never saw you."

"What do you mean you never saw me? You never looked, for

Christ's sake! Jesus Christ, I'm going to see they take away your license!"

"Oh, dear lord above, now what? I guess we have to call the police, right? Oh, my lord, my lord—"

At the mention of the police, Carla's anger seemed to blow over. "Hold on, hold on. We have insurance, right? You do, don't you?"

Millie nodded helpfully. Carla seemed to take in her appearance for the first time—the fake-looking red hair, the makeup, the five o'clock shadow, the hefty, masculine body. She glanced at the truck, with its clear Plexi bug shield on the front, the words *"Millie's Toy"* hand painted in curlicued letters. She stepped back, as if Millie were contagious.

"You know, we can just exchange information and leave it to the insurance people to deal with," she proposed. "If we get the cops involved, it'll take forever."

"Won't we need a police report?" Millie asked meekly.

"No, no," Carla said, waving a hand.

Millie nodded. "Alright. But I need to call my husband."

She caught Carla's smirk as the woman turned to get her documents out of the Hyundai's glove compartment.

Millie sat in her truck and dialed Pack, keeping an eye on Carla.

"Everything okay?" Pack answered.

"Actually, I've had a collision."

"Shit! Did she get away?"

"Thanks for your concern. No, she didn't get away. She's the one I hit."

"Oh no."

"Oh, yes." She watched as Carla came toward her, carrying a bundle of papers. "Stay out of sight until I call. Gotta go."

Millie took her time getting her papers. Then she pretended to fiddle with her ignition.

Carla was all business. Leaning on the hood of the truck, she wrote out her name and numbers on a piece of paper, then handed another sheet of paper to Millie.

"Here, write your information."

Before she did, Millie put one heavy hand on Carla's upper arm, making her jump. "I need you to give me a ride. To my garage. My truck won't start."

Carla pulled her arm away and shook her head. "Oh, no, I can't do that. I'm late already."

"Please. What direction are you going in?"

"It doesn't matter. I'm not going near a gas station."

Silently, Millie took the information that Carla had given her, checked that it was accurate, and thrust it and her own documents back into their folder.

Carla watched, confused. "What're you doing?"

When Millie spoke, her voice burned with self-righteous indignation. "I see what's going on. *You* drive like a maniac, not even stopping at the intersection, and hit *my* car. Then you don't even have the courtesy to give me a ride to a garage. I saw the way you looked at me, I know what you're thinking. Well, not everyone can be like you, a pretty little blondie. Not all of us are born the way we should have been born. But that does not give you the right to judge me."

She opened the door of her truck. "You know what, I just decided, I'm going to call my lawyer and I'm gonna sue you, I am, because you are giving me some cruel and unusual mental anguish, you know that? And you're discriminating against me. He may even tell me the collision was a hate crime."

Carla looked furious. She glanced at her car, as if she were considering a run for it. Millie saw the look and added: "And I'm going to call WTEN and tell them what happened here. They'll be very interested."

Carla could barely mask the hate. "Okay, okay, fine. I'll take you to a garage, but it's going to have to be in my direction. I can't take you any old place you want to go. I'm very late."

Millie shook her head in exasperation. "You're kidding. What's your direction?"

"Southeast, toward Massachusetts. And it's an emergency. My aunt is not well, in fact, she's dying, and I have to get there fast. So unless it's right on my way—"

Millie shook her head. "Where exactly? It might be in my direction."

Carla hesitated before speaking in a rush. "It won't mean anything to you. Someplace called New Canaan."

Millie paused, then pursed her lips and said grudgingly, "Well, since you're in a hurry, I'll show a little compassion, which is more than you did. My mechanic is in Clifton Park. Opposite direction. I'll just call a cab."

Carla looked overjoyed. "Wonderful." She found her purse in her car and poked around in it. "Here. Take this. Toward cab fare." She pushed a twenty into Millie's hand.

"Why, thank you, honey," Millie beamed. "You're a total doll." She moved as if to embrace her.

Carla backed away and opened her door. "Okay. Bye."

She hopped in behind the wheel of her car, slammed the door, and pulled away, her front right fender waving precariously.

Millie stood on the street watching her. She took her phone out of her pocket.

"What's going on?" Pack's voice was edged in panic.

"Carla's gone. Come here. You can't miss me."

"Oh no, you lost her? What about—?"

"I found out where she's going. You're not going to believe it."

"Where?"

"I'll tell you when you're here. It's too good."

CHAPTER 57

Dax was getting ready to kill Vida.

He didn't love the idea of doing it, but he didn't hate it either. That wasn't important. What he did know was that he'd seen plenty of wounded and dead, and one thing they all had in common is they were balloons of blood, entrails, bones, waste, and fluids. If he wasn't careful, any of that would be all over the place. And him. So he had to make sure he did it right.

The good news was that he was in a house in the woods with no neighbors to worry about. So all he had to do was walk her outside. Avoid any clean-up whatsoever.

The bad news was he was in the girl's father's house, and the man might come home at any moment.

Because it was peacetime, at least here in the U.S., dead bodies were not an everyday occurrence, so he had to make absolutely sure there was no trace of himself left in the house or on Vida. He'd even taken a short nap wearing gloves. Hotter'n'hell, but he had to be careful. Also, the sound of gunfire wasn't common, though he had to believe there was some kind of hunting season going on now. Maybe turkey? He should find out. Or just use a knife.

First thing was to dig a hole. It made sense to kill her right where he was going to bury her. No reason to give himself the added work of moving her body. He wished he could wait until daylight so he could see what the hell he was doing, but he couldn't take the time.

He needed a shovel. There was no shed or tool room, so he began looking through the garage, but all he found were the detritus of a family's life—toys, bikes, a plastic-coated crib-sized mattress eaten out by mice, cardboard boxes breaking open from the damp, disgorging mildewed clothing and curled up shoes.

At last he found one, or at least part of one. It was tossed in a corner, hidden under a patio umbrella. Most of the wooden handle had been cracked off, leaving about a foot and a half capped by jagged, well-aged shards of wood.

More splinters. God, he hated this place. But it was all he could come up with unless he drove to a nearby hardware store, and that wouldn't be a good idea. He hadn't been thinking; he should have bought one in Albany. He hit the end of the handle against the garage door frame, cracking off the worst of the jagged end. Then he found an old purple mitten and fitted it over the end, covering the roughest parts.

He looked in Pack's closet and found a pair of well-worn boots, a work jacket, and a pair of gloves. He put them all on and even though the boots were too small, he felt as if he'd put on another man's skin, like a uniform, and was protected. He found a flashlight in the bedroom.

Before going out he checked on the girl. She was sitting up on the couch, her eyes tracking him as he approached. She looked like shit—her eyes bloodshot, her scar purple. He picked her up by an arm and dragged her to her feet and over to the recliner. He pushed her down onto it, flipped the handle so the back went down and the footrest came up. He looked around, found the roll of duct tape on the dining table and began strapping her legs to the footrest. The tape ran out.

"Shit," he said. He threw the empty roll on the floor.

Oh, well. She wasn't going anywhere.

Outside, it was still dark, though daybreak wasn't much more than an hour away. He turned on the flashlight and climbed off the patio. He walked through the scrub of small trees and bushes, and into the woods. He was a little annoyed at himself for not thinking the plan out a little better, for not coming out here during the day and digging a proper hole. He had assumed he'd just dump the body in the woods, but now he was here that didn't seem such a good idea. Burying it would delay the finding of the body, give him more time to cover his tracks, and for evidence to wash away.

As a criminal, he was a work in progress, he admitted, as he tramped his way through the black gloomy trees, narrowly missing a low hanging branch.

Finally he found a clearing where the trees were bigger and the undergrowth sparser. He picked a spot and began digging. The earth was relatively soft, so the going wasn't too bad until he hit something hard. He shifted to the side and began again, figuring he would dig around whatever it was, remove it, and the holes would eventually all add up to one nice big one.

Forty minutes later, wet with sweat, he gave up. The flashlight had dimmed twenty minutes earlier, so he'd been working in the dark. The soil was dense clay, filled with rocks, and crisscrossed with tree roots. Now he understood the shallow grave concept: it'd take a fucking backhoe to do this right. Hey, the worst that happened is the animals would get her, right? He'd pile any loose rocks on top of the body to hide it and keep anything from dragging it away. In a few weeks maybe it would snow, the ground would freeze, and he'd be long gone. Eventually, when they found her body, her old man would take the fall for it.

Back and shoulders aching, he trudged back to the house. Once he was out of the trees, he could see that the sky was lightening. He looked at his watch. Six A.M. He had to finish what he'd started and get the hell out. That sorry-ass Pack could come home at any time.

CHAPTER 58

Vida watched Dax open the sliding glass doors and walk out onto the back patio. He was wearing gloves and in his right hand carried a shovel with what looked like a child's purple mitten stuck on it. In his left he held a flashlight. He climbed carefully off the back of the patio, turned on the light, and high-stepped into the bushes behind the house. She lost sight of the bobbing white light.

He was going to kill her. She could tell by the way he looked at her, the way he grabbed her. He'd already written her off as a human being, making no eye contact or acknowledgment of her presence. She was merely a problem to be solved.

Vida had to come up with something. She couldn't count on Pack helping her. For all she knew, Dax had already cut his throat somewhere. On the other hand, if he was alive, he could show up suddenly, surprise Dax, who would then kill him. Dax was a strong guy and could easily overpower Pack. Even so, the possibility that someone might show up at any moment must be putting pressure on Dax to move quickly. To get rid of her and move on. That had to be his game plan.

What could she do?

She felt she should have skills to deal with this. She was a trained soldier; she'd been wounded by enemy combatants. She should know what to do next. But she was overcome by a vast wave of helplessness as if, having escaped death once, she'd run out of luck. She started to tremble and her eyesight dimmed.

She began to cry. She could feel the tears as they ran down her face, tickling her cheeks.

Some part of her stayed outside, observing herself, her mouth strapped closed, reclining like the patient of a sadistic dentist. She wondered with detachment if this was PTSD, if the stress of the explosion and her injuries had weakened her core, to the point that she couldn't fight back.

The tears continued, and some of the wetness crept through a gap in the tape, into her mouth. She touched it with her tongue. It may have been the saltiness of it, or the childlike comfort of the act, but it worked as a potion. Like the voice of someone she knew and cared for, telling her to snap out of it. This was her chance, her one chance. A psycho had left her there, vulnerable and helpless. But it wasn't over yet.

Vida lifted her head and looked around. In the middle of the coffee table was the sugar bowl. She suddenly remembered Pack rolling a joint with supplies from the sugar bowl. She remembered how watching that had felt, as if the world was coming to an end, as if things could get no worse.

Obviously, she'd been wrong.

She jerked her torso forward, forcing her legs down. The back of the recliner swung upright. She leaned down, trying to see if she could reach anything on the coffee table, but she was too far away. She tried to stand up. The duct tape covered her jeans, but her legs were still able to slip down through them, allowing her feet to touch the floor.

The pressure on her shins was painful, but she managed to edge the heavy chair closer to the coffee table by inching forward, and pulling the beast behind her.

When her shins were touching the table, she sat back down, ignoring the pain in her legs as they pressed against the edge of the table surface. She inched her butt forward, from side to side, so that when she bent over her face could touch the sugar bowl. Now to break it.

With a swipe of her head, she knocked the bowl over.

She sat up and watched as it fell on its side, rolled away and rocked gently. The lid fell off.

That was it. It didn't break and the little baggie of pot was preventing the lighter from falling out. Now it was out of her reach.

She howled in frustration. It wasn't fair, she didn't deserve this! She yanked and pulled at the tape that bound her wrists, her efforts ineffectual, merely adding to her exhaustion and fear. Why didn't someone come to save her? She wanted to howl for her mother. And where the fuck was her father the one time in her damn life when she needed him?

After approximately sixty seconds of thrashing, she fell back into the chair, worn out. Once again she saw herself, whining, spinning her wheels. Get over it, she snapped at herself. And hurry, because he'll be back at any moment.

She began to move in the other direction, to push the recliner away. It was easier than pulling it, but the distances were greater and she couldn't see where she was heading.

What about the phone?

Yes, good. Pack had an answering machine and a phone. But when she looked at the table, she saw that they were both gone. Loose wires lay on the table, their recent movements visible in patterns in the dust. Dax must've unplugged the equipment while she was knocked out.

What else? She looked around. Could she break a window? With what? What would it achieve? Alert someone who drove by? Or Pack if he came back? Did he even notice things like that?

What about something in the kitchen? Could she get a knife and cut herself free?

She didn't have much time. She had to hurry, hurry, hurry.

She kept moving backwards, pushing the chair. Her breathing grew faster, then shallower, aggravated by the tape across her mouth. She tried to picture herself getting a knife out of a drawer with her teeth and having enough traction to saw through the tape on her legs. Like a contortionist or circus performer.

Fat chance. She was running out of time.

She forced herself to take a few slow breaths. And another one. In, and then out. She couldn't afford to waste energy panicking.

She looked down at her legs. All her moving around and pulling had stretched the tape. Not much, but a little. Because the roll had run out, Dax had been able to wrap it once, with only about four inches of overlap. The footrest of the chair was padded, so even though the padding was old and had mostly collapsed, it might still have a little give to it.

She sat down and began to move her legs from side to side, finding the play in it. Then forward and back. And eventually, up and down, up and down. If she could just pull her legs out from the tape that strapped her to the chair. She kept at it. Up and down. She felt a burning in her thighs. But the restraint around her ankles started to feel baggier. And finally, she leaned back in the chair and began to pull hard. Twisted. Pulled again. And again.

At last it happened. She pulled her legs out and freed them from the chair. She looked quickly out the dirty glass doors. Still no sign of him. How long would her luck hold?

Her legs were still taped together, but she could stand and she had enough movement in them that she could take tiny steps into the kitchen. Her arms were still taped behind her. She made it to the counter, nearly losing her balance in the process. She needed to look through the drawers. To do it, she had to turn and pull them out backward. Finally she found one with a few dull-looking knives in it. It was too high for her to reach into, so she pulled the drawer off its runners. It made a loud crash when it hit the floor, metal and plastic utensils skittering across the linoleum. Vida saw a black-handled steak knife and sat down, her back to the pile, and felt around for it.

All the time, looking over her shoulder, listening for footsteps on the patio, the slide of the glass door.

When she got hold of it, she squatted, then stood carefully, trying not to jab herself or drop the knife as she gripped it behind her back. On her feet, she took more mincing steps across the living room and into Pack's bedroom.

She seemed to remember that when she originally took his gun from his room, she saw her own reflection in a mirror.

Sure enough, above the yellow pine dresser was an attached, moveable mirror, stained and spotted, tilted downward. She turned around and tried to position herself so it would help her see what she was doing behind her back.

She had to bring one shoulder forward and realign her wrists to expose the tape to the knife. She had very little strength to put behind the knife, at that angle. Her hands were slippery with sweat and beginning to tremble and twice she missed the tape and stuck herself. There was a sour smell in the air; she realized it was her own. In the mirror, she saw a trickle of blood run down her wrist.

At last, she cut enough of the tape that so she could pull her wrists apart and snap the binding. "Ah," she moaned. Hands shaking, she brought her arms slowly around to the front of her body. The burning pain in her shoulders was excruciating, as the blood flow suddenly increased. She ignored it and began to pick at the tape around her mouth, and when that didn't work, she used the knife, cutting what she could, ripping the rest.

Able to close her mouth at last, she now had to free her legs. She started to saw at the gray tape with the knife.

271

"Hello," said a voice from the doorway.

Dax.

Vida jumped, as if someone had shot her through with an electrical current. She glanced up, for only for a second, to make sure he wasn't approaching. Then she kept going.

"I'll shoot you."

She looked at him again, her ankles still tied.

He was standing in the doorway, pointing a handgun at her. He was wearing work clothes, and his knees were brown with fresh dirt.

She didn't stop. If he shot her, at least she'd die with her legs free. He'd run out of duct tape. She cut through the tape and felt the wash of relief as the last thread of the tape snapped and her legs were allowed to move apart.

Now, she stood up stiffly and looked at him. "That's better," she said, her voice a harsh whisper. She looked at the gun. It was her father's.

"Drop the little knife, Vida."

She watched sadly as the knife clattered to the ground. She liked that knife. "Why are you doing this?" she said without looking at him.

"Loose ends."

"I need water. My throat is killing me," she said.

He looked irritated but he shrugged permission and pointed his chin at the bathroom. She walked ahead of him and turned on the cold tap at the sink, bent down, and drank deeply from the faucet.

She stood upright, and looked at him in the medicine chest mirror. "I need to use the toilet."

"Go ahead." He didn't move.

She realized, of course, he wasn't going to leave or turn his back. She either did it in front of him or she wet her pants. "Look away, okay?"

He didn't respond, just kept his eyes on her.

Show no fear, she said to herself, but it was an empty thought. Her legs were shaking, and she had trouble lowering her jeans. Finally she sat on the toilet and did what she had to do.

"Better?" he said.

"You like holding people at gunpoint and watching them piss?" she said, the anger seeping through the fear as she stood and pulled her pants back up.

"What's not to like?" he said. His voice had changed, and she knew he was considering raping her. Maybe if she encouraged him, she could get close enough to hurt him. The thought gave her hope. Instead, she said:

"You know Pack's going to come, right?"

The look in his eyes changed. She'd taken his mind off her body, and reminded him of the time. Which must mean Pack was still alive. "I'm sooo afraid. Come on, soldier, we're going for a walk."

Ah. This was it. "No."

"Oh, yes. You go quietly, or I'll shoot you in the shoulder." He moved aside so there was plenty of room for her to get out the door, gun pointed at her face.

She didn't know what else to do. She walked out. She could feel him right behind her.

"What about the journal?" she said, desperate. They entered the living room.

"If there ever was a journal, it's gone. Move." He gestured at the sliding doors to the patio.

She pulled one open and walked out.

Her brain was atrophying, freezing. "You can't do this, you know. They'll catch you," she said.

The sun was just coming up, somewhere to her right. It was cold, but the air was fresh with a hint of wood smoke. It was good to be outside. "Everybody knows about Haley," she said.

"What about Haley? Now move it."

She turned to him, sensing hesitation. "They know she was hooking. That you pimped her out. It's all in the journal."

Vida saw a flicker of doubt cross his face.

"There's no journal."

"Yes, there is. I remember it. And Haley recorded everything. All the dates she went on, all the money she was paid, how much you made from her."

"Lies."

He grabbed her arm and jerked her around so her back was to him and she was facing the woods. They were at the edge of the deck. She looked down and saw the planks, some black and soft with decay, others bowed up and curled.

Without thinking much about it, she lunged over the edge. He was still holding her, so for a second she had him off balance and his right foot caught one of the boards that had come unanchored from the old framework. He tripped off the deck onto her. Landing, Dax instinctively let go of her arm as he reached for the ground to break his fall. He scrabbled to catch her but she rolled away, just out of reach. She wanted to run for the trees, but she was trapped between him and the patio. She had only a few seconds before he'd manage to grab her.

Without thinking, she dove under the rotting porch and scuttled on all fours deep into the dark crawl space, back toward the house.

With a shout of rage, Dax scrabbled for the pistol in the tall grass. "Bitch."

When he found the weapon, he turned to the deck and crawled in after her, the gun held out in front of him, pointed in her direction, the other hand on the ground. He was forced to move awkwardly, like a three-legged crab.

For once, his superior size and weight worked against him in the confined space. The long, rusted nails protruding beneath the decking caught his shirt, scraping his back. When a sharp rock cut into his right knee, he grunted in pain and jerked away, causing one of the nails to jab his shoulder. He swore and pulled the trigger, shooting furiously into the dark space ahead of him.

"That hurt, bitch," he shouted.

The shots exploded wood chips and dirt back at him. He was sure he heard a cry of pain, but the noise of the revolver in the confined space was so deafening he couldn't be sure. He stopped to take a breath and listened, panting.

Satisfied, he backed his way out from under the patio. Hey, maybe it was all for the best. Who would find her under there? He checked to see how many bullets were left in the chamber. Three. That should do it.

This time, with his head and body in the fresh air, and only his arm under the decking, he methodically spaced his shots from left to right, looking ahead, carefully gauging the direction he was aiming. He was a good shot with a handgun; she didn't stand a chance.

When he'd finished, silence fell. Even the birds were quiet. He lowered his arm and stood up.

And then, pulling him back into another world, his cell phone rang a few short notes, letting him know he had a text message.

CHAPTER 59

For Pack and Millie, every second mattered. But Carla was taking her time. Before they could leave the Albany suburbs, she suddenly turned off the highway. Driving both vehicles, they followed her off the ramp. They watched as she parked outside a Denny's and went inside the diner, her arms wrapped around her body against the cold. She was gone for thirty-five minutes and came out, walking taller, arms swinging.

"Jesus Christ," Millie said, who'd been sitting in the passenger seat of the Town Car. "Look at her. Having a nice breakfast, while Vida's in the hands of her freak boyfriend. Forget that we're starving here. And look at the time. It's already five-fucking-thirty in the morning. Can I kill her?" Millie opened the car door and headed back to her cold truck.

But they had no choice. They continued, caravan-style, toward New Canaan. Their first concern was not losing track of Carla, at least not until they could figure out exactly where she was going. They could stay a good distance behind her most of the way, but as they approached New Canaan they'd have to get close enough to see where she turned or stopped. It wasn't great, but it was the best they could do.

On the drive down, Pack tried to solve the puzzle of why Dax had picked New Canaan. Did he know someone there? Had he rented a place in the area? Could he possibly know that Pack lived there? It seemed unlikely, but . . . Or what if, and this thought really frightened him, what if Carla's trip there had nothing to do with Dax? What if she actually did have a dying aunt, and was going to visit her? Hours had passed since Dax took Vida, and this destination of Carla's was all they had to go on.

So back to the original question: if Dax was actually there, why New Canaan? It was a small, rural community that covered a lot of acres. Even he, Pack, didn't know many folks there, and he'd lived in those woods for years. What reason could Dax have for taking her there? And, for that matter, keeping her alive?

Millie, on the other hand, was thinking about guns.

She had three handguns, a shotgun, and a boatload of ammo in the truck. She was ready for war. Just give her the chance, and she'd take the fucker's head off. And little Miss Carla's, too, if she got in the way. What did Dax want with Vida? He must be afraid that she'd remember something important. Which meant he must've killed the girl, Haley. Millie picked up her phone and dialed as she drove, her truck weaving from side to side as she divided her attention between the road and the number buttons.

"Yeah?" Pack answered.

"He killed the roommate."

"Why do you say that?"

"Why else would he take Vida? It's not about the pimping. He wouldn't risk this much over the pimping. He must be afraid she'll remember something a lot worse."

"That makes sense. Sure. So you think he just wants to shut her up?"

"I'm afraid so."

Pack was silent, fear cramping him. He closed the phone and dropped it in his lap. He'd just found Vida, and now he was close to losing her.

As soon as he thought it, he realized how selfish he sounded, even to himself. Why the hell couldn't he figure out where they were? He slammed his hand against the steering wheel, as if that would jar it free.

By the time he turned off the highway, he could see Carla's vehicle up ahead. He was too close—she was bound to see him at this rate. He put on his signal and turned off at the Hess station. He could grab a cup of Rusty's coffee to keep himself going, meanwhile putting a little distance between himself and her, all at the same time.

Millie pulled in next to him and rolled down her window. "What's up? We're going to lose her."

"You stay on her, I'll be right behind. But don't stay too close. She knows your truck. I need coffee."

Millie nodded and pulled out of the parking lot.

Inside, the place was empty. He could see Rusty through one of the glass side doors, smoking a cigarette outside, talking on the phone. He caught sight of Pack and waved. Pack waved back, poured out a coffee, fixed it with milk and sugar, and brought it to the counter. As he was digging some change out of his pocket, Rusty came in. "You again."

"Hey, Rusty. How goes it?"

"Nearly time to go home, so I'm good."

"How's the little guy?"

"A shining light. Oh, that was him on the phone—he told me to tell you, he knows where to get you that hood ornament for your car. Won't cost you a nickel."

Pack shook his head. Enterprising little bugger. "Tell him thanks, but I'm fine. I like mine just the way it is."

Outside, he walked toward his car. He was about to get in, when he stopped. What had Rusty said? Something about the emblem on his car? He looked at his hood: the emblem was there. Some of the chrome was peeling off, but it was still there.

He put his coffee on the roof of his car and ran back inside. A customer was talking to Rusty, but Pack interrupted. "Rusty, what did you say? About Jake? He said he'd get me a new ornament? Because mine's old?"

Rusty looked up, confused. "No. He said he noticed this morning that yours is missing and—"

"Thanks, man. I love you." Pack ran out the door, pulling his phone from his pocket as he ran. Millie answered on the first ring.

"I know where he has her, Mitch! The bastard's at my house!"

"How'd you figure that?"

"Because of my car—the kid next door, he—doesn't matter! Pull over somewhere and let me get ahead of you, okay?"

He backed out, and the coffee cup was jerked forward, rolled down his windscreen, splashing brown liquid on the glass. Ignoring it, he squealed out of the parking space and back onto the road.

CHAPTER 60

Carla drove leaning forward in her seat, hands gripping the steering wheel. She felt much better since she'd eaten. Now she was eager to get to her destination, to the showdown. She watched for the exit sign off the highway, then turned toward Massachusetts. She drove straight east, glancing occasionally at the mileage counter. One stoplight in a small village, but otherwise she clipped along, only looking in her rear-view mirror when she needed to. She never saw Millie or Pack behind her.

As she got close to the twenty-mile mark, she began looking out for the New Canaan Post Office. The first time, she drove past it and kept going for a couple of miles before she had to admit to herself she'd made a mistake. She turned around and went back. This time she saw the flag flapping overhead.

But when she got there, the post office was closed down tight. Of course, it would be. It was the middle of the night. She looked at her watch. Well, not quite night anymore, being close to six A.M. Still, she had at least two hours to wait before it opened. Damn.

The parking lot was built against a night-black hillside and she could imagine the hungry predators creeping down to find her—coyotes and bears, eyes bright in the deep shadows. She locked her doors.

To keep her mind off the lurking dangers, she turned on the radio to a country-western station, where a peppy DJ played the usual songs about love and loss. Carla knew she should turn it off, but she couldn't: she loved country, but it had an unhealthy effect on her. Sure enough, within minutes she was back to rerunning the images of Dax and Vida, Vida and Dax. Her agitation level began to rise.

She took out her phone and dialed Dax's number. It rang and rang. She hung up before the voice mail message got underway.

"Snake," she said aloud.

She knew what she could do to get him to talk to her.

He'd read a text, she was positive. And if she made it interesting enough, he'd answer. She pecked out: "man looking for u and girl." That should wake him up. And then, unable to resist, she added: "where r u u fukr?"

She pushed SEND.

CHAPTER 61

Just as they were approaching the post office parking lot, they saw Carla turn in, coming from the other direction. "Why'd she come from there?" Millie called Pack to ask him.

"I don't know, but hopefully she's going to sit tight." All Pack could think about was getting to his house. And pray Dax was still there, and Vida was still alive.

A hundred yards further on he turned right, Millie's truck close behind him. They drove for two and a half miles until they reached the un-surfaced road that led to Pack's. A short way in, they got to Rusty's log cabin. There were no vehicles in the area in front of the house and Pack knew that if he left his car there, Rusty would figure he had good reason. He pulled in, turned off the engine, and ran back down the driveway to Millie's idling truck. She'd already opened the door for him, and he pulled himself up into the passenger seat. They took off before the door swung closed.

CHAPTER 62

Carla was right. Dax called her within minutes of getting her text. "What do you want?"

"Hey, you can't just disappear, you know, Dax? I'm not someone you can do that to. I deserve bett—"

"Shut the fuck up. Who's looking for me?"

"Don't talk to me li—"

"Carla, I'll hurt you, I swear. What men, and what did they want? Tell me now, or next time I see you—"

"What are you going to do, huh? I'm not scared of you, you know. I'm going to call the cops the next time you do anything to me."

Though she couldn't know it, the adrenaline was pumping wildly through Dax's veins. If Carla'd been standing next to him he'd have effortlessly put his hands around her neck and pressed the life out of her. He took a deep, shuddering breath and forced a softer tone into his voice. His mind, meanwhile, kept bouncing back to Vida's body, riddled with bullets under the deck. He knew she was dead, but he was going to rip up the planking to make sure.

"Carla, honey, I love you, you know I do. But I'm in a real bind. Do you think I *wanted* to leave you? There are people trying to kill me. I gotta know what's going on. I swear, next time we're together you can get as mad at me as you want."

"You just say that—"

"Tell me now. Right now. Or you'll never see or hear from me again."

She started to cry.

"Please, babe. Talk to me." His grip on the phone tightened, his knuckles bloodless.

"I don't know, some old guy with white hair."

"What did he say, baby?"

She cried out, her voice like a child's: "He says he's the father of that girl who came to see you in the cafeteria, he says you kidnapped her. I went along with it but I know that's not true, I know you're having a thing with her, I know you don't love me any more. I saw the two of you together. And I'm so tired here, I just want to sleep. But the flagpole keeps banging."

Dax envisioned her parked outside the VA hospital. "Come on Carla, you know I love you. Are you about to go into work?"

"Nuh huh."

"Because you're too upset."

"No. Because I don't feel like it."

"You'll feel better once you're inside."

"I'm too far away to get there on time. I had a pre-op call, you know."

"What're you talking about? Where are you?"

"At a post office. In the middle of nowhere."

Suddenly, Dax's world tightened up. He held his breath as what she was saying sank in. "You're where?"

Carla realized she'd made a mistake, but it was too late to rectify it. "A place called New Canaan. At the post office. But they're closed up, I—"

"How did you end up there?"

Carla knew that she couldn't tell him the truth. If she told him she had made a key to his apartment, he'd kill her for sure. She said: "The guy, Pack. He let it drop. Yeah, he said you might be here, so I drove out. But now I'm here, I don't know where to find you."

But Dax had already hung up.

Shit. They were coming. He had to move quickly.

CHAPTER 63

Pack and Millie drove the last half mile to the house in a cloud of dust. When they were within fifty yards, however, they could see there was no vehicle in the driveway. If Dax had been there with a Town Car, he was gone now.

Millie pulled up on the road. "He could still be there. Here, take this," Millie said, reaching into her glove compartment. She handed Pack a black 9mm semi-automatic. It was one of her favorites, her Browning Hi-Power. "Trigger is tough, so nice and steady. Also, look out for the bite—if you get sloppy, it can chew up your hand."

"Great." Pack took it gingerly, checked to see if it was loaded and the safety was on. Millie reached behind their heads and lifted her Beretta 12 gauge shotgun off the rack. She loaded it, and they both climbed out of the pick-up and moved quickly and quietly to the house.

Pack pointed down the ramp toward the raised garage door. He bent over and went in, stood in the darkened space and moved through it as silently as he could, looking for Dax, Vida, or any sign of either of them. When he came out, he signaled to his cousin that he was going around the back.

Millie nodded and walked silently up to the front door. Standing to one side of it, she turned the handle as gently as she could and pushed the door open with the tips of her fingers. It swung back. She waited, listening. When nothing happened, she stepped cautiously inside.

Pack searched the backyard, giving a cursory glance under the deck. He peered through the windows, seeing nothing but Millie standing in the living room. He raised his hand. She nodded.

He slid open the back door and joined her inside. Saw the recliner in the middle of the room.

Millie was now in the kitchen area, checking behind the counter. She registered the drawer and its contents upended on the floor.

She caught Pack's eye, pointed at the short hallway, and moved down it, shotgun held against her right hip. Pack followed.

Bathroom was empty, as was the second bedroom. They moved into Pack's bedroom.

Pack realized he'd been holding his breath, expecting to find Vida's body.

On the floor of his bedroom, he saw the strips of bunched-up duct tape, dotted with blood. "Aw, shit," he said. He bent down to pick them up.

Millie grabbed his arm. "Don't touch 'em."

Pack pulled his hand back and scratched his forehead. "You're right. Oh, Christ, Millie, he's still got her. Somehow he knew we were coming, and he's run with her."

Millie turned toward the front door. "So? We catch him. Let's go."

Pack followed her out and they ran to the truck.

As she fired up the engine, Millie said, "Tell me about this road. Where does it go?"

Pack stared ahead, visualizing the turns. "It dead-ends in about three miles at Blueberry Hill Road."

"If you were him, would you turn left or right?"

"Shit, how should I know?"

"Okay. Does one way lead uphill and one down?"

Pack thought about it. "To the left it's level and then goes down. To the right it gets narrower and goes uphill."

Millie pulled her nose, thinking. "I think he'll go to the left." She put the truck in gear and pulled away from the house. "It leads downhill and north, so it'll feel like he's heading in the general direction of the highway. He'll feel like he's escaping, heading down to the real world. Is he?"

Pack attached his seat belt. "Not for a while. The road levels out and goes through Meizinger's farm. After that it dips down and meets up with the main road. But it takes a while to do it."

Millie nodded and pushed down on the gas. "We just have to follow him, assume he's gone that way, and hope he gets stuck in the mud or something."

She drove hard, focused on avoiding the ruts and holes in the road.

Suddenly, Pack said: "Slow down. Up here, on the left, you can barely make it out." He gestured to a clump of trees by the side of the road.

Hidden among the trees was a track. "What's this?" Millie asked.

"Meizinger's logging road. He doesn't use it much anymore, but it leads right to his farm. Save some time."

"Let's do it." Millie threw the wheel round and the truck bounced onto the uneven surface.

The truck had high clearance and big tires, and it ate up the narrow trail, which was nothing more than a pair of tracks, visible now because the summer undergrowth had died off. A month earlier, it would've been impossible to follow.

Before too long the path smoothed out and they came to the edge of a pasture, enclosed in sagging electrical fencing. The track circled around the outside of the field and they stayed on it, heading toward a ramshackle cluster of buildings visible on the rise before them. Millie sped up, the tires skidding on the muddy track. Pack was thrown from side to side in the cab, his head slamming against the window. The cows in the pasture raised their heads and looked at them. Cresting the rise, they drove into the courtyard of the farm. The road they were heading for divided the buildings of the property in two, the house on one side, the barns and sheds on the other.

There, parked by the house, was a muddy black Lincoln Town Car. A tall, sandy-haired man was standing next to it, talking to the farmer, who was gesturing down the far stretch of road. Both men looked at the filthy red truck as it barreled toward them and slipped to a stop twenty feet away.

Dax was the first one to start moving. At the same time, Millie grabbed the shotgun and Pack threw himself out of the truck yelling: "Get him!"

"Out of the way, move!" Millie yelled as she raised the shotgun. The farmer ran for the house as Dax flung himself into the Town Car and Pack veered to the side, shouting, "The trunk, look out for the trunk!"

The slug burst from the shotgun, just as Dax began to accelerate away. A split second later the left rear tire exploded, throwing shards of black rubber into the air. The Lincoln skidded into a semi-circle and kept going, as Dax tried to right it.

Pack and Millie started running toward the vehicle.

The farmer, who'd made it to the porch of his house, called out: "Pack, he's climbin' out the other side."

Pack nodded. Now they could see Dax emerge, making for tree cover.

Pack said, "Fuck him for now. Let's look for Vida."

He slowed down as he got to the car, and tried to see into the interior, through the tinted glass. He threw open the back door. Nobody on the floor inside. The trunk was locked. In the driver's seat, he pulled the trunk release and Millie opened it.

Pack got out, went to the back of the car, and stood next to her, looking in.

But there was nothing. Empty.

"The bastard already got rid of her." Pack had to fight back despair.

Millie grabbed him by the shoulder. "We're going back to the house. We'll find her there." And to the farmer, he said: "That guy's bad news, he's abducted and possibly harmed Pack's daughter. Call the cops and lock yourself and the family in. You got a gun? Load it. Oh, and disable this car. Shoot it or something."

The farmer nodded and hustled back into the house, looking toward the tree line where Dax had disappeared.

The cousins climbed back in their truck, doors slamming. Millie reversed and turned it around. She drove as fast as she could back to Pack's house.

CHAPTER 64

Dax ran until he knew no one was following him. The trees had become thick and if he turned to look behind himself, he could no longer see the pastures of the farmhouse he'd just left.

Panting, he wished he had something to drink or even a hard candy. A Life Saver, he thought, and didn't see any irony in the thought. He touched his pockets, hoping to find something, and that's when he thought of his phone. How could he forget his phone? He pulled it out of his pocket and checked for service. There were three bars. He smiled. Service, for the woodchucks. Now that was progress. He thought for a moment, then hit Carla's number.

CHAPTER 65

Back at Pack's house, Millie began to search every corner in the house, while Pack tore apart the garage. He dug through the boxes, ripping open anything that might be big enough to hide a small body. He moved mattresses and toys, looked in the crawl spaces near the water heater and pump, but came up with nothing.

Outside, he walked around the house, searching for telltale signs. At the rear of the house the weeds had been flattened around the back porch, but that was probably how Dax had first broken in, so it didn't mean much. He also noticed a freshly split board, where someone may have climbed on or off. He thought of the worn duct tape, pulled off and left lying on his bedroom floor. He wondered if Vida had attempted to escape out the back door. Maybe.

He climbed onto the patio and looked around, hoping to find something, some little detail that would tell him what had happened.

Millie appeared in the French doors. "Anything?" she said. Her red wig was tangled and her smudged blue eye shadow made her look sickly, but her gaze was hard and fixed on Pack.

Pack shook his head. "I can't figure out what went down. I think she got free, but did she get away—and if she did, where the hell is she? Wouldn't we have found her on the road?"

"Not if she went to someone's house looking for help."

"True. Or she could have headed out there and then gotten

lost." Pack stood with his back to the house, looking out over the woods. "We've got to call the cops."

"Meizinger already did. They're on their way."

Pack was still staring at the trees and the dead and tangled growth behind his house. "Look at that. Do you see where it looks paler?"

"No." Millie squinted at the trees, trying to see what Pack saw. "Why would it get paler?"

"There, see?" Pack grabbed her shoulder and pointed. "As if someone walked through there, flattening the weeds; it looks different from the rest."

"I don't see it, but let's check it out." Millie went to the edge of the porch and hopped down, grunting as she released herself from the planking. "Hey, look at this." She squatted down on the ground. "Casings."

Pack climbed down next to her and stared. There were two spent shells in the ground. They searched the ground for more, found another one, and finally, a fourth. "No blood that I can see," Pack said. "He was shooting after her. They're close to the porch, maybe he was standing on the edge here, firing into the trees. Which might mean she got away. Come on, let's go."

He started toward the woods, trying to keep track of the faint shadowing he'd seen in the shrubs and weeds. Millie followed, looking from side to side.

"Vida!" Pack called. But in the silence that followed, all they heard was the low hum of the woods around them, the rustling of leaves, distant birdcalls. About a hundred feet in, the trees changed from leafless deciduous to a stand of white pine. Under the dark cover of greenery, the undergrowth thinned down to nothing. Their feet crunched on the bed of brown needles and the air seemed cooler, smelling of warm mulch, a woodsy decay.

"What're we looking for?" Millie asked, her voice low.

"Anything. Doesn't matter. Maybe she dropped something,

maybe we'll find footprints."

"We should walk side by side, about twenty feet apart," Millie suggested. "It'll give us a wider range."

"Okay," Pack nodded. He moved over as Millie caught up with him. They could now see each other and comb the area around them.

They walked for about five minutes, until Millie pointed at something. "Hey, look at this."

"What?"

"Pile of rocks," Millie said, walking a few feet out of her way.

She stopped by a mound of freshly turned earth and stones. It was next to an indentation in the ground that looked like a giant's footprint, about four feet long by three across and maybe a foot deep.

Pack dropped to his knees and touched the bottom of the hole. It was hard and root lined, obviously the bottom. He began pulling the stones and earth off the pile next to it. He flung them to the side, digging under the soft soil. Millie quickly joined him. But they soon reached the hard untouched earth underneath.

"Scared the shit out of me," Pack said.

"He was going to bury her here." Millie stood slowly, pushing off from her knees.

They spent twenty minutes zigzagging in the woods around the house, calling out for Vida and listening for an answer. Finally, they headed back. When they broke out of the trees, they were met by two burly young police officers standing on the rotting back deck, weapons drawn and pointed at them. "Don't move!"

Millie raised her hands above her head. "Hey, hey, I called it in. Call Major Houser in Albany. Tell her Officer Mitch Jedd and his cousin are trying to save a young woman and apprehend a kidnapper. Do it now—please."

The officer stared dumbly at her. "What's with the hair?"

Millie shut her eyes. "I'm undercover." She lifted her wig. "See?"

Pack had returned the Hi-Power to Millie, who had unloaded it and tucked it away into a holster under her waistband. Her wig was stuffed carelessly in her pocket, her expression dark. "I want him. It's killing me. He's nearby, but he's getting away."

Pack nodded. "Yeah, and if he decides not to talk, we may never find where he stashed her. There may be a way to get him if it's not too late. Go after the girlfriend, Carla. You know he's contacted her—probably why she's around here in the first place—she's come to pick him up. If she hasn't already."

Millie nodded, an ugly glint in her eye. "Yeah, of course. We could force her to team up with us, and then we'd wait for him to appear." She dropped her voice. "Or the cops could wait for him. I could go in after him."

Pack loved that look in his cousin's eye. "If anyone can do it, you can."

"With luck, he's still in the woods, Officers," Millie said, turning to the two young men who were emerging from a search of the house. "We have a plan you might like to be part of."

"Yeah?" The heavier, red-faced officer sounded suspicious but his partner looked at Millie, eyes bright with interest.

"It entails a two-pronged ambush. The guy has a girlfriend who's waiting down the hill for him, at the post office. You all wait with her, grab him when he shows up. I wait at the Meizinger farm at the top of the hill, just in case he decides to double back to his vehicle."

"Sounds reasonable," said the suspicious one. "Let me speak to the chief."

While the two cops were out of hearing, Millie turned to Pack. "What about you?" she asked.

"I've got to stay here and keep looking. She's gotta be somewhere near here." He grabbed her shoulder. "Get him, okay?"

"With pleasure."

CHAPTER 66

Millie drove back to the Meizinger farmhouse. Dax's Town Car was where he had abandoned it, resting lopsidedly on one wheel rim, the trunk still open. The hood was up, too. She guessed the farmer had disabled it.

The officers had agreed to call when they located the girlfriend. While she waited, Millie reloaded her Hi-Power and her shotgun, filled her pockets with spare shells, and locked the truck. She'd told the officers she wanted to stay there so she could keep an eye on the woods, in case he reappeared. She hadn't told them she was going in after him.

She knocked on the farmhouse door, and when the farmer unlocked it and stepped out, she said: "I'm going to try to find this guy."

The farmer nodded.

"What direction would you guess he's going to take?" she said.

The man rubbed his nose, then pointed across the dirt road toward his barn. "There's a creek runs right through the property, nearest point's right about there, past that big oak. It heads down to the valley. If you follow it, you can cut off a lot of time."

"How do I know which direction he'll take?"

"When you first drove up, he was just askin' me how to get to the main road. That's where he's headed. Where he went in," and now he pointed the other way, where they'd last seen Dax, "there's an old trail. For hunting, mostly. He's most likely goin' to follow it. It makes a big loop, then meets up with the creek. Day like today, cloudy, he won't know he's not going straight. But once he gets to the creek, he can follow the water all the way down to the road. Of course, he may do somethin' different, but I'd bet on him following that trail."

"What about the road? What if he made it over to the county road and followed it down?"

The fellow shrugged. "He'd get there. But he'd have to cross the creek to get to the road. Creek's a lot faster."

"Got it. Thanks."

"I hope to hell you get him. I can't stay inside much longer, I got chores that won't keep."

Alone, Millie leaned on the front of the truck and waited. Four minutes later, her phone rang.

It was the red-faced officer.

"Did you pick her up?" Millie asked.

"Man, that woman is difficult."

"Did she tell you about Dax?"

"Yeah."

"What did she say?"

"We threatened her a bit, you know, nothin' serious. Finally told us he phoned her a while back, said he'd call her again as soon as he made it out of the woods to the road."

"So he's still out there."

"Seems likely. I figure we get a couple more cars out here, put extra men along the road, and just wait for him to show up. Then we grab him. Easy."

"I hope so," said Millie. "But don't leave that woman alone with her cell. She'll try to warn him."

"I got that little sucker right here in my pocket. When he calls, I'll be breathing down her neck."

"Hmm. Hey, if someone comes out of the trees, look before

you shoot. It might be me."

"Why you? You said you're just waiting up top for him."

"Yeah, well I can't sit around here, doin' zip. Oh, by the way, the farmer here says, if Dax finds the creek, he can follow it smack down to the road. So you might want to find out where it comes out."

Without waiting for a response, she closed the phone.

CHAPTER 67

Dax was no outdoorsman, but he was strong and confident. How could there be anything he couldn't handle in a small wooded area forty minutes from a major city? He wasn't in the middle of the Rockies. He'd do fine.

After his initial sprint into the cover of the trees, he'd waited, listening for pursuit. But once the voices at the farmhouse had died down, he started moving again, hearing nothing but his own footfalls as he rustled and crunched through the layer of dried leaves and scrub that blanketed the uneven ground. Before too long, he found what seemed like a path—or at least a kind of trail less overgrown than the rest of the woods.

Though it was early morning, the sky was heavy and overcast and the trees, some leafless, some evergreen, created a dark, cavernous world. Occasionally, his way was blocked by a fallen trunk or limb, and he had to avoid sharp branches that seemed to lunge at him like pitchforks. The air was musty, with pockets of dead animal stink.

Good thing he had Carla waiting for him down the hill. He'd forgotten how angry he'd been at her, and was beginning to think of her appearance as a piece of the larger plan, one he'd purposefully set in motion.

He looked forward to getting behind the wheel of her car and driving back to Albany. If worse came to worse, they could get money out of her ATM and spend the night in a hotel. A few days to find a good lawyer, and these jokers wouldn't be able to touch him. Hell, there was no proof he'd killed the girl—it was going to be Pack's word against his. Pack's gun, Pack's daughter. Anyway, Pack was a much more likely candidate—living in squalor like that. A misfit, no question.

Half an hour later, the ground began to slope downward. Must mean he was heading to the road. Great, he was on his way. His stride was long and relaxed, and he was making good progress. The only problem was Pack's shoes squeezing his toes in a death grip and rubbing his heels raw.

God, he was thirsty. Hungry, too. But it was no big deal, he'd eat when he got home. He just really needed some water. This made him think of Vida, leaning over the sink and drinking from the tap. The picture intensified his thirst.

Ten minutes later, the land leveled out. There was still no break in the trees and he was beginning to feel a little low, a touch light-headed.

Maybe it was the shoes, or maybe his flagging energy but, not stepping high enough, he jammed his foot, full force, against a rock hidden under a soft pile of dark red leaves. Suddenly off-balance, he stumbled and fell hard, his shin making contact with the rock as he hit the ground.

He lay there, curled up, hands on his leg, the pain excruciating. All he could do was moan through clenched teeth. His hand was hurting too; he must've broken his fall with it.

At last the worst wave passed and he was able to relax the muscles in his neck and face and take a breath. He allowed himself to lie there, eyes closed, resting.

He must've passed out. A tickling on his arm woke him. He scratched it. His side was cold where he'd been lying. He pulled up his pant leg, gently, and examined the gouge in his shin. Nasty looking, a little pulpy around the edges, still white, but would soon change to dark red. He prodded it, then wiggled his toes. He pulled the fabric back down to cover it.

He groaned and stood up slowly, weight on his good leg, brushing off the dirt and crud. He put his foot down and shifted his weight, testing it. Nothing serious, he thought with relief. No big deal. In a few hours he'd be somewhere he could ice it and disinfect the cut.

He looked at his sore palm. It was the same one that had been pierced by a splinter four days earlier at Pack's house, and he wondered if he'd hit the same spot. He pressed it and was amazed at the jolt of pain. Looking carefully, he saw the redness was centered around the place where the splinter had gone in. A streak of red ran from the center of the wound, up the inside of his wrist.

Great. Blood poisoning, of course—from all that foul rotten wood. He felt a flush of rage at Pack and his cheeks began to heat up. "Fucking slob," he said out loud. If he had Vida here, he'd kill her all over again. And if Pack were watching, he'd do it slowly.

Regretfully, he broke out of his fantasy. Time to get moving.

He walked on, this time more slowly. Was he still on the path? He looked around. Nothing but shitty trees everywhere. He wasn't certain which direction he'd come from. He looked up at the sky. If the sun were out, he'd be able to figure out which way was north. Maybe. But it wasn't, and the sky was a dull, uniform dark gray.

Just then he felt a drop of rain on his face, as if someone in a tree had spat on him. Fuck. He wiped it off and stared at the wall of green.

And then he noticed the trees seemed a little thinner, a little shorter, off to his right. Was it a clearing? He moved cautiously toward it and found himself standing on the low bank of a shallow creek. The bed was all rounded rocks, and the water, though only about a foot deep, was moving along it at a good pace. It looked clear and clean.

He squatted next to it and tried to shovel a handful of water into his mouth. When it leaked out his fingers, he was forced to lean over and lap it up like a dog. Humiliating, he thought. But no one was watching. He just hoped it wasn't full bacteria and organisms. He'd have to get on a course of strong antibiotics when he got back to the real world.

When his thirst was quenched, he sat back, pulled up his pant leg again, and dabbed water on his cut shin. Then he made himself comfortable and held his sore hand in the cold running water. Ahh. The relief. He put his other hand to his forehead. He was a little warm, probably from the running.

After a minute, his hand grew numb. He stood up, stiffly.

He'd follow the stream. Water flowed downhill, so it had to be the most direct route down the hill. Unless it was going down the wrong hill, but he couldn't worry about that.

And then, from somewhere upstream, he heard the loud reverberating snap of wood. A dried branch cracking underfoot. Something or someone was moving toward him. Okay, he should reload the handgun he'd taken from Pack's house. He'd grabbed a handful of extra bullets, so he was fine. But when he reached in his pocket, the gun was gone. Damn. He thought back. It must've fallen out when he tripped.

Fucking Vida and her fucking old men. Fucking rock.

Chapter 68

Millie was no tracker, so she took the farmer's advice and stayed with the creek, rather than trying to follow Dax. He had close to an hour's lead on her, and she'd never make that up without a shortcut.

She didn't know if he knew much about the outdoors, but he was a combat veteran, armed with a handgun that might or might not be loaded. Plus, he was a lot younger than her. So she had to go carefully.

She kept her eyes moving and looked for overturned vegetation, crushed leaves, and broken twigs—any fresh disturbance that might be a sign someone had recently passed through.

The creek went downhill steeply for a while, creating small whitecaps when it broke around rocks and boulders. It had been a wet fall, and all the waterways were running, even those that had been dry most of the summer.

After a while, the ground leveled out. Millie cursed herself when she unwittingly stepped on a branch and it snapped noisily. She paused, letting the silence gather around her, hoping no one was close enough to have heard.

Eventually, she started moving again, this time more cautiously, watching where she put each foot.

The stream took a detour around a cluster of large pine trees, roots partially exposed by erosion. Millie could see, past them, where the stream reappeared on the other side. She headed straight for it.

The pines were thick, with small saplings filling the gaps between the mature growth, making the whole stand dense and impossible to see through.

Though she was being careful, she was certain Dax was far ahead of her, hurrying down the hill to freedom. It didn't seem possible she might've already caught up to him. So, coming around the pine outcropping, she had no warning he was waiting for her—a heavy limb in his hands like an ungainly baseball bat, pulled back and ready to swing.

As soon as she cleared the last tree he struck at her, too low to hit her in the face, but across the top of the chest. Her torso was propelled back, her legs forward. She lost her hold on the shotgun and it flew to the side.

CHAPTER 69

As soon as she went down, Dax ran to Millie. She was winded and gasping for air. He hit her again, and she stopped moving.

Who the fuck was this guy? It wasn't Pack. He'd been driving the truck earlier. Could be the cousin. Big son-of-a-bitch. He dragged her, unresisting, to the stream and rolled her into it so she was face down in the water. This way if he dies, Dax said to himself, it'll look like an accident. How had the cousin known where to find him? If he knew, the cops knew too. Dax pulled out his cell phone and called Carla. The phone rang and rang, and just as it was about to go to voice mail she answered, her voice going in and out, as if the phone were moving away from her, then too close. What was she doing?

"Carla?" he said. "That you?"

There was a pause. What was that noise in the background?

"Yes, Dax, it's me."

"What's going on?"

And then suddenly she started shouting into the phone, "Run, run, the cops're here, run," and Dax could hear a man's voice, raised, followed by a cry. Then the phone went dead.

With a roar of anger, Dax flung the phone away as if it were a hot coal. It ricocheted off an old maple and disappeared in the underbrush.

What was he supposed to do now? He gave Millie a vicious kick, then reached down, rolled her over, and searched her pockets. He found the keys to the truck and the spare shells for the shotgun. When he found the magazines for the 9mm, he searched her again until he found the Browning. "Shit, tried to hide that, didn't you?" he muttered, checking that the safety was on before he shoved it into his waistband.

He put the ammunition into his pockets and held the keys, thinking, clenching and unclenching his hand around them. The action seemed to calm him. Retrieving the shotgun, he checked it: loaded. He trotted over to where he'd seen the phone hit the tree, and searched the grasses, but no luck. Fuck it.

Dax hefted the shotgun and held it diagonally in front of him. His nerves were still jangling from Carla's warning, but a sense of calm and goodwill began to spread from his arms through the rest of him. It wasn't as fulfilling as his old rifle, but still, holding it made him feel like a better man—righteous, powerful, someone you don't mess with—like the soldier on that first recruitment poster he'd seen.

He stepped back into the water and started moving upstream, in the direction Millie had come from. Leaning forward, he moved agilely from stone to stone. He'd learned that dogs couldn't track a scent across or through water. He didn't know where he'd picked it up—some dog TV show, but it made sense. So bring on the hounds—it didn't matter, they'd never catch him.

Millie opened her eyes just in time to see Dax disappearing upstream, hopping from stone to stone. Shit. Her Beretta. She loved that shotgun. Where the hell was he going?

Achingly, she hoisted her body out of the water and looked in her pocket for her phone. Not there. She went to the spot where the bastard had ambushed her and searched the ground, but it was nowhere in sight. Her entire chest ached and she pressed her fingers into it, wondering if any ribs were broken.

She was still wearing her holster, so she didn't realize the Hi-

Power was gone until she reached for it. Her heart sank. She'd really fucked up. But she had no choice, she had to go after him.

She wasn't quite sure why he was walking in the stream, but he had her keys and he must have figured her truck was at the farmhouse. And however fast he could stone-hop, she could go faster on solid ground, no matter how rough the terrain. At times she had to clamber over rock piles and fallen trees, but it didn't take long before she was close enough to see his bobbing head ahead of her. She widened her distance from the edge of the water and circled around, ducking and weaving between the trees, trying to be as quiet as possible, and still close the gap.

Dax made it up to the farm in a fraction of the time it had taken him to get down. He stood for a moment at the tree line, assessing the situation. The place looked deserted. The only vehicles he could see were his car, obviously out of commission, and the red pick-up that had come after him, driven by the big man he'd left downstream. He didn't waste any time on his car, but made his way as quickly as possible to the truck, taking the keys out of his pocket as he moved.

The lights flashed as he unlocked it remotely, and once in the cab, the powerful engine started without a hiccup. He backed out quickly and pulled away from the farmhouse. He wouldn't go down the hill to the main road, he'd go back out past Pack's house and leave in the opposite direction. They'd never expect him to go that way or move that fast, so he had a good chance of getting away.

CHAPTER 70

Pack had been out in the woods and searched and called until he was hoarse. At last, back at the house, he stood on the edge of the patio and scratched his head vigorously, with both hands, as if to shake away old ideas and allow new blood into his brain.

He climbed down and stood next to the shell casings on the ground. He looked carefully at them, looked at the house, out at the woods, knelt and looked under the porch a second time. That's when he saw the heavy crawl marks, crushed weeds, and furrowed ground.

He stood for a moment, lost in thought.

Excited, he walked quickly around the house and down the ramp into the garage.

He shoved his way through the cartons and possessions, heading for the back of the garage. At the far wall, he came to his last obstacle—a tall shelving unit, thick with dust and stacked with half-empty cans of paint, rusted tools, jars of nails. He dragged it away from the wall, and when it caught on the floor and toppled over with a crash onto a stack of boxes, he ignored it.

He had uncovered what he was looking for: a small rectangular awning window, about a foot high by two feet wide. It was high up on the cinderblock wall, originally put in to provide cross-ventilation for the garage. The top of the window was just below ground level—he remembered it had a small well in the earth in front of it.

The porch had been added a few years after the original construction, covering the window and blocking any daylight from coming through it. As time went by, the opening, buried behind shelves and unused possessions, was forgotten. It was thick with cobwebs and the small pane so streaked with dirt, visibility through it was impossible.

Pack pulled an old chair up to the wall and stood on it, testing his weight so he wouldn't break through the seat. His eyes were level with the window. He rubbed at the dirt with his hand, cleaning a small circle. He moved his head away, trying to adjust his vision.

He would have expected there to be enough morning light filtering through the wide gaps in the old deck to enable him to make out a faint glimmer, but he couldn't see anything. Maybe the window well had filled with debris. He enlarged the circle, and when that didn't work, he tried cranking open the window. Nothing. It wouldn't budge. But then, it had probably been stuck for years, he thought, angry at himself for letting everything go to hell.

And then, suddenly, he saw it. Like one of those magic eye tricks, it was all in how he looked at it. What appeared as a looming depth of darkness out the small window wasn't actually what it seemed. In reality, it was black fabric, pressed against the glass. Which made no sense, except it was what he was looking and hoping for. A black piece of clothing, maybe a t-shirt. Pressed hard against the glass, because there was a person in it.

Vida lay curled in the window well. And her back was three inches from Pack's face.

Pack went to work tearing up the section of deck that was nearest the house. It wasn't hard, given the condition of the lumber. He worked fast, trying to keep the fear at bay, heaving the long, rotting boards aside as they came free.

It took him ten minutes to rip a hole big enough to reach his daughter. He found her curled in the window well, her clothing sticky with blood, her eyes closed. She looked bad.

His own heart seemed to slow down and, though he'd been sweating, his fingertips were icy cold. He rubbed his hands together, trying to warm them, before putting them on her neck, looking for a pulse.

He couldn't find one.

Fighting panic, he pulled out his cell and called 911. Then he hoisted himself up to the open sliding doors, ran into his bedroom, and tore a blanket off the mattress. Outside again, he placed it on the ground next to Vida. "It's okay, everything's going to be fine," he murmured, trying to believe it.

He knew it was dangerous to move her, but he was more afraid of leaving her in there. Maybe he couldn't feel a heartbeat because she was curled up so tight, her chin tucked against her chest. Hell, he was no nurse, but she looked like she could suffocate, jammed in there.

Jesus, she was so damn small.

Taking a deep breath, he knelt over her and, as gently as he could, slid his hands under her body and pulled her slowly out. Then he laid her on the blanket and wrapped it around her, cocooning her. Carefully, he picked her up and carried her to the front of the house to wait for the ambulance.

He heard an engine in the distance. That was fast. Thank god.

But once it crested the rise, he realized it wasn't an ambulance. It was Millie's truck, hurtling down the road toward him.

His heart soared. Trust Millie to save the day.

Dax took the dirt road as fast as he safely could, aware that if he made it to West Bantam he had a good chance of getting to the highway. He had to distance himself from this mess, and then he'd be in the clear. With Vida dead, they had nothing on him—other than taking this truck for a joy ride. A good lawyer would find some way around that. He'd pay a fine, maybe.

As he came over the last hump in the road before Pack's house, he saw a white-haired man standing by the mailbox, his arms full with a long bundle. Actually, it looked like a body. Looked like Pack, Vida's father. Shit—he must've found the girl. She couldn't still be alive, could she? Dax slowed down, trying to think.

He saw Pack grin and raise his arms, as if presenting the body to him. He looked like he was moving into the road, as if to meet the truck partway.

And then Dax watched his expression change, as the truck drew closer and as Pack realized the man driving it wasn't who he expected. His smile collapsed, replaced by surprise and shock. He started backing up to the house, still holding the girl.

Shit, Dax thought again. Now the fucker would get on the phone and call the cops and they'd know exactly where he was, what he was driving, and what direction he was heading in. Without giving it much thought, Dax turned the wheel, stepped on the accelerator, and headed straight for the man and his bundle.

Millie sat in the passenger seat as the farmer backed the old Taurus out of the barn. His truck was at the shop, so Millie's choice had been to be driven in the old sedan, or ride on the back of a tractor. When she'd insisted he bring a weapon, Meizinger had produced an old Remington bolt-action rifle.

"God Almighty. This the best you got?" Millie asked.

"Hey, you want it or not? I'm not usually lookin' to chase killers, you know," the farmer grumbled.

In the car, she worked the bolt, making sure it moved smoothly, then loaded it.

"My dad got that at Montgomery Ward back in the sixties." Meizinger shot it a glance as he drove, as if he were afraid Millie might toss it out the window.

"And you haven't used it since, right?"

They were headed in the direction of Pack's house. She figured, because Dax knew that road, he'd go back that way. If he didn't, he ran the risk of getting lost on the winding back roads, and at this point that was something he couldn't afford to do. Or that's what she hoped.

She was furious at herself for losing control of the situation. She's promised Pack she'd handle the guy, and instead the man had made off with her truck and her weapons.

"Can you give it some gas?" she asked Meizinger, doing her best to keep the impatience out of her voice. He nodded, and when they turned down Pack's road the worn tires slipped before they regained traction. "Woops," said her driver.

"We've got to stop at Pack's house," Millie said.

If he was still there, Millie planned to let him know what was going on and make a call to the troopers waiting pointlessly at the post office. Then she'd find the bastard, no matter what.

Ahead of her, she saw the red of her truck. She'd guessed right. Good. "There he is," she said, pointing.

The farmer nodded. He was leaning forward, clutching the wheel. He accelerated. The Taurus rattled harder.

Pack had been so focused on Vida, first on finding her and then on getting her to the people that could save her, that he couldn't take in what was happening right in front of him.

When he first saw Millie's truck, it seemed like all the pieces were coming together. He'd found Vida, now Millie was showing up. The paramedics had to be only minutes away. Luck was beautifully on his side.

So it took him slow seconds to understand that the red truck was not being driven by Millie, but by the man who wanted his daughter dead.

He looked at the fast-approaching face of the man behind the wheel, his mouth open, an expression on his face that looked like excitement and he got it, finally. The son-of-a-bitch was going to run them both down. He turned and started to move awkwardly toward the house, Vida tight to his chest.

Behind him, he heard a loud crack as Dax hit the old, tilting mailbox. He didn't turn back to look. He heard the roar of the truck gaining on him and leaped to the side, out of its path. He could feel the heat from the engine as it passed him, inches to spare.

The air was filled with the smell of exhaust. Quickly he lay Vida down on the ground, butted up against the side of house. The truck would have to ram the house to touch her.

Desperately, he looked around for something to use as a weapon.

The truck had braked, and was now backing away fast in a smooth curve.

Pack knew what was going to happen. This man wouldn't drive away. He wanted to kill them. In a few seconds, he would put the truck in gear again and take another run at them, and if he had to ram the house, he would.

He had only seconds left. Pack started chasing after the truck. Just as it slammed to a halt, ready to go forward, Pack grabbed up the old mailbox post that was lying on the lawn, the box still attached to the cracked 4 x 4 post. Without hesitating, he ran to the truck and smashed the box down into the driver's window.

The window was partially open, and Dax yanked his head out of the way as the old metal cylinder came into the opening after him. His foot must've slipped off the brake, because the truck began moving backward again.

Pack hit the window a second time, harder, and now the mailbox broke off inside the cab, hitting Dax on the forehead.

Dax reached up to protect himself, and Pack, still running next to the truck, which was now moving across the road, was able to grab the handle and wrench open the door with his left hand, still holding the post with his right. Blood had welled out of the cut on Dax's forehead. Pack swung and hit at Dax again, this time getting him on the shoulder. Dax cried out and leaned forward, his head down, hands out of sight. Pack felt a rush of pleasure at the sound. He wanted to hit him again, and hear him cry out, and then do it over and over until there was no sound left in the fucker. He pulled his arm back, getting read to strike him across his back.

And then something was driven into his stomach, and he doubled over, knocked from the door of the cab. He stumbled away, gasping. Dax had picked up the shotgun from the floor of the cab and had rammed it, stock first, into his middle.

From where he was, Pack could see Dax was trying to turn the shotgun around, so the killing end would be facing him. He scrabbled to his feet and made a lunge for the weapon. He had to reach it before Dax could fire it. He saw Dax's finger curl around the trigger, but he ignored the warning and lunged for the barrel.

Just in time, he grabbed it and shoved it away from his body. The gun went off with a blast. For a second, both men seemed to reel from the explosion.

Pack's hands could feel the heat in the barrel, but he didn't let go. He had to believe there was a shot left. Before Dax could recover, he pulled the barrel, hard, catching Dax off-balance and yanking him out of the truck and onto the ground.

Dax howled in anger and held on to the weapon, managing to pull it into his body so he had more control. He swiveled on the ground, trying to get enough traction so he could stand, while kicking out, trying to move Pack into the range of fire.

When the shotgun went off a second time, it rocked them like a cannon. The stock had recoiled against Dax's rib cage, and he let go of the gun, pulled his knees up to his chest, and rolled onto his side, groaning.

Pack got shakily to his feet, looking around for a rock big enough to smash the man's head in, oblivious to the old gray sedan that had skidded to a stop forty feet away.

It didn't have to be sharp, just heavy. Dax's head would crack like a rotten egg. He saw one, right by the side of the gravel road.

Millie was already out of the old sedan. She rested her elbows on the hood, and peered down at the sight. She took a steadying breath.

Dax opened his eyes. He saw Pack pick up the rock and carry it awkwardly toward him. He struggled to free the Hi-Power from the waistband of his snugly fitting jeans. When he had it in his right hand, he used his left to fumble for the safety.

He took aim and started to squeeze the trigger.

But he didn't know how stiff the old pistol was and before he could pull it all the way home, Millie fired the hunting rifle.

Dax jerked, grunted, writhed once, and lay still.

A second later Pack, unstoppable, dropped the rock onto the dying man's head.

CHAPTER 71

The State Troopers were the first to arrive, followed by the ambulance. Vida was taken to Albany Med, a paramedic beside her. Pack and Millie were hustled off to the barracks to give their statements.

By the time Pack made it to the hospital, Vida was being wheeled out of surgery.

The ER doctor said that Vida had been lucky—the bullet had gone through the muscle of her upper arm; no bones shattered, no important blood vessels torn. She'd lost blood and had a variety of lacerations and other minor injuries. A night or two in the hospital, barring complications, and Pack could take her home.

Vida slept most of what was left of the day while Pack sat in the chair next to her, an open paperback in his lap, watching her sleep. She had bruises on her wrists and the skin on her face was raw and chapped where Dax had taped her mouth.

Vida opened her eyes in the early evening. She saw him reading next to her and said, her voice a croak: "What's the book?"

"Hey, welcome back, sweetheart." He paused, embarrassed by his own endearment, then turned the book over and read the back: "*Luck of the Moon:* A werewolf with a heart of gold wins the lottery and sets out to help all the people who stood by him during his early years."

"Wow," she said. "Did you pick it out?"

"Found it in the waiting room. How're you doing?"

"I'm okay. A little out of it."

"Any pain?"

"Not much. Did they dope me up?"

"Yup. Gonna be sore when it wears off."

"When can I get out of here?"

"They want to keep you at least one night, make sure there's no infection. Maybe tomorrow."

"That's good." Her eyes drifted shut again and she slept.

At six P.M. an orderly brought in a tray. Pack helped her sit up.

She looked at the food and grimaced. "Can't you get me something good, Pack?"

He found a diner a few blocks away and picked up a hot pastrami sandwich, a cheeseburger, mac and cheese, and a Greek salad. He figured whatever she didn't want, he'd eat.

When he got back to the hospital room, Millie was sitting on the edge of Vida's bed. She was wearing a clean skirt and a sleeveless yellow top that showed off her muscular arms. Her wig was back in place, brushed and neat.

"Hey!" Pack said, putting down the large take-out bag. "How did it go?"

Millie was pale and her face seemed less elastic than it had before. The grooves on either side of her mouth seemed deeper. She didn't answer, just looked at Vida.

"What's up?" he asked, looking at his daughter.

"Dax is dead. Millie shot him," Vida said, and started to cry quietly.

Pack hesitated, unsure of how to comfort her. "I know. She saved my life. Hey, I tried to do it, but I only dented him." He turned to his cousin. "You okay?"

Millie thought for a moment, then nodded. "No regrets. He'd have killed you both."

"Most likely."

"I'm glad he's dead," Vida said, wiping her eyes.

Awkwardly, Pack reached over and patted her shoulder. "I know. Me too."

"I mean it. I do."

"Yup. I'm just sorry we had to do it. Well, Millie, really."

After a moment of silence, Vida added, "If only he'd hit a land mine."

"Amen to that," said Millie.

Just as they were about to eat, a couple of detectives from the BCI, the plainclothes branch of the troopers, showed up to interview Vida. Millie took a walk and came back with a six-pack of beer packed discreetly in a brown paper bag. When the detectives finally left, they each popped a can and shared the cold diner food.

After Millie had gone home, Pack made himself comfortable on the chair next to Vida's bed. The nurse on call tried to make him leave, but he said, "Hey, look at it this way—I'm doing you a favor. She needs anything during the night, I'm here to get it for her. All I need is a blanket. D'you have an extra blanket?"

Sure enough, during the night he helped her to the bathroom, got her a glass of cold water, and gave her a pill for the pain. When she groaned and tossed, he held her hand. Softly, he sang:

> *"Hush little baby, don't say a word,*
> *Papa's going to buy you a mockingbird,*
> *If that mockingbird don't sing,*
> *Papa's going to buy you a diamond ring—"*

It was all he could remember of the song, so he sang it over and over again until her sleep became less agitated.

By morning, Vida was pale but clear-eyed and ready to go home. She turned down the routine pain killers, saying she'd take an over-the-counter pill if she needed it. The nurse looked skeptical, but left her alone. The doctor came to see her, looked at the wound, and told her she could go home if she wore a sling and didn't move for a week.

"I love doing nothing," she said.

He also told her that it was a gunshot wound, and he'd had to report it to the police. So she couldn't leave until she cleared it with them. "I love doing nothing," she said.

By the time they pulled into the driveway at Millie's house, Vida was pale and worn out. The red pick-up was nowhere in sight.

Inside the house, everything was as Pack had left it when he'd driven up to Albany, looking for John Dax. It was strange to think that was less than forty-eight hours earlier. It seemed like a slow-moving year since he'd set out.

He got Vida comfortable on the crushed velvet sofa in the living room, the small television on, rabbit ears perfectly positioned for one of three available channels. "You need anything?"

"Nope."

"Hungry?"

She thought about it. "Can I have pancakes?"

"Pancakes?" he said, feeling a wave of panic. He didn't know how to make pancakes. "Sure, fine."

He went into the kitchen and looked around. He opened the cupboards, one at a time, looking for a mix. He found cans of peas and beans, he found jars of sauce and pickles, and in the freezer he found popsicles. But no pancake mix.

Finally he turned to the bookshelf. There was no help for it. He was going to have to find a recipe.

When the doorbell rang twenty minutes later, he had eggs and flour and milk and baking powder and salt and sugar, all lined up on the counter. He needed a mixing bowl. He went to answer the door.

Standing on the step was a middle-aged couple, both in jeans; the woman was small and slim, with short hair, a little brown left in the gray, her face lined but still attractive. The man was tall, with a thin, rangy body. His long gray hair was tied in a thin braid; he had deep lines on each side of his mouth. A large, pale blue suitcase rested on the step between them.

"Hello, Pack," said Shelley, Vida's mother.

Pack stood in the door, speechless, looking at his ex-wife. Her husband broke the silence, held out his hand, and said, "I'm Bill. Nice to finally meet you."

Pack snapped out of it. "Shit! Yes! You too." He took Bill's hand.

Shelley said: "Are you going to let us in? We've come a long way."

"Sorry, sure." He jumped aside, holding the door wide.

"Mom!" A cry from behind him made Shelley stop dead, and then Vida appeared, pale as the sling that held her arm close to her body. She started sobbing, and Shelley started crying, and they went for each other and Pack yelled, "Look out for her shoulder, she's been shot! Christ Almighty!"

And Bill was laughing as he came in the door, lugging the blue suitcase.

The pancakes weren't forgotten. The recipe had to be tripled, however.

"We'll need it," Vida said, sitting at the kitchen table next to Bill.

Shelley had agreed to help Pack. "But I won't do it for you," she added, forestalling any plea of ignorance. "And start heating the frying pan now, don't wait until everything's mixed."

Pack nodded obediently. Vida took Bill's hand and held it. Together they watched Shelley and Pack work.

They didn't hear the front door, so no one knew Millie was

home until she was standing in her kitchen door. "Hello everybody," she said. She had on freshly-applied eye shadow, and was carrying a bag of groceries.

"Millie!" Vida said, delighted.

Pack smiled happily. "Great. Hungry? I'm making pancakes."

"Starving."

Shelley stared at Pack's cousin. "Millie?"

Millie nodded, and said, "Was Mitch. Now Millie."

It was Shelley's turn to be stunned. Bill, who didn't seem to be thrown easily, recuperated sooner than she did. Standing up, he held out his hand and said, "Pleasure, Millie. I'm Bill, Shelley's husband. If you tell me where it might be, I'll get you a mug and fill it with coffee."

CHAPTER 72

That night, Pack went home to New Canaan. Shelley and Bill were going to stay for the rest of the week while Vida convalesced, so the house in Goose Creek was crowded.

He walked into his home and stood in the living room, looking around. The old dirt was now layered with new dirt, the kitchen drawer still overturned on the floor, the back door open, all the windows so dirty they looked opaque. Through the French doors, he could see the gaping hole in the back porch, boards uprooted and thrown aside, as if a small hurricane had passed through. The threadbare red and white deck chair was lying on the pile of debris, its seat finally torn through and fluttering in the breeze.

What a dump.

He could finally see it for what it was—a neglected, dismal space, unloved and uncared for. He walked into his bedroom. The police had already been through, taking pictures and fingerprints. The duct tape used to restrain and imprison his daughter was gone. He sat on the edge of his unmade bed. He bent his head and began to cry, at first slowly and gently, eventually in big, gulping sobs.

After about ten minutes, it was over. He went into the bathroom and splashed cold water on his face. The towels looked dirty, so he shook his hands dry. Then he went into the kitchen and hunted around for a garbage bag. Time to get to work.

A week later, Millie drove Vida up to Pack's house. A large green dumpster was parked in front of the house, next to the Town Car.

"Well, what d'you know," Millie said.

"What's going on?" Vida said.

"Not sure."

They both got out of the truck and walked toward the house, stopping near the dumpster. The overhead garage door was open all the way and they could hear noise coming from inside it. It was Pack. They watched as he carried an old bicycle tire and a black garbage bag up the ramp.

He started when he saw them. "Shit!"

"Hi," Vida said.

He threw the bag and the tire into the dumpster. "You shouldn't creep up on people like that." He went back down into the garage.

"What're you doing?" she asked.

Millie got a foothold and peered into the dumpster. "Looks like he's cleaning house."

Pack picked up a large, torn cardboard box and brought it outside. A small, scuffed sneaker fell out en route.

Vida picked it up. "You know, you should get your landlord to do this. It's not your responsibility," she said.

Pack stood, listening to her, holding the box. "You think so?"

"Also, if it's not your stuff," Vida added, "you could get in trouble for throwing it out."

"True," he said. "So what do you suggest I do?"

"Get hold of your landlord and tell him that you've had it with living like a slob and you want to use the garage. Go on a rent strike."

"Okay." He put the box down. "Vida, I'm tired of living like a slob and I want to use my garage."

She rolled her eyes. "Save it."

But Pack nodded. "I'm serious. Vida, I'm tired of living like a slob, and blah blah blah."

Millie looked on, interested.

Vida was getting irritated. "What're you doing?"

"Well, you told me to have it out with my landlord, and since you're my landlord—"

"What d'you mean?"

"What I said. This is your house, Vida."

"What're you talking about?" she said, lost.

"Not complicated. I bought this place when you were first born. When your mother left, I put it in your name."

Vida looked around. "This is where we lived?"

He nodded. "You don't remember?"

Vida shook her head. "You gave it to me? Why?"

"It had to belong to somebody."

She looked down at the small shoe in her hand. Her eyes filled up with tears. "Is this mine?"

Pack nodded. "Unless you had a friend over and she forgot it."

"All I do is cry these days."

Pack hoisted the waist of his jeans. "Hey, it ain't much, you know, just a lousy little split-level. Mosquitoes in the summer. Skunks in the winter. Hey, come on, Pip, stop. Stop, okay? Come on, honey."

CHAPTER 73

Shelley and Bill had gone home to Alaska that morning. The house in Goose Creek felt empty and still. Vida didn't have much to pack; when she was done she sat at the foot of the stairs and waited, glancing occasionally at her watch.

She had tried to say goodbye to Millie, who'd left thirty minutes earlier to teach a class at the Rod and Gun Club, but her father's cousin had brushed her off. "I hate goodbyes. Just remember to pay attention, okay? That's all I ask. Pay close attention."

"To what?"

"Everything. Details. You're a good girl, Vida, and I'll see you soon."

Pack was due to arrive any minute. Vida was nervous. The plan was for them to drive to Fort Drum, where she had an appointment at the JAG office. With Pack's help, she'd found a lawyer in Watertown who would meet them there and help her plead her case. The lawyer didn't think clearing things up would be too hard, given what had happened to her in the last ten days. But still, her stomach was in a knot. This was the Army, and in the not-so-distant past, she could have been shot as a deserter.

She moved her left arm, slowly, feeling the ache in the shoulder. She'd be offered an Honorable Discharge, the lawyer guessed. Vida wasn't sure yet if she wanted to get out or rejoin her unit. If they gave her a choice, she'd decide when she got there.

Through the lace curtains, she saw a black car turn into the driveway. There was a short blast of a horn. She grabbed her bag and went out, pulling the front door shut behind her.

The Town Car was sitting in the driveway, engine rumbling. She could see Pack in the driver's seat, his eyes hidden behind sunglasses, tapping his fingers on the steering wheel. He turned his head toward her, then lifted his hands, palms up, in a "what's taking you so long?" gesture. Vida made a point of walking extra slowly down the steps.

To get to Fort Drum, which was near the Canadian border, they had to drive through Albany, head west to Utica, then turn north. Traffic was minimal as they approached the capital. They sat together in companionable silence until they reached the southern outskirts of the city.

They were coming up to an exit when Pack suddenly announced: "Detour." And without explanation, he veered off the highway.

"Come on, no!" Vida didn't want to stop. They had close to four hours driving ahead and she wanted to get going. Old Man probably had to pee. God, this was going to be a long ride.

But Pack just said, "Something's missing."

"With what?"

"With the whole thing."

"What're you talking about?"

"I'm not sure, but just let me do this, okay?"

Within minutes she knew where they were going. They were in Delmar, and then they were turning onto Birchwood Lane, the street where Haley grew up and where Mrs. Flynn had been murdered. A suburb she wanted to forget.

"Hey, Pack, I don't want to be here," Vida said, panic in her voice.

"I know."

And then they arrived. The street was empty. Pack pulled the car next to the curb across from the drab little Flynn house. Pieces of torn crime scene tape still decorated the yard. He turned off the engine and looked at her. There was compassion in his eyes, but not much hesitation.

"You can wait in the car, if you don't want anyone to see you." He opened the door and climbed out.

The wind was hitting one of the remnants of yellow tape just right, making it whistle like a blade of grass held to a child's lips.

Vida followed him, not ready to be left behind. "You think I'm going to hide? I didn't do anything wrong."

Pack looked at her. "That's the ticket."

The green house to the left of the Flynns had no cars in the driveway. Unlikely anyone was home.

Parked in the driveway in front of the house to the right were two vehicles, a vintage yellow Camaro with rusted wheel wells, and a silver minivan. A pink plastic tricycle lay on its side on the grass.

They crossed the street, walked past the cars, and Pack went up to the front door and rang the bell. The sound of rock and roll leaked out of the front windows. Vida hung back, turning away as if she were admiring the street. After a delay, a woman's voice called out: "Coming!"

While he waited, Pack dusted off his scuffed leather shoes on the backs of his calves, one after the other. He was wearing jeans and an old tan canvas work jacket, darkened at the pockets and collar. He brushed the sleeves.

The peephole darkened. He pretended not to notice.

"What d'you want?" A woman's voice, high and anxious.

"I have an appointment with your next door neighbor, Mrs. Flynn. Do you know her?"

"She's not available," the woman's voice answered.

"Any idea when she'll be back?"

"No, no. She had an accident. She doesn't live there anymore."

"I'm sorry to hear that. Where can I reach her, do you know?"

A pause, then: "Look, she's dead."

He heard a man's voice at the back of the house, the words not clear, rising at the end in a question.

The woman responded: "I don't know. I didn't want to open the door." More arguing. "Fine. You do it then."

After some scuffling, the door swung open. A young guy stood there, tall, probably mid-twenties. He looked suspicious and irritated. Possibly a permanent expression. "What do you want?"

"Sorry to intrude, but I bought a piece of furniture from Mrs. Flynn about three weeks ago over the Internet. A credenza."

"So?"

"Well, see, today was the day I was supposed to pick it up. I hear from your wife Mrs. Flynn's passed away, and I'm real sorry, but do you think anyone, a relative or a close friend, might be able to help me with this?"

"No." He glanced past Pack at Vida. "All her stuff is going to probate—house and everything. You can't take anything out of there."

Pack nodded. "Wow. Sure. Of course. Maybe there's someone I could talk to. Leave my name with. A friend of hers?"

The neighbor seemed to let go of some of his irritation. "I don't know. We're just getting settled in. You could ask the old lady across the street. She's a family friend." And then he turned into the house and yelled: "Sal, we're gonna be late, hurry up!"

"Coming!"

Pack turned to look at the houses across the street. "The white house or the yellow one?"

"White."

"Thanks for your help." But the door was already shut.

"A credenza?" Vida shook her head in admiration as they crossed the street.

"Yeah. I don't even know what a credenza is."

Vida stood next to him on the old lady's porch when Pack rang the bell. As soon as she opened the door, Pack recognized her—he'd talked to her briefly on the day Lorna was murdered.

Her eyes went from him to Vida, hand still on the knob. "I'll tell you right now, don't try selling me anything, I'm not interested."

Pack decided the credenza story wasn't going to fly. "I'm here about your neighbor, Mrs. Flynn."

"Who're you?"

"Reynolds Packard. This is my daughter Vida. She was in Iraq with Haley Flynn."

"You look like a spy," she said, indicating his dark glasses.

He took them off. "I'm not. A spy."

"Hmm. Do I know you?"

"No, ma'am."

"Is that your car?"

"Yes, ma'am."

"Don't ma'am me." She switched her attention to Vida. "You're the girl who was staying with Lorna, aren't you? The one they were looking for?"

"Yes," Vida said, glancing at Pack, wondering if this woman was going to start screaming for help. "But it's all been cleared up."

"I know that. They shot that bastard. Good riddance." The woman looked at Pack, weighing him. She seemed to be making up her mind. "I'm Mary Calhoun. What d'you want?"

"We have some questions about Haley. We were hoping you might be able to answer them."

"Why'd you come to me?"

"We heard you were a friend of Lorna's."

"From who?"

As if on cue, across the way the front door opened and the young husband emerged. He was holding the hand of a little girl in a pink windbreaker, who in turn was carrying a stuffed animal. Behind them came a plump blonde. While she stopped to lock the front door, the man opened the passenger door of the Camaro and moved the seat forward. He kissed the little girl and slid her inside. He bent in, possibly to buckle her seat belt, then walked around to the driver's side.

"Ah, yes. Young Jordie," Mary said.

They watched in silence as both adults got in, shutting the doors in quick succession. The yellow car pulled noisily out of the driveway.

Mary said, "Okay, do it. Ask me what you want. I've got things to do."

Vida said, "Any chance we could look in Lorna's house?"

Mary Calhoun frowned. "I don't know if that'd be right."

"Is it still a crime scene?" Pack asked.

Mary shook her head. "No, no, they're done. In fact, I said I'd help go through some of her personal things, clothes, papers. Do a little tidying up. Police have most likely left a terrible mess." She looked at Vida. "Why would you want to see her house again? Haven't you had enough?"

Vida's gaze found the drab building across the street, the yellow tape the only bright spot. "Definitely. But I think I need to say goodbye properly."

They waited on the porch while Mary Calhoun went inside to find the Flynn house key. As they crossed the street next to her, she confessed, "I've got to say, I'm relieved to have some company going in. Last time I stepped foot inside this house was two weeks ago. I had coffee with Lorna." She shook her head. "I've known her for eighteen years, give or take. I still can't believe it."

Inside, the place felt very different. The first thing Vida noticed was the odor—of dirt, disinfectant, sweat. Oil, too, for some reason. The frumpy, closed smell of before was gone, with its cleaners, polishers, and old air.

The carpets were muddy, a path of footprints from the front door, splitting off to the stairs and going back to the kitchen. Mary snorted. "Look at this. Lorna is spinning in her grave."

Pack looked around, taking in the drab, serviceable furnishings, cleaner versions of those in his own home. "Did Haley grow up in this house?"

"Yes. They moved in when she was a bitty thing. Cute as a bug in a rug, but she was a biter. Oh, my dear, do you think they cleaned the upstairs? I can't go up there if they didn't."

"I'll check it out." Pack looked at his daughter, who was still standing by the front door. "Vida, stay with Mrs. Calhoun, okay?"

"Check what out?" she asked, as if her thoughts had been far away.

"I'm going to see if they cleaned up the crime scene. Mrs. Flynn's bedroom."

Vida shook her head as if to clear it. "I'll do it. You don't know which room."

"You sure?" he asked protectively.

She nodded. "Sure."

"Want company?"

"No. I'm good."

He watched her walk upstairs, her footsteps slow, as if a weight were pushing her down. She looked tough, but he wondered if she should go back into that room alone.

"I'm sorry, I've never seen a crime scene before. I don't think I can face it." Mrs. Calhoun's face look twisted with worry.

To distract both of them he asked, "What do you mean, Haley was a biter?"

"She bit other kids when she got excited."

"I bet she didn't have a whole lot of friends."

"Oh, she grew out of it. And then she had too many. That boy, for instance."

Pack couldn't do it. He couldn't leave Vida to face it all by herself. "I'll be right back." He took the stairs two at a time.

He found Vida in what had to be Mrs. Flynn's bedroom. The room was airless, ground zero for the powerful antiseptic smell that permeated the house. The bed had been stripped, mattress and box spring leaning up against the wall. The center of the carpeted floor was decorated with a large, dark stain. Vida had her back to him and was struggling with one of the storm windows.

"You okay in here?"

"It's so hot," she said, her voice tense. She was pushing and wiggling the latches, trying to simultaneously hold up the sash with her elbow. "It's stuck," and she slammed a hand against the window frame, hard. She hit it again and again, until Pack walked over to her and grabbed her wrist. "Hey, your shoulder. Careful."

She yanked her arm away. "I can't breathe in here."

"Go easy, okay?"

"I should be able to do this. I didn't help her, but at least I can open the fucking window."

"You tried to help her," Pack said.

"No, I didn't. The thing is, I was so sick of her, sick of her tantrums, of her bitching and moaning." She leaned on the sash, her head on the glass.

Pack was confused for a moment, until he realized she wasn't talking about Lorna Flynn, but about Haley.

"What tantrums, when?"

"All the time. There was always some catastrophe when you were around her. We were at war, but that wasn't enough drama for her. No way."

"When did she need help? The day she died?"

"The night before." She lifted her head, as if she were looking at something that was replaying in her mind's eye. "She came in late and woke me up. She was a mess, like she'd been roughed up. I asked her what was wrong but she wouldn't say. I was so tired, I didn't ask very hard. I fell asleep while she sat on her bed. Crying."

"What had he done, do you think?"

"My guess is he raped her. She had scrapes and welts on her face and arms."

"What else?"

"That's it. I woke up a little later and she was writing one of her letters. She wrote a lot of letters."

"Maybe she decided to turn him in."

"If she threatened him, it would explain why he killed her."

Pack thought about it. "Who'd she write to?"

"I don't know. She never told me and I didn't ask."

Mrs. Calhoun was standing in the doorway holding a couple of dark green garbage bags. "Her little girl. She wrote dozens of letters to her. To explain what she was doing over there. So her kid would understand, be proud of her. In case something happened to her."

Vida looked at her in surprise. "I didn't know she had a little girl," she said.

Mrs. Calhoun looked around. "Oh, my gosh." She saw the discoloration on the carpet. "Oh, no, look at that. Oh, what a smell! What happened to the mattress? No, no. Don't explain."

She crossed the room, being careful to avoid the darkened center. She opened the closet then turned to Pack and Vida, who hadn't moved. "You'll stay with me, won't you, while I put her clothes in bags? I won't be long."

Pack nodded. He worked on the storm window until he got it open. At last, a cool breath of air circled into the room. Vida breathed deep and closed her eyes.

"And then we'll make a cup of coffee. There's only instant, but I don't think it'll matter. Not today, anyway."

"What did you mean when you said Haley didn't have any friends, and then she had too many?"

The three of them were sitting at the kitchen table. They each had a steaming mug of coffee in front of them. A little color had returned to Vida's cheeks, but she still looked dazed.

The old lady hesitated. "Well, there was something off in the family dynamics, and Haley, of course, paid the price."

"Her father, right? I bet it was her father," Pack said.

Mary glanced at him. "He had something to do with it, that's for sure. They were a religious family, and that can be good, or it can be bad. In this case, I don't think it did the girl any good. Anyway, she was daddy's little angel until she turned about thirteen, and then the screaming started. She became very hard for them to control, ran with some rough kids, had an older boyfriend, that whole thing. Her mother was heartbroken."

"What about the father?"

"He went Old Testament on her, as far as I could tell. If he hadn't died, he'd have locked her in the basement."

Pack thought about raising a daughter. He'd sidestepped all that responsibility, all those arguments. He felt a stab of regret. "What happened?"

"He fell off a ladder one day, cleaning the gutters. Classic, wouldn't you say? Came crashing down and hit his head. Haley was the only person at home. He survived for a while on life support, but eventually they pulled the plug and that was that."

"Mrs. Calhoun," Vida said. "You said Haley had a boyfriend, older than her. What happened to him?"

"Nothing. He's the one you met, across the street. Jordie. That's the house he grew up in, though he left a long time ago. His mother died a few months back and Jordie inherited the house and moved back with his wife and the little one."

"Cute little girl."

Mrs. Calhoun looked at Vida. "That's Haley's daughter."

"You're kidding."

"Haley gave him custody when she joined the military."

"Why did she do that, give the father custody?" Pack asked.

"He insisted, said if anything happened to her, he wanted to be sure he didn't lose the girl. Also, he'd get benefits."

"He sounds terrible," Vida said.

"I don't think he is, really. He seems to love the child."

"It's weird, Mrs. Flynn never mentioned any little girl to me."

Mary Calhoun sighed. "She didn't know. I only just found out from Jordie."

"How's that possible?" Vida asked.

"Remember, Haley left home at sixteen or so and never came back. She and her mother didn't speak and she had the baby in Arizona, I think. So it was easy not to tell Lorna. And Jordie went along with it, though I know he planned to tell her soon, once they were settled in. He figured that the little girl needed a grandmother. Free babysitting, too, is my guess."

Vida shook her head, trying to absorb all the information. "What kind of a mother was Haley?"

"Jordie said she was pretty good, actually. She wrote letters to the little girl all the time, with drawings in them. And while she was in Iraq, she managed to send surprising amounts of money for the child's college fund. I guess that can happen in the military, if you live frugally. I mean, everything's free, isn't it?"

Before leaving they helped Mrs. Calhoun lug down the garbage bags full of Lorna's belongings and pile them up by the front door. They said goodbye to her in the driveway.

"I don't even know that little girl's name," Vida said thoughtfully, once she was in the car.

"You can always meet her again when she's a little older," Pack said, as they turned off the quiet street.

"Like you did with me?"

"I didn't mean that."

Vida leaned back, closed her eyes. "No, but it fits. Maybe I could just appear one day, save her life, give her a house, and then, I don't know, get to know her a little. What d'you think?"

Pack shook his head. "Sounds ass-backwards to me."

Vida smiled faintly, her eyes still closed. "Yes, it is."

ABOUT THE AUTHOR

Julia Pomeroy was born in Okinawa to a Foreign Service family, and spent her childhood in Libya, Somalia, and Italy. She first moved to the States at nineteen and wound up in New York City, working as an Italian interpreter and an actor. She graduated with a Lit/Writing degree from Columbia University, invaluable for writing the menus when she and her husband opened a restaurant in the town where they still live, in upstate New York. Her previous books are *The Dark End of Town* and *Cold Moon Home,* both in the Abby Silvernale series.

Julia's website is www.juliapomeroy.com; you can write to her at juliapomeroy@aol.com.